Love's Heirloom

Adam J. Ridley, Blake Allwood

Blake Allwood Publishing

Content Warnings

Gang Violence

Violence

Drug Dealers

Abandonment

Assault

Kidnapping

Join Blake's email list to get advance notice of new books and receive his occasional newsletter:

www.blakeallwood.com

<table>
<tr><td>

MM Romance
By Blake Allwood

Transitions Series
Aiden Inspired
Suzie Empowered (MF Romance)
Bobby Transformed

Chance Series
Love By Chance
Another Chance With Love
Taking A Chance For Love

Romantic Series
Romantic Renovations (1)
Romantic Rescue (2)
Romantic Recon (3)

Melody Series
Melody of the Heart
Melody of the Snow

Road to Rocktoberfest Anthology
Changing His Tune - 2022

Coming Home Series (2023)
A Long Way Home
Family Home
Down Home
…and many more

Novellas
Tenacious
Moon's Place

</td><td>

Romantic Fantasy
By Adam J. Ridley

Big Bend Series
Love's Legacy (1)
Love's Heirloom (2)
Love's Bequest (3)

The Witch Brothers Series
Emerald Earth
Diamond Air
Ruby Fire
Sapphire Water

</td></tr>
</table>

Acknowledgments

A special thank you to

Bryan Seranas – Developmental Editor
Jo Bird – Line Editor
Renee Mizar – Developmental Editor II
Ann Attwood – Final Editor
A special thank you goes to all my friends and family who supported me, I couldn't have done it without you.
John Gilchrist
for his work on the family tree and being a great Beta-reader.

And of course, a big thank you to my husband who encourages me to keep going down these rabbit holes never knowing where I might end up.

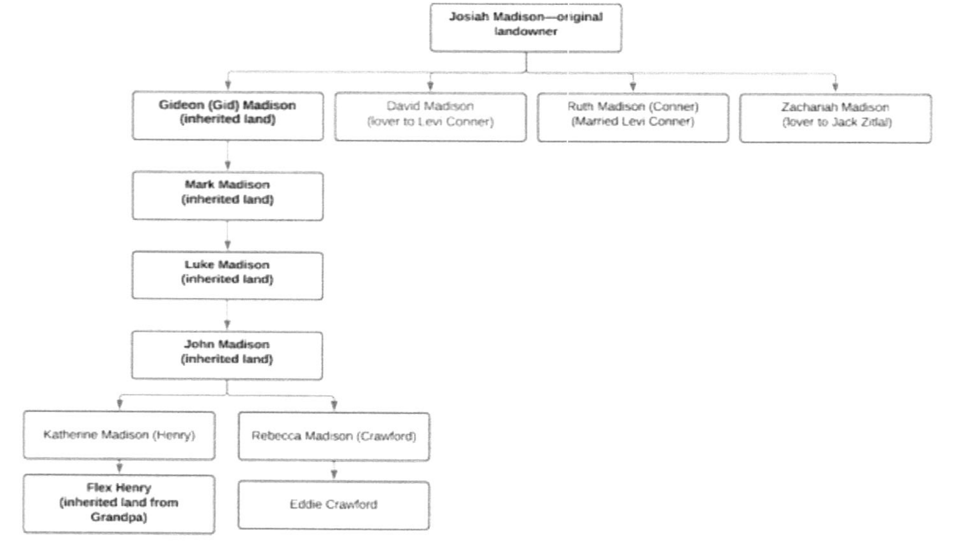

Josiah Madison—original landowner
Gideon (Gid) Madison (inherited land)
David Madison (lover to Levi Conner)
Ruth Madison (Conner) (Married Levi Conner)
Zachariah Madison (lover to Jack Zitlal)
Mark Madison (inherited land)
Luke Madison (inherited land)
John Madison (inherited land)
Katherine Madison (Henry)
Rebecca Madison (Crawford)
Flex Henry (inherited land from Grandpa)
Eddie Crawford

1

Eddie

I JUMPED WHEN I heard the movement in the bushes just over to my right. Fearing it might be a mountain lion or a bear, I immediately jumped off my horse, Red, and pulled my rifle out of its holster on the saddle. I slowly crept around the bottom of the mountain toward where I'd heard the sound. Normally, I'd have ridden away from the sound, but we were all wary since Flex, my cousin, had been shot and almost killed.

Once again, I felt my heartbeat quicken when I rounded the corner and found some random man sitting on a boulder. Staying out of sight, I watched him for a moment to get my bearings on the guy, before confronting him.

He seemed to be dressed in old-time clothes, but he was so covered with dust I couldn't quite tell what he was wearing. "Hey, you can't be here," I said forcefully, as I walked around the mesquite tree, hoping to catch him off guard. The guy just turned toward me and smiled.

"Well, I was a wonderin' when y'all would be coming this way. Been meaning to talk to you."

"Who are you?" I demanded, completely suspicious of the stranger.

"Diamondback Jack," the stranger replied, then said with a wink, "You can call me Jack, though."

I looked closer at the man and guessed he was in his mid-forties. He was handsome under the dust and grime with a long thin frame and high cheekbones. His hair was coal-black and hung below his shoulders.

"Where did you come from?" I asked, determined to find out who this guy was, and why he was here.

"Oh, your grandparents hired me long ago to keep an eye on this place, been doin' it ever since," he said. I could hear a slight Mexican accent then, giving away the man's origin.

"My grandpa's been gone for over five years. You probably shouldn't still be here," I said.

"Well, I don't leave no job half done," he replied. "Besides, I have something you need to see."

The guy got up then and walked into a thicket directly behind where he'd been sitting.

I kept my gun at my side, ready if I needed it. Diamondback Jack didn't particularly feel dangerous, and having dealt with the riff-raff my drugged-out wife hung out with, I'd come to listen more with my gut than my head when dealing with people.

When I came through the thicket, I was shocked to see that the mountain curved inward here. This was the mountain my granny used to call the volcano, and of course threatened us with its eruption if we misbehaved. Flex, Eric, and I had grown up climbing this mountain, and I'd never seen this part of it before. It was clear this had been where ancient lava had flowed in such a way it'd created a natural crevice in the mountainside.

"How did we miss this?" I asked out loud, then remembering I wasn't alone, quickly looked around to find the guy who'd shown this to me.

The man was nowhere to be seen. "Hey, mister," I yelled, but there was nothing. He'd totally disappeared. I cautiously walked around. Clearly, the place hadn't been used for a long time. There was some old rusty cooking stuff sitting near the mountain wall that looked like it'd been used to hold a coffee pot over a fire.

The entire area caused the hairs on the back of my neck to stand up, like I'd walked through a time warp and had been transported over a hundred years into the past. I quickly slipped out of the clearing and back through the thicket.

There was still no sign of the man, so I called out again. There was no answer so I quickly climbed onto Red's back and sprinted back toward the ranch house. I kept looking over my shoulder in case I was being followed, but as far as I could tell, I was by myself.

When I got back to the house, Flex was sitting on the porch swing across from Emma Jean and Jimmy.

Flex was my first cousin, but was more like my brother and best friend. He and I had been forced apart when my mom had sued him for the inheritance of this property. She lost and luckily, we'd been reunited. Emma Jean and Jimmy were the ranch caretakers my grandparents had long-ago hired. They'd also been taken for a ride by my mom, but luckily, they hadn't held me accountable for her actions. Now, they were acting as surrogate grandparents for my two boys, Drake and Luke. On the porch sat three of the most important adults in my life, and I'd fight like a mad dog to protect them.

I dismounted, tied the reins to the hitching post that'd been there since before I could remember, and went to stand with the group.

"I just had a really strange experience," I said. "And we probably need to let the law know about it."

Flex sat up when I spoke. No surprise since he'd been the one to almost lose his life when an uninvited stranger last came on the property.

I told them about riding out by the volcano, and the man who'd shown up saying he was called Diamondback Jack. When I said the name, Emma Jean and Jimmy give each other a weird look.

"Like an idiot, I followed him into a clearing behind a thicket, where the mountain opened up in such a way you couldn't see it unless you knew to look. It was a perfect hiding spot," I said. "I can't be sure he wasn't the guy who shot up Flex, and it was sure a perfect hiding space."

I told them I was gonna call the sheriff when Jimmy held up his hand. "Can you describe him to us?"

I shrugged and did the best I could. "Tall, well over six feet, longish dark hair, definitely Mexican descent, but there was native there too, he might be Apache?"

"Or Aztec," Emma Jean said.

"Well, could be, but I haven't met a lot of people who are Aztec, so I can't be sure. I'm gonna let Sheriff Walker know," I said, and walked toward the door. This time Emma Jean stopped me.

"Before you do, you'd better sit down."

I looked at her funny, and noticing my cousin was perplexed as well, I crossed over and sat next to him.

Jimmy smiled and a gleam shone in his eyes. "The legend goes, yer first white ancestor in these parts, Josiah Madison, discovered a vein a gold around the ol' mountain y'all call the volcano. Even though it weren't big enough to turn into a major gold mine, it was significant enough that it could'a become dangerous for the folks on the ranch if outsiders found out." Jimmy's accent always got stronger when he was telling his stories. The more he liked the story, the thicker his accent got. He must like this one a lot cause he was laying it on really thick!

So, yer ancestor did what he saw fit. He found the meanest, toughest, nastiest man around these parts to patrol the area. It didn't take long for the man to figure out he was protecting gold, and he got mighty mad that your ancestor hadn't been completely forthcomin. 'I deserve part of the gold,' he argued, and he wasn't wrong, as that was the way things tended to be during those times. If'n you wanted to hire somebody to protect your claim, you gave them a bit of the gold in exchange."

I leaned back knowing Jimmy was just getting into his stride, when the man started to spin a tale, wasn't much you could do but sit back 'til he spun it out.

"Your ancestor tried to convince the guy he had no intention of mining any damned gold or anythin else, but that were just the same as talkin into the wind.

'Course, the no-good SOB didn't believe it, and next thing he knew, the lowdown sorry... well, you know what I'm sayin..." Jimmy said and winked before he got back to the story, "He left the ranch and recruited his brother. Now them men wuz the leaders of a notorious outlaw gang. Course, he and his men signed right up, considerin there was gold involved.

Well, y'all know, back then, the law weren't really up to keeping things settled, so it was up to yer ancestor and his men to keep the peace on their land.

As it turned out, the whole thing blew up into some sorta mini-war. One of the brothers ended up killin one of the old rancher's kids who worked in town, not to mention several of the men runnin the ranch. Finally, it got sa bad the Texas Rangers stepped in. That drove off the outlaws, but the Ranger's involvement was only superficial, and everybody knew it wuz just a matter a time fore them bandits returned."

As was Jimmy's way, he leaned back then and chewed on what I could only assumed was a memory of the tobacco chew he used to use, but Emma Jean had long ago forced him to stop. When he finally leaned forward again, the gleam had returned to his eye, as he continued, "As luck would have it, the old man's daughter had married Alamito's first lawman, the one Flex saw in his dream and the man that'd been killed by the brothers. After the lawman's death, his half-brother showed up looking for work a' keepin the peace here on the ranch."

Jimmy looked around gathering the suspense with his expression before continuing, "Ol' Mr. Madison was suspicious, a course, and didn't really much like the man. For one thing, the man was a northern officer in the war and your ancestor had fought for the south. The old rancher and his daughter were also estranged. He didn't much trust her neither, and since she'd been married to this guy's brother, he wuz wary of this one. So, thinkin he'd get rid of him once and fer all, the rancher decided to offer the man a strange deal."

Jimmy chuckled as if he was recounting the story firsthand, "'If'n you can find the gold mine on yer own, then I'll hire ya.' The fella just laughed, 'I'm of the Aztec people. We are blessed with the gift of findin and protectin gold. I'll find the mine, and you'll hire me,' he said."

Jimmy shook his head then, like he was perplexed by the next part of the story, "The man left, but was only gone for a day. When he returned, he asked to see your ancestor in private. He took his saddlebag off his horse and after they walked into the house, he pulled out a stone laced with gold. 'I've found yer mine, now will ya hire me to take care of it as we agreed?' he asked. Your ancestor was amazed. He had no choice since he'd agreed, and so the man wuz hired to manage the mine just as the old rancher had promised. 'What's yer name, stranger?' your ancestor asked."

Jimmy looked over at Emma Jean as he asked the question, then when he made eye contact with me he finished the story, "The man turned around an' told him, 'Diamondback Jack.'"

I sucked in a breath, then laughed. "You're telling me I saw a hundred-plus-year-old man out there? I'm telling you he couldn't have been over forty-five. Who all knows this legend?" I asked.

Jimmy thought for a bit. "Well, reckon it could be any number of folks. It was a popular story among the hands. Although, none of 'em ever saw him, and your ancestor never talked about him to anyone as far as I know. 'Sides the only real mine found in these parts was the Shafter mine, which mostly produced silver. Only a tiny part of what they dug out of the mine was gold, so the story was chalked up ta legend. But, son, Imma tellin' you, if'n you call the sheriff and tell him you done met Diamondback Jack, you're gonna need to prepare for some serious skepticism."

I sighed. "Well, ain't that something?" I asked. "But, it stands to reason this person knew about the story, and for sure was leading us on with it. Regardless, I want the sheriff to know someone was out there, and we need to be prepared just in case."

"Yer gonna get some shit fer seein ghosts, but yer right," Jimmy agreed.

I hadn't known the boys were up and listening to the story, until Luke, my youngest son, blurted out, "Ooh, Uncle Jimmy said shit!"

"Luke," I admonished, while trying not to laugh. "Just because Jimmy said it doesn't mean you can."

Luke pouted. "He needs to get in trouble too."

Emma Jean smiled at Luke. "Don't you worry, young man, I'll get him later. Have you two done your morning chores?" When he and Drake, his older brother, nodded, she added, "Well then, get your school clothes on and I'll set your breakfast out." Both boys took off up the stairs.

Emma Jean had been a blessing. She'd taken on the responsibility for most of my boys' day-to-day activities, which had been a total lifesaver. I'd had a-hundred-percent responsibility for the boys since their mom, my *unwife* as I'd come to refer to her, had left.

Now that Emma Jean had started working with the boys, I'd noticed their self-esteem had increased. That was accompanied by an uptick in their grades as well. The woman was a natural, and I knew they'd already begun to think of her as their grandmother, something they'd never experienced in a positive way before.

My mother had ostracized us when I wouldn't join her in the lawsuit against Flex for the property. She'd come back into their lives only after Flex had moved in with us temporarily, while we were all preparing to move out to the ranch.

Theresa, the boys' mom and my unwife had parents about as good as mine. Her parents disowned her when she married me. They were convinced I was the reason she was a drug user. I thought bitterly of the arguments we'd had over the years. Me trying to get her to stop using, her becoming more and more resentful. I guessed it was just easier for her parents to blame me, rather than face the reality that their daughter wanted to be how she was.

In the end, that's what caused her to leave. I felt the telltale signs of anger and frustration course through me, and had to unclench my jaw and my hands. Theresa still saw me as self-righteous and uptight, because I didn't want her doing crack or meth around the boys.

She was probably right about me being uptight, but at least one of us was able to keep it together for our sons. No matter what I did, I would never win when it came to Theresa, and as always that thought made me feel hopeless.

Right before Flex got shot, and our lives were turned upside down, Theresa had asked me for a divorce. In fact, that's where I was when Flex had been shot, dealing with my final fight for our relationship. I still hadn't agreed. It wasn't like I thought she'd get her life together or anything, it's just I'd made a commitment. I didn't like breaking my promises, even if she was more than happy to break hers.

I sighed with relief as I thought about Emma Jean and her involvement with the kids. It had been both strange and a bit funny how much of a relief it was to have someone else looking after the kids with me. I once again had to shake off the feelings of loss when I thought how Theresa had never been that. Until returning to the ranch, I'd been their only parent. I technically still was, but at least with Emma Jean, Jimmy, and Flex, I had that village people always talked about kids needing while growing up.

We'd connected a phone up in the master bedroom, since mobile service out here sucked and occasionally I'd need privacy when I had a phone call to make. I climbed the stairs and went there to call the sheriff.

When I was finally connected, I told him what I'd seen. "Someone seemed to be impersonating the guy from the gold-mine legend they used to tell here on the ranch. He was even dressed in period costume and everything," I said.

"Do you think it could be our shooter?" he asked me.

"I'm not sure," I admitted. "Could've been a prank too, but you know how things are. We probably need to keep an eye out and I figured any strange occurrences needed to be reported."

"I appreciate it," he told me. "Keep an eye out and I'll try to get out there this afternoon to see if we can spot any footprints or other evidence to point to who this guy is."

He showed up right before dinner, and Emma Jean demanded he join us before we all traipsed off leaving all her hard work to get cold. The sheriff was a wise man, so he didn't argue with her.

When we'd finished eating, Flex, Jimmy, the sheriff, and I drove the old pickup truck out toward the area where I'd seen the man.

It took a moment for me to find the little thicket again, but it was just as I remembered when we went through the gap. "Split up and walk lightly," the sheriff said. "Try to find footprints or anything that's been used..." he looked around the old campsite and added, "...anything that's been used in the last century."

We circled the camp, but there was no evidence of footprints other than mine, or evidence anyone had swept the area to hide them. When we were done, the sheriff just shrugged. "Whoever did this was either an expert or a ghost."

I looked at the sheriff with narrowed eyes. "Don't go thinking I made this up, Sheriff. I never would've found this if someone hadn't shown me, and I don't believe in ghosts," I said.

I turned to leave when the sheriff laughed. "I ain't calling you crazy, Eddie, but you tell this story to anyone else, and they might."

I ended up flipping him and the others off, causing all of them to burst into fits of laughter. "Fuck all of you," I said as I stalked back to the truck. "I saw what I saw, and I don't need nobody telling me otherwise."

They had the decency not to harass me too much as we all drove back up to the homestead, although I could feel they were questioning my experience.

The rest of the week passed without incident. For over six years the property hadn't had a cow on it and that seemed wrong. Before our grandpa had died, there'd been cows here continuously since my ancestors had come to settle here like a hundred years ago, well, probably closer to a hundred and fifty, to be honest. So, it was a big deal when the cattle were delivered over the weekend.

Flex and I worked on an old windmill that brought water up from an underground stream. We had the water next to the house, but it couldn't hurt to have a source further away for when the cows were grazing out on that part of the property.

It felt right to have the cows back where they belonged. They were such a big part of my childhood that when I thought of the ranch, I could almost smell them from my memories.

2

Alex

F uck," I said to myself as I drove through the pitch blackness from the Big Bend National Park to the little motel my assistant had booked for me in the neighboring town.

For the tenth time I asked the universe why she hadn't booked me into the hotel here in the park? My guess was it was my father's intervention. He didn't want me to look like I was favoring the United States national park over Mexico's. Having our family's hacienda in El Paso and working in Juarez had always been a point of contention between the two governments. Luckily, we'd owned this land and the hacienda since the early nineteen hundreds, so we had a good excuse for living and working on the different sides of the line. Still, how people perceived things was something we were always keenly aware of.

That night, when I *finally* got back to the motel, I collapsed, falling asleep the moment my head hit the pillow. The next morning, I checked out of the motel and greeted the handsome man who waited on me behind the counter. If I'd had more time, I would've pursued him as a possible hookup. Sometimes, the locals in an area were the best part of a visit, and this guy certainly pinged my gaydar.

I sighed as I drove off, thinking I'd given up one more opportunity on this loathsome trip.

The little motel and picturesque town were too modern for this film, but because it was so nicely renovated and accommodating, if all else failed, I could use the little motel as a headquarters. I might find some uses for that motel guy also.

As had been arranged at the party the night before, I walked into the restaurant in Alpine and found my group had already arrived.

During the gala at the national park, I'd managed to meet several of the town's local leaders, including the mayor, sheriff, and the local university's president. I was particularly interested in speaking with him since his school had a bachelor's program for film. If I was lucky I could offset the costs of working in the states by having several students help with the process.

We all got down to business almost immediately, and things were going really well. The university president had even offered his film department's support, which boded well for me. "If they have the skills to help with some of the grunt work, that would be a real boon," I admitted.

The sheriff assured me there were various ranchers and landowners who would be excited to have me film on their property, and he could introduce me to them. We were making good progress, and I was excited about where we were going, when a rather attractive man about my age came over and asked the sheriff if he could speak to him.

Despite my immediate attraction to the stranger, I didn't pay much attention to the man. Instead, I forced myself to focus on the conversation with the councilman, who'd just announced he had a large parcel of land himself that bordered the parks that he'd love to have us use. I really needed land on the river, but I assumed I'd have to use the Mexican side for that, since the park would likely have too many people and new building improvements for me to make the time periods work for the film.

The sheriff came back with a concerned look on his face. He looked back at the ruggedly handsome man who'd initially come over to speak with him and then back at me. He cleared his throat and interrupted my conversation with the councilman. "Mr. Zitlal, may we speak to you for a moment in private?" he asked.

Strange, I thought, but in Mexico I had fans asking for autographs frequently enough. I hadn't acted in my own films in years, but maybe the man was a fan. His blond hair and light skin made me think probably not, but who was I to judge this book by its cover.

The sheriff and man led me outside the building and behind the sheriff's vehicle, which was very private. My immediate thought was this was going to end up being a racist issue. *Shit* was all I could think, before the sheriff spoke.

"Mr. Zitlal, when did you arrive in the area?"

I was confused and shrugged. "I checked into my motel room around noon yesterday. Why? Is there a problem?"

"Well, maybe," he said. "Have you been to the area before?"

"No, this is my first trip to this part of West Texas. I usually work in Mexico, as you know. We are just now considering a film in the US."

The sheriff nodded and looked a little sick at his stomach. That couldn't be good.

He cleared his throat and looked at the man with him again. "Are you sure, Eddie?"

The guy nodded curtly and looked at me in a nasty way.

The sheriff sighed again. "Mr. Crawford here has alleged he saw you on his property the day before yesterday. Said you showed him an area on his ranch he didn't know existed."

I cocked my eyebrow at the man, and shrugged. "My story can be corroborated by my assistant, my family and various people who work for me. It can also be verified by the motel attendant in Alamito. Do you need to speak to them?" I asked.

This time I returned the man's nasty look. I must admit, working in Mexico, I'd avoided the racism that my fellow Latino brothers and sisters had to deal with in the states. This was a first for me, and the experience made me livid.

The sheriff nodded. "If you could, that would help to put this to rest," he said. "Eddie, I'll be in touch as soon as I've verified Mr. Zitlal's story."

The man looked at the sheriff and turned to leave.

As soon as he was out of earshot, I said to myself, but out loud, "Asshole."

The sheriff looked at me. "You've never seen that man before?"

"No, what an ass! Sheriff, how much of this crap..." I waved toward the man. "...will my actors have to deal with here? I'd hoped since this film will bring significant revenue to your area, not to mention increase tourism on both sides of the border, that we'd be given a break from this kind of thing."

The sheriff shook his head. "Mr. Zitlal, I understand how this looks, and I apologize, but you have to understand Brewster County is about fifty percent Latino. Besides, Mr. Crawford's family are Latino themselves, or at least partially. The family is fiercely proud of their heritage. I doubt racism is behind his reaction."

I shook my head. "Then what is it? I sure as hell never went on his land."

"My guess is, he thinks he saw you on his property," he said matter of factly, then he led me back to the table.

After the meeting, I went with the sheriff to the station, and gave him my contact information for the company in Juarez, as well as my assistant and family in El Paso. He also spoke to the motel guy where I was staying. Once they all confirmed my whereabouts up until last night, the sheriff shook his head and apologized. "I'll let him know, but again, these are good people, Mr. Zitlal. They've had a really nasty bout of luck lately. Eddie's cousin was shot last year, which very nearly killed him. The attack seemed completely unprovoked, and could've been a robbery gone bad, but regardless, it's shaken them up quite a bit. I'm willing to bet that's what's behind this."

Then, the man looked at me and shook his head. "Not that my excuses make you feel better. What I'll say to you in no un-certain terms is that you and your film crew would be welcome and even embraced here. You'd bring a little excitement to an otherwise quiet little town."

I nodded, but this had really quashed what little desire I had to work here. I had to admit I'd be lobbying to avoid this place if possible. Not only did we have the pitfalls of government relations, but now some crazy redneck thought he saw me tres-passing on his property.

That afternoon, I went on the tour with the university pres-ident. I didn't let on about the meeting, or problems with the man who'd made the ludicrous allegation. It was always best to be a diplomat in these situations.

The film department was everything I could've hoped for, with numerous students wandering in and out of classes, and plenty of work examples to peruse. Yes, this would've been a dream come true, and when I made my report to my father and the rest of the board, I figured the incident with this Eddie character would be ignored or given less weight quickly enough. Besides, I was just the producer. Most of my work would involve running the behind the scenes aspects of the film. I had people who managed most of the ins and outs of the local issues. Once I had the setting shored up, I'd be able to take more of a back seat.

3

Eddie

SHERIFF WALTERS CAME OUT to the ranch later that day, and asked me to walk with him for a moment. "We checked out his alibi, Eddie. He's telling the truth."

"He's lying, they're all lying. I know what I saw..."

He interrupted me. "No, not all those people are lying, none of them knew we were calling. They all told me the exact same story, Eddie. Even Mitch, at the Alamito, confirmed his story. The only story that doesn't make sense is yours."

I stopped walking and looked at him. "You can say what you want, Sheriff, but I know what I saw. That man was on this damned property, or someone who looks a hell of a lot like him. He was just sitting there when I came around the corner, then he said he had something to show me and took me back into that group of trees. I know I'm a lot of things, but one thing I am not is crazy."

The sheriff laughed. "I don't think you're crazy, maybe a little confused, but you're not crazy. Listen, here's the deal. That man owns a very large production company, and they're looking to do a documentary type film that supports a relationship between the two national parks between Mexico and Big Bend here in the US. This is an international issue, and you interfering could bring a lot of problems down on you and your family."

When I looked at him, he put his hands up, and said, "Not from me. I'm here for y'all and want to catch the son of a bitch that fucked y'all over as much as anyone, but if you cause the area to lose what will likely be a multi-million-dollar deal, not to mention the tourism associated with it, you'll have more enemies than you can shake a stick at."

"What kind of production company?" I asked.

"A film company, they make movies."

I nodded toward the sheriff and we walked back toward his car.

The game began to make sense now. He must've been in costume, and for some reason had picked us as his place to play make-believe. I quickly connected the dots and figured he must have heard the story of Diamondback Jack, and decided he'd play out the scenario himself.

I looked at the back of the sheriff as he walked in front of me, and knew I was barking up the wrong damned tree. No way could I convince him, or even my own family at this point of what I'd seen, so I decided to keep my mouth shut. Well, for now at least, but God help me, I'd keep that scoundrel as far away from my family as I could. I had no idea what devious plot this guy might be cooking up, but I'd be damned if I'd let him take us down. For all I knew, the guy could've been the one who shot Flex, and that made me all the more determined to keep him away from us.

4

Present Day – Eddie

TWO YEARS. TWO LOVELY uneventful years had passed since Flex had been shot. Well, maybe not uneventful. First there was the weird Diamondback Jack incident, but I was convinced now that was just a heartless prank by the film company jerk.

Lander Diez from the *Texas Cowboy* had come to visit, and convinced us to rebuild the old workers' lodge as a hostel-type arrangement for visitors to this part of the world.

Luckily, because Flex hadn't spent all Grandpa's seed money on cattle, there was still plenty of money left to fund the improvements. We began working on the lodge first, which utilized the old foundation from the workers' housing. This created a long narrow building with multiple bedrooms. Of course, nothing was simple when using old things, and we found out almost immediately the sewer system for the entire structure was dead. After renting a backhoe and digging out the old plumbing, we realized it'd be just as easy at this point to add an additional set of RV lots on this side of the building, which would bring us to well over fifty sites.

It was amazing how fast the building went up, and the RV lots were ready for use. Less than six months after beginning work, the lodge was completed. I'd honestly thought it would take a lot more work, but it was pretty cut and dried, and with Flex's boyfriend Mitch's very capable hands, we swept through the building like wildfire.

We decided to christen the lodge late one summer night with a big party. We invited Landon and anyone he wanted to bring with him from the magazine to be our inaugural guests. There was so much whiskey drunk that night, I was happy Mrs. Ruth, Mitch's assistant, had agreed to keep my two boys with her at the motel.

I had just sat down on the porch next to Mitch and Flex, when I looked up just in time to see Lander running across the lawn, naked as the day he was born.

"Whoa, dude, put your fucking clothes on!" I yelled, but the man was too drunk and having too much fun to hear me.

I quickly turned to see how Emma Jean was taking it, but the woman was lying across the swing, literally in Jimmy's lap, laughing so hard, tears were streaming down her face. If her puritan ways could accept this wild party, surely so could I.

I joined the party then and let myself fall into the festivities. Although I kept my clothes on, I enjoyed the stories of how Lander and his friend had visited the clothing-optional Faywood Hot Springs near Deming, New Mexico. Apparently, some dude who looked like a freaking model showed up with his girlfriend, and when she ended up passing out drunk, the model boyfriend rushed over with his ass in the air. "With all the queens in that pool, you'd have thought he'd have been at least aware of what he'd done…"

One of Lander's buddies called out, "I still say he did that on purpose, freaking closet bottoms!"

It was all in good fun since the story ended with the girlfriend recovering, and the model boyfriend winking at the group as he escorted her back to their RV.

I left that first day and joined my kids in one of Mitch's motel rooms. I didn't think the ranch was really an acceptable place to have the boys hanging out, considering how wild it had gotten. I'd need to have a serious conversation with Flex about boundaries for our guests.

When Lander and his crew left, it was with great fanfare. It wasn't more than a few weeks later that the article describing the party in painful detail came out in the magazine. We started getting calls and bookings almost immediately.

After the third big party had occurred spontaneously, I sat Flex, Emma Jean, and Jimmy down for a serious talk about the boys. "I can't have the boys in the middle of all this," I said. "Hell, I walked up on a threesome the other day just outside the house. I personally don't care what people do, but seriously, the boys gotta have some separation from all that."

They all agreed and said they had similar concerns. When I told them I wanted to look at putting a house on the far side of the homestead, just down the road, but still within walking distance of the main house, they all agreed wholeheartedly. Besides, we never planned on keeping the boys under the same roof as Emma Jean and Jimmy anyway. I was sure they wanted to get back to living their own lives.

Surprisingly, Jimmy had other plans. "We've been talkin' about movin' too," he said. "Flex, this property should be somethin' for you and Mitch. You've been generous lettin us stay, but we want to move on and give you yer space."

Emma Jean chimed in, "The only reason we didn't suggest getting a trailer is because I couldn't stand the thought of not having the boys to look after, but Eddie, if you're really gonna consider building your own home, would you consider building it as a duplex? Jimmy and I could pay to have our part built with the money we got back from you mom." She cringed a bit like she always did when she had to discuss her with us.

My mother had taken rent money from them when the property was in dispute with Flex, and the judge had just ordered her to pay them back. I could almost hear her screaming from here.

"We could also pay rent," Emma Jean continued, "now that you're paying us for working here. This is where we'd like to spend our final days anyway, and now that the two boys are back here, we can't imagine not being a part of their daily lives."

I looked at Flex and back at Emma Jean and Jimmy. "I-I would love that, but I thought you'd be tired of us by now."

Emma Jean looked confused. "Why would we be tired of you? You're the best thing that's happened to us in a very long time. Honey, we thrive on the life of this ranch. Now that you boys have turned it into a place where people can come and enjoy it, that's something we can't imagine not being a part of. Ain't that right, Jimmy?"

Jimmy was grinning from ear to ear. "It's like watching one of them ol' shows where they renovate an old house and turn it back into somethin beautiful. We sure do wanna be a part of that," he said.

"Well, if that's for sure what you want, we'll start looking up designs and maybe hire an architect to draw them out. If Mitch can help, I'm sure he and I can build it."

That was how the magic began. My heart was filled with joy every freaking day as I woke up in the mornings, excited to be back here and putting my own touches on the place. I caught myself singing as I prepped for the morning chores, and would come back just as happy as we got the boys off to school. Life was finally what I'd hoped it'd be. I was so content, it was hard to keep myself from singing at the top of my lungs day and night.

Flex would officially take over our grandparents' house, and manage the day-to-day movements between the RV park and the lodge. Jimmy and I would manage the cattle, and keep an eye on people who were in the backcountry.

Since business was also booming and revenue flowed into the property from visitors, we were able to put aside a huge chunk of profit to ensure we remained financially solvent. That ended up being a wise decision, because after the success of our first year, Lander Diez got a job writing for one of the larger gay magazines in California. Our source of free promotional articles about the gay outdoorsmen's paradise had dried up.

Our bookings fell from full with a waiting list, to less than a third full. Maybe our luck had dried up, and although the new duplex was finished and we had a nice nest egg, we found ourselves back at square one.

5

Alex

THE ISSUE OF FILMING across the two national parks became a war between my father and me. I argued, albeit unconvincingly, that trying to film in both countries would be a logistical nightmare.

I did manage to distract my dad with two other films that had been in the works for a while. One in the jungle surrounding the Mayan ruins of Palenque, and the other, a sort of follow up to that one, on Cozumel Island. Luckily, this allowed me to avoid the Rio Grande project, as my father called it, for quite a while.

However, after finishing that last film, my father met me on the island with the Minister of Natural Protection, as well as the new minister for the Canon de Santa Elena park. The Canon de Santa Elena minister wanted the film to be a way to ease relations between the two countries.

"¡Es exactamente lo que necesitamos en este momento!" he said emphatically.

I repeated it in English. "Exactly what we need at this moment," I said, aware I'd already lost the fight. Not only did I have one of the most influential politicians in Mexico, the Minister of Natural Protection, putting pressure on me, but I also had my father, owner and CEO of the company, riding my ass over it. I might as well put my cowboy boots on now and get it over with. I was gonna film in West Texas, like it or not.

Our strategy meeting went well. I shared with them that we'd need to find a place to put our headquarters, and hopefully do a lot of filming there too. We'd likely be able to use the studio at the university, but those resources were limited as well, and the area was way too modern to film on location.

I warned my team to be on the lookout for any international tension. Things had gotten worse since I'd visited the region. Deportation was at an all-time high, and we expected to deal with some chaos from the border patrol. Hopefully, none of my stars would get deported. Mexicans were very tolerant of the US, but send one of their beloved stars home in disgrace, and it could lead to war.

I mentioned the crazy cowboy, and several of my assistants nodded. They'd all had to deal with them on both sides of the Mexico/US line. "We'll be fine," they told us.

"We're used to navigating the international line," my assistant, who worked primarily in Juarez, told me. "Just trust us to navigate them. If we have a problem, we'll come find you."

I nodded. They were probably right, I wasn't experienced in this arena, but if shit hit the fan, I'd be the man to climb the political chain, on either side of the line.

Next was my trip back to the park. I had my assistant book me into the same motel, mostly to keep me on neutral ground between the two countries, then I set up all the appointments.

I also needed to secure the relationship with the university. We'd do most of our filming over the winter break to take advantage of the students being on break, but also the heat of the summer.

I called the sheriff and asked if he'd be willing to introduce me to those ranchers of his. I assumed we'd have to set up tents, since I doubted there'd be any accommodation suitable for this kind of production out in the countryside.

He was genuinely pleased to hear from me, which was a relief. I needed local law enforcement on our side, in case anything got out of hand. After my first visit, that was a distinct possibility.

With my itinerary lined out, I packed my bags, mourning the fact that it'd be a long time until I found the comforts of my own bed again. If all went as planned, I'd have a few months to find accommodation, negotiate agreements, and get contracts signed.

The same little charming motel greeted me upon my arrival. This time a totally different man met me at the front desk, taller, darker. I could happily roll in the hay with this one as well.

I flirted, testing my gaydar vibe, which had always been one-hundred-percent correct. The guy did smile at me, but as he rummaged through the paperwork for me to sign, he said, "My *boyfriend,* Mitch, will be here this afternoon. He's the owner. I'm just filling in for him."

It was an off-the-cuff comment, but the message was clear. *I'm taken.*

Well, shit. Zero for two. I'd already opened my Grindr and laughed when first there was little to no coverage at all, and when I finally got the app to open, well, let's just say there was more than one kind of desert out here.

I left the handsome man alone and decided to walk around the little motel. I could see us setting up camp here, but I doubted the owner would want us to monopolize the entire motel for the time we were filming. Usually, those situations ended on bad terms with the owners. They were flush with our cash for a time, then when we left, they were deserted. Not only that, but actors were pains in the ass. They often needed significant attention to be happy, and small motels didn't have the necessary capabilities to stroke overly inflated egos with their often over-the-top demands.

The motel was very nice, though, with cute gardens using native species. More rooms had been renovated than I'd seen during my last stay here. The RV court attached to the motel was off to the side, and really couldn't be seen by the other guests.

I laughed when I walked up to the chicken pen. Dang, you might be able to take the Texas out of Mexico, but you couldn't take the Mexico out of Texas. I'm sure there were plenty of Texans who'd disagree, but a motel with chickens was more Mexico than Texas for sure.

I liked the little place, and if by the time we were done filming, if I didn't hate the area, I'd consider filming a more modern piece here. This motel, for example, was a perfect setting for a telenovela. I could almost see the dialogue between distraught lovers under the arches leading into the cute courtyard, or a bitter slap backdropped by the old covered wagon.

I walked back into the courtyard just as the handsome boyfriend and the guy I now assumed was the motel's owner, came out hand in hand. It really was sweet, the two of them moony-eyed over each other. I wondered if I could somehow incorporate them into my story. Two men, one very Anglo-Texan, the other definitely had signs of Latino in his family's history.

"Do either of you speak Spanish?" I asked as they approached me.

Both men laughed and the motel owner stated in Spanish, "Everyone here speaks Spanish, or else they alienate half the community."

I cocked an eyebrow. "I'm from El Paso, and it's right on the border. Most Anglo-Texans can't speak much."

"Things are different here, we've been more... integrated," the owner, Mitch, said smiling.

I returned his smile. "As you know, I'm Alexandro Zitlal. I'm here scouting out locations to film our next movie."

Both men looked at each other shocked. "You're going to film a movie in Alamito?" the tall, dark one, I don't think he told me his name, asked.

I laughed. "No, probably not. The setting is the Mexican and US national parks both across the Rio Grande from each other. I'm hoping to find a location where I'd be able to film without having to navigate all the red tape. Do either of you have any suggestions?"

"Did my cousin set you up to this?"

"Um, no. I'm not sure who your cousin is," I replied. The clearly thought this was a joke. "I assure you, I'm not joking, my primary job over the next few weeks is to identify a location where we can film, hopefully over the holidays."

"I may have something that'll work, but I'll need to know more about your needs," he said. "Will you be needing a large facility? What are your ideal accommodations?"

"Usually, I'd find a nice hotel to put my staff and actors in, I was considering this one, but I'd prefer to be on location, if at all possible. If there was a place that met our needs, I could possibly incorporate a tent camp for my crew. However, I'll warn you, I've only just begun my search. The ideal place would be bordered by the river, so we can take the river scenes on private land instead of in the park."

Both men laughed again. "Are you sure you weren't sent as a joke? Is there a hidden camera somewhere?"

I shook my head, and this time reached inside my pocket, pulled out my card and handed it to the tall man. "You can see, I'm legit."

"I'll tell you what, meet us tomorrow morning for breakfast at an address I'll give you. You can tour the property I own, and if it meets your needs, we can talk further."

I smiled, might as well jump in the deep end of the pool. "Sure, that sounds good. What's the address?"

I typed it into my GPS as the man spoke. "What are your names?" I asked.

"Oh, sorry, I thought we'd told you. I'm Flex Henry and this is Mitch Armstrong. Mitch owns the motel, and I own a ranch between here and the national park."

"And you have land that borders the Rio Grande?" I asked.

The man nodded. "It's technically shared between the Texas Wildlife Preserve and us, but I have use of the property, as long as I don't go duck hunting without notifying them."

I laughed. "Well, if what you say is true, this may be serendip-itous."

The guy shrugged. "Maybe. You can see tomorrow."

"Oh, make sure you have the directions downloaded because there is absolutely no mobile coverage on the ranch. In fact, you'll have to go up to the hotel in Big Bend if you want cov-erage after leaving here. Keep that in mind if you're considering bringing in a large number of actors."

I laughed. "If I could get rid of their mobile phones, I'd prob-ably get done filming in half the time."

Both men nodded as if they understood, then saying their goodbyes, disappeared back into the office.

I had serious doubts the place would meet my needs, but it was good to be looking for a location right off the bat. I still thought, besides the political headache between the two governments, the next biggest issue was finding a location. If this property was indeed bordered by the Rio Grande, I could see if we could do the river scenes there. That alone would save me an intense headache.

6

Eddie

F LEX AND MITCH DROVE up to the house and honked. The boys ran out to meet them, pulling them both into a bear hug. Since we'd moved into the duplex, the boys had really missed spending as much time with their uncles.

"Hey," Flex said, pulling me into a hug as he walked up to me. "Where's Jimmy and Emma Jean? I have some news that might be worth hearing."

"We're here," Emma Jean said, as they came out of their side of the newly built duplex.

"Which of you want to host a party? I have news to share."

Emma Jean smiled and looked at the boys, then up at me. "I'm guessing you'd like us to host, since you and the boys still look like you're living out of your boxes," she said.

"Hey, not fair judging, I have a lot more to unpack and these rug rats aren't very helpful," I said, rubbing their heads.

I nodded toward Emma Jean and Jimmy's side of the build-ing. "If you don't mind, Emma Jean, it'd definitely be more comfortable there."

As we settled in, Flex leaned back in Emma Jean's comfort-able, yet dated, couch she'd pulled out of the storage shed when they moved into their side of the duplex.

"We invited a movie producer to come see the ranch tomor-row morning," Flex began. "He's looking for a property that borders the Rio, but doesn't belong to the park service."

I immediately became suspicious. "What does this producer look like?" I asked.

"I don't know," Flex said. "About my height, Mexican-Amer-ican, really attractive."

I stood up and walked toward the door. "Where're you go-ing?" Flex asked.

"I think we're being played," I said. "That's the son…" I looked at the kids catching myself. "That's the guy I ran into that'd been traipsing around our property."

"You mean when you saw Diamondback Jack?" Jimmy asked.

"Allegedly, however, as I told y'all then, when I saw him at the diner in Alpine, I knew then and there, that was the guy I saw."

Flex looked at Mitch, and asked, "Did you get any weird vibes from him?"

Mitch looked at the kids and then back at us. "Not those kinds of vibes."

Flex laughed. "Oh, well, yeah, he was definitely a player, but he turned out to be harmless."

"Perception isn't always as it appears," I argued.

The kids had already lost interest, and both got up to leave, as they'd become accustomed to doing lately. Emma Jean was trying to break them of the behavior, encouraging them to excuse themselves, but sensing we needed to have an adult conversation, she let them wander off.

Jimmy waited 'til they were gone, and asked, "I thought it was the general belief that the guy who shot Flex was probably that ol' Baptist pastor from Alamito."

"That hasn't been confirmed yet, and I'd rather be too safe than sorry. I have precious cargo here to protect," I said, looking back at the door my kids had just walked out of.

Flex sighed. "Well, I agree we need to be careful. Since last time you met the guy, you and he left on less than friendly terms. Let's just play this by ear. Jimmy, Mitch, and I can meet him in the morning. We'll take turns asking him questions and getting a better handle on him. If he likes the property and wants to rent it, we'll go through all the proper investigative channels to make sure he is who he says he is."

Emma Jean smiled too. "Y'all need a woman in on this too. Men always underestimate what a woman can learn from a man, especially if he's hungry. I'll go over to your place tomorrow morning, Flex, and prepare breakfast. I'll be able to get a handle on him as well.

I didn't like it. I'd have preferred they kicked the man to the curb and be done with it, but same as last time, I was clearly outnumbered. That didn't mean I wouldn't be a stubborn mule when it came time to defend my people, even if the man wooed them like he had the townsfolk.

I went to bed right after settling the boys into theirs. Now that we were in our own homes, I'd begun missing the companionship of Emma Jean, Jimmy, and Flex. Living together had been a blessing to me and the boys. I'd watched them blossom under Emma Jean's care and having Flex back in their life was like a boost of caffeine. For the first time in a very long time, I could tell my boys were feeling like they fit somewhere, that they had a place where they belonged.

I fell asleep thinking about them and about our situation here on the ranch.

It seemed as if I'd just dropped off when I saw it slithering around the back part of the ranch. I couldn't quite make it out, it was dark, and the creature was black, but I knew from Flex's description of the dream he'd had before that the thing in my dream was the same large serpent he'd described.

I squatted in the underbrush downwind of it, hoping it wouldn't know I was watching. The moon was out, and I was able to tell where I was. The clearing. I was in the clearing I'd found when that movie guy had shown me where to look. I could see in through the thicket, but the snake didn't seem to know I was there.

Behind me a man whispered, and I startled. "He's back, but this time he's not alone."

I turned around and saw the guy from before wearing the same clothes he'd wore that day, but instead of a young face, his was older, mid-fortyish. I forgotten that part when I'd confronted the movie guy.

"You'll need his help. You can't fight this level of hatred alone, trust the one who comes today, he said as he slowly vanished before me.

When I looked back toward the serpent, it too was gone, and I was alone in the clearing beside the volcano.

I woke up thinking about the dream. What did this mean? I was sure when Flex told me about his dream that it was one of the premonitions my grandmother used to talk about. Whoever owned the land was given the gift of prophetic dreams. It was what she called our heritage gift. But, I wasn't the owner of the property, I was Flex's contractual partner. The land belonged to him.

I got up, knowing I was pretty much done with sleep for now, and made a cup of coffee. I sat and thought about the dream. *"Trust the one who comes today."*

It didn't click who that could be. I shrugged it off. More likely than not, this was a symptom of having too much on my mind, worrying about my boys losing what they'd learned to treasure. Hell, what we'd all learned to treasure since moving here.

I took a deep breath and decided to welcome the early morning with a horse ride toward the volcano. If there was any sign of the man who'd hurt Flex, I'd like to know that right now. I had a few hours before I had to be back to get the kids ready for school.

I saddled old Red, who'd become my horse. When we built the duplex, I'd talked Mitch into helping me put up a makeshift stable to keep a horse here close to the house. I was continually thankful I'd thought of that, because I ended up using Red more and more to work the cattle. I also kept an older bay we bought the same time we'd purchased Red to keep her company, and for the kids to use as they learned to become horse owners.

I neared the volcano and dismounted Red, tying her to a branch out of sight from the hidden clearing next to the mountainside.

I crept around to where I'd seen the serpent in my dream. There were no footprints and no evidence that anything had been here. The early morning light from the rising sun wasn't that bright, but it was enough that I could've seen evidence of any recent activity in this part of the property. Not only was the ground dusty, but it'd been a very long time since we'd had any rain. So, footprints would've shown well.

"Guess it was only a dream," I said out loud.

"Dreams are often valuable things," the voice said, and I startled, angry I'd left my gun back with the horse, and ready to defend myself with my hands if I had to. "Settle down, man, you act as if you're facing a ghost," he said, and chuckled.

When I turned, the same older man from my dream stood before me.

"Who are you?" I asked, my heart beating out of my chest.

"I told you, I was hired by your grandfather to guard the place. I'm doing my job." I looked down at the ground where the man stood, but there were no footprints. He followed my gaze and laughed. "You know my secret now," he said, and chuckled again. He looked at me then and squinted against the sun that had just crested the ridge. "You don't trust many people, *campion*, but the time for you to learn is now. If you don't accept the changes coming and don't let yourself trust, both yours and mine will be in danger. Mine will come today. You *must* let him in!"

He looked over at the sun again and when I followed his gaze, I saw it had crested the top of the ridge just enough to shine across the earth toward where we stood. When I looked back, the man was gone. A chill spread through me as I looked at where he'd stood moments before. There were no footprints in the dust. I'd either just seen a ghost, or I was going insane. At this point, I was pretty sure either could be the case.

Everything in me wanted to run from the place, but the spirit had told me to trust. Trust began with the entity, I got that, but did he mean I should trust the guy I thought looked like him—the one I'd have been willing to bet money *was* him?

"Diamondback Jack," I said the name out loud, but got no response. Even the strange sensations that had surrounded me moments before leveled out, as the newly-risen sun's rays began to warm the earth around me.

I walked toward my horse, climbed up, and looked back again toward where I'd seen the serpent in my dream, and where I'd seen Diamondback Jack moments before. Something told me I'd see no evidence of either, no matter how hard I looked. So, I pulled Red toward the front paddock and did my morning chores, riding the fences before I went back to the house and my kids. Seemed like I had an appointment with our guest after all.

Flex would be pissed that I'd shown up, but after he heard about my morning visitor, I was sure he'd forgive me. Now, the man I'd accused of trespassing, that was a different story.

7

Alex

I WOKE UP IN a great mood, like something important was about to happen.

I showered, brushed my teeth, and instead of wearing the Armani suit I preferred when visiting potential partners or vendors, I threw on my favorite jeans and a button-down shirt I'd decided would fit in better with this part of Texas.

I stopped by the front desk, and when I saw Mitch coming out of the office, I asked if he'd like to ride out with me this morning.

"I'd like to, but I have a ton of crap to catch up on here. Flex could probably give you a ride out there, though. He's just getting ready to leave. I think he's planning to come back here this afternoon anyway. He owes me several favors after he worked my ass off down at his ranch. I plan to check in one of those favors tonight," he said, and winked at me.

I was a man who loved sex. I blamed the Latin blood in me for also being an avid romantic. I tried to keep my life full of love and beautiful men, but the way this man winked at me caused me to blush. Seeing the kind of love that was obvious between these two, seemed more intimate, more private than the kind of stuff I got up to.

Flex came out of the back office almost instantly, and my blush deepened when he winked at and kissed his man in front of me. Something inside me churned, seeing this kind of affection. Almost—not quite, but almost—making me crave something similar for myself.

I shook my head dramatically. "You two are making me have strange, uncomfortable thoughts about getting tied down. I ask you to stop that instantly, before I catch whatever illness has caused you to be all... committed."

Both men chuckled. "Love has a tendency to slip up on you, don't be surprised if it isn't lurking around the corner even as we speak," Mitch said.

I jumped, again being dramatic, and glanced quickly outside, like there was someone coming to get me.

Both men laughed as I hoped they would.

Mitch asked Flex when he planned to be back, and Flex smiled. "Don't worry, I'll be back soon. A promise is a promise, my love."

Mitch blushed this time, and asked, "Do you want to drive our guest here to the ranch and show him around? You can bring him back with you unless you have a lot of chores to handle before you return."

Flex looked at me. "I do have a few things to attend to. We have a party coming from Houston this weekend, and I need to make sure the lodge is up to par. Maybe Jimmy, our caretaker, can give you an extended tour, though, while I work on getting things ready."

The lodge was an interesting twist on things. Last night they hadn't told me much about the place we were going to. I didn't assume there'd be much in the way of accommodation, but if they had a lodge and guests coming to stay in it, that could improve the prospects of using the ranch.

"I can happily entertain myself while you finish your chores," I said. "It'll be good to see the countryside we're going to be filming in. I'll just go back to the room and change these shoes for some hiking boots."

"We have horses," Flex said, as I turned around. "If you have cowboy boots, that'd be even better."

I laughed. "I should've brought a pair. My hiking boots do hang up in the stirrups. Maybe I should wear these, after all. I foolishly didn't come prepared to ride."

"Well, if you're gonna be looking at ranches, you may need to get a pair of proper riding boots. Most ranch owners have switched to ATVs, but some of us still prefer the horse for getting around, especially in the mountainous areas."

I nodded and agreed to meet him at his truck, which he'd pointed out to me before I left.

I went to my car, pulled out my water bottle and found a hat in the back seat. No, it wasn't a cowboy hat, although that would've probably been better out in the searing heat, the ball cap would have to do for now. I'd have to have my assistant send more appropriate gear out to me. I didn't know why I didn't think about what would be needed. I'd grown up in West Texas, and even though we spent most of our time traveling around Mexico, I still understood the need for a wide-brimmed hat and cowboy boots in the desert.

Flex and I chatted all the way to the ranch. The countryside was as beautiful as I remembered from my visit before. Desolate planes interrupted by the occasional mountain. Most of them on the smaller side, but some of them quite significant. All decorated with various desert colors reminiscent of the Southwest.

When we got to the ranch, I was already transfixed by the beauty of the place. The small house sat nestled in among cottonwood trees, which was unusual for this part of the country. The contrast between the tree-surrounded house plot and the nearby desert made it that much more appealing to the eye.

I noticed off to the side, and further back behind the home, a long structure that looked like a modern version of the buildings used to house cowboys in the past. I'd seen several of these around El Paso, but they were always dilapidated, and most had long ago been torn down.

There was a large, modern barn structure behind the home as well, but the sides had been covered in old wooden slats that helped it feel like it belonged in among the older buildings. I turned after getting out of the truck, and could see various old outbuildings, some in rough shape, but most still appeared to be in use. The entire look made the area feel welcoming, like it all belonged in this arid part of the world.

Flex walked toward the door of the main house, a structure that looked like it'd been built in the early part of the twentieth century, with a wide front porch and beautiful wooden front door.

Once on the porch, I heard the cows moo just as a woman opened the door. She wore an old-fashioned dress and apron, and I felt as if I'd slipped back in time. So far, it felt perfect for what I was looking for.

The woman's smile was broad and welcomed us in. When we were in the main room, she introduced herself and her husband, Jimmy, then she looked at Flex, and said, "The other owner will be coming by to meet you later this morning. He has to get his kids off to school first."

Something passed between the woman and Flex which I couldn't quite read. I was sure it had to do with the other owner, but I wasn't sure what it meant.

We had a huge breakfast with biscuits, gravy, and all the things you'd imagine a ranch cook on this side of the border would cook. The food was good, and I was stuffed by the time we were done.

We helped the cook—Emma Jean, she said her name was—clean up, and then Flex took me over to the long building out back to show me what he called the lodge. I was shocked when I walked in. The lodge had been built to look old on the outside, but when you went inside, it was modern and clean. There was a big room in the middle, with tables and a big television over what appeared to be a gas fireplace.

On either side of the main room were hallways that led to rooms of the same size, each filled with bunk beds. Some had two, others had three or four.

"We're technically a hostel, and cater to people who want a place to sleep before going into the backcountry to explore. Most of our visitors who use this building tend to hike the park, though, and not our ranch.

We looked into several of the rooms as we walked toward a door that led outside. When we exited, Flex showed me they had over fifty RV spots available to rent. Each one was graveled, and he assured me they were all full hookups with fifty-amp service.

We walked over to what appeared to be an old shed, but when he opened the door, I saw it was a shower house, separated for women on one side and men on the other. "These are rough ac-commodations," he said. "Most of our customers are gay men, to be honest, or have been up until recently, so we didn't really need to divide the stalls out as much as we will now. Each area has a communal shower and three bathroom stalls. Mostly, it's where our backcountry folks can come in and shower, and clean up after they've been out exploring the territory. We also have several people who've been staying in the park use this to clean up as well."

I was already mentally placing my crew in various sites around the property. I could easily rent several luxury RVs for my actors. The lodge was more than adequate to fit the needs of my other staff, though we might need to upgrade the mattresses and get some higher grade sheets and blankets, but we'd stayed in far worse over the years in Mexico.

I had to figure out where to put the main headquarters, and technically, that could be a tent. I could put it next to the shower house, so we had restrooms. Now, I needed to see the property itself to determine if I could use it as a place to film some of our other scenes as well. Of course, since over half of the movie was going to be filmed on or around the Rio Grande, I hoped this area would be adequate for our needs. I'd need to see that first before I began any negotiations.

We walked toward the main house, my mind buzzing like it did with plans to fit my crew in and make the accommodations work, so I wasn't paying much attention to everything around me.

When we came up to the porch, I saw Flex pause, then walk up toward the house. I looked up, and right into the face of the man who'd accused me of trespassing when I'd come to the area just over a year ago.

"Fuck," I said out loud, not giving a damn if either of the men heard me.

I looked at Flex and asked, "Is this the other owner your housekeeper was talking about?"

Flex nodded.

"Does he live here?" I asked.

Again, Flex nodded.

"I'll be in the truck," I said, and turned to head back toward the vehicle. *Damn, I should've driven myself.* Why did I let this happen? Well, I could just sit in the damned truck all day if I had to.

8

Eddie

W ELL, THAT WENT BETTER than I expected." Well, all except for the look of contempt my cousin was sending my way.

"We agreed you wouldn't show up until we had a chance to get to know him better," Flex said under his breath. The way Flex's jaw clenched, and the fact that he had to force himself to open his fist, told me my cousin would really love to lay into me.

"I know," I said as we watched the guy walk toward and then get into Flex's truck. "I had... well, I had a dream. I'll explain later, but it caused me to, um... change my mind. I had to come today, Flex. Give me a chance to make this right. You can bust my nose later if you want to, provided I don't convince him to trust us."

Flex gave me a final look, then walked into the house. "You'd better fix this, Eddie," he said.

Never in my life, at least that I can remember, had Flex called me Eddie. It was always Effie, the nickname I got when we were both little, and he couldn't pronounce my name. The fact he called me by my name and not the nickname sent shockwaves through me. I don't think he'd ever been that mad at me before. "Diamondback, you'd better have my back on this one," I whispered, as I walked toward the truck.

The man ignored me as I stood outside the vehicle. The temperature was nearing a hundred, but he sat behind the glass. It would've been funny if I didn't have so much at stake.

"Listen, I understand why you're angry with me. Hell, I'd be pissed if I were in your shoes, but you don't understand how bad things were back then. I'd seen a stranger on my property who looked a hell of a lot like you, and that was after my cousin had been shot and almost killed."

The guy said something that I didn't quite grasp behind the window.

"Sorry, I didn't catch that," I said, and the man opened the door.

"I said, you think all Mexican people look alike?"

I laughed in spite of myself. "You can't tell it, but my grandmother was Mexican, as was my grandfather's mother, so no, that isn't really my problem."

The man looked at me funny. "So, you're telling me, you really thought I'd come onto your land?"

"That's exactly what I'm saying, and, dude, the man looked just like you, except he wore old-fashioned clothes and was dirty as hell. When the sheriff told me you were with a film company that just made me more suspicious. I'd decided you were wearing a costume. I was convinced you were my guy, until recently."

"What changed your mind?" the guy asked me.

"Well, let's just say the spirit moved me," I said. "Anyway, I'm sorry, and if you'll let me give you a tour of the property, if you still hate me when we're done, I promise I'll stay as far away from you and your production the entire time you're here."

"You probably just want to take me to the back of your ranch and throw me face down into the Rio."

I laughed. "You have a vivid imagination."

"It's what I'm paid for," he said as he climbed out of the truck. "But, here's the deal. I don't trust you and I don't like you, but since I'm stuck here without a vehicle or mobile service, I'll have to take my chances. However, if you try anything, know I'll fight back, and I intend to hurt you, even if you're able to take me down."

I laughed. "Okay, I promise, you will get back in one piece. I'll guard you with my life, Scout's honor," I said, holding up three fingers.

"Scout's honor? I'm sure that's what all the serial killers say."

"Come on in the house. Can you ride a horse?" I asked.

The man looked me up and down. "Texas State Equestrian Champion. Twice," he said, stressing both words as if I'd challenged his manhood just by asking the question. Well, arrogance was never something that bothered me, luckily.

"If you want to go inside and hang out, I'll saddle your horse for you."

Again he looked me up and down. "Not likely, I'll saddle my own horse, thank you very much."

I let Flex and the others know we were leaving, and grabbed a radio just in case. Flex said before I left, clearly still miffed, "Take care of him, Effie. He could be a gold mine for us, and we need the income. He wants to see where our land meets the river. Take him there first, then around toward the buttes. That's one of the most picturesque areas we have on the ranch. On your way back, take him by the volcano. Those could all be nice sites for him to film on the ranch."

The mention of the volcano sent chills up my spine, but I nodded.

As I headed out, Emma Jean said, "Take plenty of water. It's supposed to be a scorcher today."

"I'll fill four of our canteens," I told her. "Two for him, two for me."

She nodded. "Should be enough," she said.

Jimmy came over, a worried look on his face. "Want me to ride out with ya?"

Jimmy's back had been hurting him lately, and we all agreed to try to reduce the amount of riding he'd be doing. "No, Jimmy,

I'd rather you stay here and keep the radio close in case I need to call you about something."

He nodded, but I could tell he was relieved I didn't need him. It always sucked to see your heroes get older.

I came back out with the canteens filled with water and handed two to the already-mounted movie man and took two over to Red, securing them next to my saddle. I was a bit surprised that he found his way to the stables behind the house and saddled his own choice of the horses there.

I decided not to comment on his making himself at home with the horses. I'd left Red saddled after the morning ride, thank goodness, or I'm sure he'd have decided to pick her, since she was the best-looking animal in the stables, I was about to climb on Red when I noticed the man was only wearing a ball cap. "If you go out there in that, you're gonna have a nasty sunburn before we get back," I said.

The guy looked at me with scorn. "I didn't bring a different hat. I'll be fine."

I walked Red toward the barn, and came back with a relatively new cowboy hat we'd bought for our guests to wear when they were headed out into the backcountry. It was straw and cheap as fuck, but it'd keep the sun off his neck and ears, the two areas that wouldn't fare well if he didn't wear it.

When I took it to him, he shook his head, but I didn't move until he put it on.

"Much prettier," I teased, getting another nasty look from guy. He clearly wasn't used to being teased, nor was he used to wearing cheap-ass cowboy hats. Something about that gave me a perverse joy, although I was supposed to be making nice.

"I'm Eddie," I told him as we rode down the main road that skirted the border between the national park and our property. He didn't respond with his name which also made me chuckle to myself. I knew he was Alex from talking to Flex about him the night before.

This area wasn't particularly picturesque, but it had a higher elevation, so when we got closer to them, he'd get a good view of the buttes off in the distance. I thought it would be good for him to see them from a distance *and* close up. This was also the best route to the river.

When we crossed into the preserve, I explained that we had a partnership with the state for this part of the property. "Back in the twenties, my great-grandparents had gone to war with the state. They were trying to take this part of the land in eminent domain. They settled by making it a partnership. My family have always been conservationists, even before it became popular. So creating this part of the property as a preserve made sense to them. We still officially own the land, and can give you permission to use it if you want, although it's also linked permanently with the preserve."

We rode a piece further and the Rio Grande came into view. From up here, it looked like a snake winding itself through the desert. We'd ridden almost as far as the river, when I pointed out the little adobe building off to the side, under an old cottonwood tree. "That's the original homestead on this property. I don't even know how many great-relatives it is, but way back there, my ancestor came here, married an Apache woman and built this little adobe hut on a little stream that seems to come and go when it chooses."

We got off our horses and I warned him to keep an eye out for snakes. "This place has always been bad for rattlers. The adobe's roof long ago fell in, and one of my ancestors or their workers must have removed it, but you could look inside the front door. With a new roof, it could still be used as a home, if you didn't care about any modern amenities."

I looked around the homestead and sighed happily, "I used to come down here and sit inside the little building and think about all my ancestors who used to live in this place. Sometimes it's like their spirits are lurking around, but it feels good, like they're happy to see you."

When we walked in, the man sat down on the cool floor, and looked up and around the little room. I sat across from him, enjoying the space as well. I hadn't been back down here since we'd come to live at the ranch. For the life of me, I couldn't think why I'd left it so long. It'd always been my favorite place on the ranch.

"So, your roots are deep in this part of the world?" the guy asked me.

"Yeah," I replied. "Been here since after the American Civil War."

"You said your ancestor was Apache?" he asked.

"Yeah, story goes both of my ancestors were captives of the Comanche, who pretty much ruled the place at the time. They fell in love while in captivity, and when they were released they took ownership of this land, and we've been here ever since."

"Damn," the man replied. "And I thought my family history in West Texas was long."

"Really, what part?" I asked.

"El Paso mostly, but in this area as well," he said. "Mi abuelo told stories of a man who lived in these parts. He was hired to guard a gold mine from some nasty bandits. They ended up killing him in the end, but of course, in typical old Western story style, he killed them before they did him in," the guy chuckled, but I had a feeling I knew who his ancestor was.

"By any chance was your ancestor's name Diamondback Jack?" I asked.

The man stopped laughing and looked at me strangely. "Why do you ask?"

"Well, let's just say my family has a similar legend, but it was our gold mine he was guarding."

The guy stood up and walked toward the little room's front door. I got up to follow him, ran into his back, and had to put my arms around him to keep from pushing him out the door.

That's when I heard the threatening rattle. I eased him back into the little room and behind the wall.

Damned if it wasn't a giant diamondback rattlesnake staring me right in the face.

I spoke quietly to the snake, moving back as I did. "When did you come up?" I asked. Through the years, I'd watched both my grandfather and even Jimmy practice talking soothingly to a rattler as they moved away from it—almost a Texas-style of snake charming. I modeled the same behavior as I scooted away from in front of the door. When I was out of the snake's view, I realized I was standing right in front of the man. He was taller than me, but he was still close enough that I could smell coffee, mixed with a minty aroma that must have been his toothpaste. The fear of the snake caused my heart to beat faster, but being this close to him had racked the beats up significantly more.

I had been celibate since my wife had left four years earlier, my only companion being my right hand. In all that time, I hadn't felt even the slightest attraction to women or men, until now.

I pushed away, thinking I'd be better off facing that rattlesnake than this, whatever this attraction was.

When I looked back around the corner, the snake was gone, like it'd never been there. Something told me my friend Diamondback Jack was having a little fun at our expense, but I kept that thought to myself.

9

Alex

I HADN'T THOUGHT THE guy was gay or bisexual or any-thing really. My anger at him had hidden any gaydar that might've given me a warning before we took to the horses.

The snake had scared the shit out of me, but the second that man had slipped in front of me, my fear shifted to lust. He moved me safely out of the path of the snake, distracting it with himself. Had the animal struck, it would have gone for him instead of me. That was an act of chivalry that you only saw in the movies.

When he eased himself in front of me, I'd already turned around, and found myself looking down at his pouty, delicious-looking mouth. I almost leaned down to kiss it. Maybe it was the mix of emotions, fear to anger, then to curiosity. I'd been angry that maybe he was manipulating me about my ancestor, then my fear of the snake, but I wanted to taste this man more than I thought I'd ever wanted to taste another man's mouth in a long, long time.

He pulled away, though, and after looking outside and seeing the snake was gone, he disappeared fast enough to let me know he didn't fancy a roll in the hay, or cacti, or whatever they rolled in in this part of the world.

We climbed on our horses again without speaking, and rode less than a mile up to the Rio Grande. I'd never been to this part of the river before. The part that ran through El Paso was mostly empty, and I guessed I'd figured it'd be about the same here, but instead it was beautiful. The river flowed like a proper river, almost like a mountain stream. From where we stood, it ran into the national park.

Before I knew what was happening, Eddie was stripping off his clothes, and I just caught a glimpse of a perfectly formed ass before he leaped into the water.

"Come on in and cool off," he said, and fuck if I was going to wait for him to ask again. I was in the water in less than ten seconds, and moving as fast as I could to get over to him. The moment I reached him, I thought about pulling him into a kiss. I was still pondering it when he splashed me with water and swam away. The water wasn't deep, but there were deep spots, and you could tell at times the river ran deeper than now, but it wasn't something to be too concerned about. I swam after him, and before long we were splashing each other and laughing like a couple of schoolboys. There was a nice rock ledge that lined the water's edge, and Eddie crawled out onto it and lay back, his gorgeous, runner's build, muscular body sprawled out for me to see. It was almost like looking at one of the European sculptures of male nudes, except this one had an ample package.

I looked away, knowing if I had a hard-on, I wouldn't be able to hide it very well when I came out of the water stark naked, and I didn't know if this guy was straight or gay, closeted or... well, there were too many unknowns.

I came over, but not too close to him, and lay out on the rock myself.

"I had no idea this area was so beautiful and serene," I said.

"My favorite part of the world," Eddie replied. "Not that I've seen that much of the world."

I leaned up on my shoulder, willing myself not to look at his perfectly formed cock. "You haven't traveled much?" I asked.

"He looked over at me and smiled. "Nope, I became a father at eighteen and a husband before that. I haven't done much but try to make a living, so I can support my kids."

"What about your wife," I asked, before I thought about what I was saying, then wanted to kick myself when the expression on his handsome face changed to sadness.

"Well, that's complicated," he said. "She left a few years back. I saw her a couple years back, but only briefly, when she and her new boyfriend were asking for a divorce."

"Did you give it to her?" I asked.

He shook his head. "No, I should, but no."

"Why not?" I asked, realizing I was asking for personal information I didn't deserve.

The man stood up and began putting his clothes back on.

"It's complicated," he said as the sadness poured off him. I watched him dress as he told the story of his failed marriage.

"We were high school sweethearts. When she got pregnant with Drake, our first son, I was so happy. I know a recent high school graduate shouldn't have been happy about having a kid and a wife that early in life, but it all seemed to fit with what I wanted most in my life. I had naïve visions of her moving to the ranch with me, and living with our grandparents, raising our kids, and learning to work the land."

He was trying to play off the emotions now, but I could see by the way his mouth turned down and the sad look in his eyes, it was difficult for him to talk about.

"What happened?" I asked.

He shrugged. "Life... reality? She had no intention of living in the middle of nowhere. In fact, the only thing she really cared about was getting her next fix. She didn't use while pregnant with Drake, I convinced her that it'd damage the baby, but as soon as he was born, she went right back. We were already having difficulties a few years later when she got pregnant with Luke. I caught her just as she was about to shoot heroin, and put my foot down, saying I wouldn't allow her to destroy our baby because of some fucking addiction."

Eddie swallowed hard at the memory, before carrying on, "She cried in my arms all that night, and I managed to get her to agree to attend rehab. I don't know how we managed it, but she stayed sober for Luke also, but after that, she looked at me differently. She'd tell me I was judging her like her parents used to do. It was just a little after Luke turned three that she took off with her dealer."

I sighed. Being in the film industry, especially in Mexico where drugs were easier to access than in the US even, I'd seen more than one of my friends lost to that nasty habit.

"I'm sorry," I said lamely. No words I could say would help, and I felt like a heel even trying.

He smiled at me. "It's good to have someone to talk to about it. Family and friends are too close, so they judge me or her or the situation. Life can suck, but the truth is, the boys and I are happy here. Things are good for the most part, or at least will be once we find the guy that shot Flex."

"About that," I said. "What's the deal there?"

"Don't know, just some whack job came out here one night quoting scripture and shit, then shot and almost killed Flex. If it hadn't been for Flex's boyfriend Mitch, he'd have gotten the second shot in and killed him."

"How's that?" I asked. "Mitch saved him, how?"

"Mitch came out and shot the son of a bitch before he could finish Flex off. Struck him in the shoulder, we believe, but he's not been seen since then."

"Any idea who it is?" I asked.

"Two possibilities. One is someone my mom hired. She and Flex were embroiled in a legal dispute over this property after my grandfather left the ranch to Flex. The other is some random Baptist preacher from the local town who disappeared about the same time.

I looked at the guy, perplexed. "So you think your own mother could be involved in trying to kill your cousin, her nephew?"

"I'd be willing to bet money on it," he said.

I'd almost finished dressing and had sat back down on the rock to put my socks and shoes back on. "You and your mother must not be close."

He laughed a bitter laugh. "No, my mom never cared much about me, but when I got Theresa pregnant, she was really pissed. Her sons were supposed to be upstanding people, not trash like the people she grew up around, meaning her parents. When I refused to help her destroy Flex by spying on him and all, she pretty much kicked me out of her life for good. I saw her for the first time right before we moved out here. She was angry because Flex and I moved in together." He chuckled again. "My mom is a certifiably insane, bitch," he said, and climbed back on top of his horse.

"Sounds like a telenovela," I said, and went to climb on top of mine.

I heard him laugh as he led us away from the river.

10

Eddie

OKAY, SO THINGS GOT a little weird. I needed to cool off, and damn if the river didn't seem like the right place to do it. Unfortunately, I didn't think about seeing the man's package out in the open when I stripped and went into the water.

As soon as I was in, I knew I was screwed. The guy stripped, and his perfectly trimmed, dark, tanned body with the perfect abs followed me in seconds after I was in the water. He came at me and I knew exactly what he had in mind. Damn, I didn't mind it in the least, so I splashed him and ran away like the chicken shit I was.

It was not like I was that shocked. I'd always had a bit of an attraction to guys, not that I'd ever acted on it. I met Theresa in high school, and she was my first and last sex partner.

I could honestly say I hadn't really thought of anyone else, male or female, since I got married. Well, maybe that was not true, I had watched porn some before leaving Houston, and I quickly learned I preferred gay porn over straight, but even that hadn't really convinced me I was gay. I just didn't really think about it.

The sexual heat between us had cooled down enough then that I crawled onto slab rock, as we referred to it as kids, and let myself dry off. I wasn't at all sure what would happen when he came out, so I kept my eyes shut and waited. Here was the deal, I'd made a commitment to my wife, and I meant to keep it as long as we were married. Yeah, she'd cheated on me, like almost the day after we were married, but her integrity and mine were totally different things. When I committed to someone, it was a commitment and I'd honor it 'til it was no longer a commitment.

That didn't mean I didn't want this man. He lay next to me, and although he was at least three feet from me, I could feel his sexuality radiating from him. Somehow the topic switched to my wife, then my mom, and the feeling passed. I was both relieved and disappointed. I was sure I'd have generations of fantasies that revolved around him taking me while lying out on that rock, or in the adobe cottage, or in the river.

Okay, enough of those thoughts, time to focus on the job at hand. Damn, thinking of his hands didn't help matters.

He rode up next to me, and I told him Flex wanted me to show him the buttes, where he thought they might like to film, but it was several miles away. The horses drank water at the river. "Do you mind picking up speed?" I asked.

"State champion, twice," he said again, and let the horse take his lead. I kicked Red, who was always happy to go for a run and took off. Red could've been a racehorse, she loved to run, and since she and I had been practicing together, it only took a moment to pass the horse in front of us.

"Looks like I'm taking your crown, state champ," I said as I passed him.

"No fair," I heard behind me, but I didn't look back, instead letting Red keep up her pace.

When we were almost halfway to the buttes, I slowed Red down and was glad to see the man had stayed close behind me. "We're about halfway there, I assured him, but let's give the horses a break. Damn, it must be a hundred and five out here."

We both dismounted and walked companionably down the trail.

"You know, I don't know your name yet. I keep thinking of you as the guy or the man."

He laughed and said, "Alexandro, but people in the States call me Alex."

"Alexandro feels more like you." I chuckled. "You're a bit refined for this area."

He laughed. "Well, usually, I'd be in a suit and not jeans, so your assessment might be accurate, but I grew up in El Paso, riding horses and tormenting my sisters at every opportunity."

I smiled. "How many sisters?"

"I have two older sisters. One is now the de facto president of the board, although my father still has the official title, and my other sister is an attorney, who defends the company in both the States and in Mexico."

"Ouch," I said. "They sound intimidating."

"I'm sure they are, to anyone who isn't their little brother," he said. "It was my life's most dedicated purpose to create as much havoc in their lives as I could."

I chuckled. "You have that same ornery feel about you, so I can imagine they wanted to destroy you."

He nodded. "I'm sure they still do, but they love me too much to kill me. However, I do sleep with one eye open when I'm home."

"Probably wise." I smiled.

"So, you're close to your family?" I asked.

"They are my life. I love running the production side of our company, but it takes me away from my home more often than not. When I'm away, I miss them."

"That must be nice. I feel the same about my cousin, Flex. He's more like a brother to me than a cousin. We spent almost every day in each other's company growing up, mostly at his mom's house, since my mother always complained we were too loud. We even went to school together, even though I'm a year older."

"Wow, that's amazing. You grew up here then?" he asked.

"No, in Houston, but my aunt and mom lived less than two blocks from one another. They love to hate each other, so they moved as close as they could without moving into the same home."

"Again, with the telenovela theme. I'm going to have to interview your mother and aunt for a new miniseries."

"Dear God, please don't. They're enough to handle as they are."

We came to where one of the hills dropped off into a canyon-like area, and at this time of day it offered a bit of shade. I walked Red down the incline and sat on a boulder. Memories flowed through me of the countless times Eric, one of our friends from high school, Flex, and I had sat on these same boulders. It brought back good memories of our childhood.

I pulled my canteen off the saddle and took a long drink of the water, some of it pouring down my t-shirt.

Alex sat next to me, and I assumed he was drinking water himself, but when I put the canteen down, his eyes remained on my lips.

"I can't tell if you are gay, bi, or straight," he said. "But, I have a feeling you wouldn't push me away if I were to kiss you."

I turned away. "Please don't," I said. "I'm still married, and that's important to me."

He looked away. "I can't promise if you do another sexy thing like spilling water down your beautiful chest that I will be able to resist, but I'll try."

I looked over at him, and suddenly wanted him to stop trying. It seemed as if someone had taken over my body. At that moment, I wanted to feel his lips on mine. It was almost like possession, but I knew it was just pure attraction. Fuck, I was going to do this, wasn't I?

I leaned over and kissed him myself, slowly letting my lips touch his. He instantly returned the kiss, putting way too much heat into it than I was ready for.

I pulled back and stood up. "Alex, I-I..."

He held up his hand and smiled. "It's okay, *campion*," he said, and stood up.

"That's what he called me," I said out loud, because of the surprise of hearing the word come out of his mouth. "*Campion*, what does that mean?" I asked. My Spanish had always been lacking.

"Champion, but we use it as an endearment. Who called you that?" he asked.

My face turned red, fuck if I was going to admit to this man that I'd just told not to kiss me, then kissed him instead that I'd seen the ghost of his ancestor this morning.

"Never mind," I said, uncomfortably. "I like you, Alex, which surprises me, because I haven't been attracted to anyone since my wife left. I thought I'd basically lost interest in anyone else... but you... I can't really explain it."

He stood up and walked toward me. I put my hand on his very firm, well-defined chest, and asked him to stop.

"I am married. I will not be one of those people who ignore what that means. I'm sorry for leading you on like that, but until I no longer wear this ring..." I showed him my wedding band. "...I'll not be fucking around with anyone but the person it belongs to."

He stared at me for a long moment, before asking, "So, are you bisexual, or just got into a bad situation?"

I laughed. "No, I loved intimacy with my wife, but we were young. I think I prefer men, but we can safely say I'm bisexual. If my wife hadn't left, I'd have been faithful to her my whole life."

The man sighed. "I could show you a very good time, but I admire a man who can keep his commitments. Let's go see this butte your cousin says is worth the trip, then I really must be getting back to the motel."

I could tell this was him shutting whatever this was down, and I couldn't blame him. I must seem like a total freak coming on hot and cold like this.

He was back on his horse, waiting for me before I could mount Red. When I was finally up, he laughed and kicked the horse into a gallop. *All's fair in love and war*, slipped through my mind as I kicked Red into a gallop, so I could keep up with them.

Alex's ass seemed to mold itself perfectly to the saddle. There was no doubt he'd been riding for years, and he was elegant to watch, bouncing more like a British showjumper than a cowboy.

We reached the rise where the buttes shot up. You couldn't really see them until you were over the ridge, so it was a breathtaking experience. Alex drew his horse in and stopped on the ridge, taking in the view.

"Madre María, ¡la vista es hermosa!" he said.

"Es verdad," I said, happy I knew enough Spanish to know what he'd just said. "It is one of the prettiest views around."

"I understand why your cousin recommended the spot. He's right, this would be a perfect spot to film several scenes in the movie."

We sat on the vista, looking out for a long time. The guy seemed deep in thought.

"Can you take me back to the ranch house?" he asked abruptly. "I would like to make an offer to use your property for our film. It's perfect in every way," he said.

"I have one more place to show you. Well, technically, Flex wanted me to take you down to the buttes, because they would be good for filming as well, but you can go there another day. I think you'll want to see this, though, before you agree to anything."

The man nodded cautiously, and I led Red back down the way we'd come, so we could take a shorter route to the volcano.

"My family have odd traditions," I told him as we rode next to one another. "We have lots of native blood in us, as well as typical West Texas roots. So, things other people would think are ridiculous, we accept as normal."

"Like what?" he asked.

I thought for a moment, trying to figure out how best to frame my thoughts, so I didn't sound totally insane, but was still being honest with him, nonetheless.

"Well, for one thing, our grandmother, who I told you was Latina and Indian, would tell us that whoever owned this land would be plagued with dreams, anytime it or someone on it was at risk."

"Do you believe that?" he asked

"I do. Flex had two dreams about a snake trying to attack him before he was shot. His last dream showed him that his lover would save him."

Alex nodded as if wary of where the conversation was going. We arrived at the volcano, and I let him take in the surroundings before I continued. I led him to where the clearing was hidden behind the thicket, the place where I'd seen his ancestor just hours before. I was about to dismount, when I got a call on the radio.

"Effie, come in." Flex's disembodied voice sounded strange in the serene quiet of the volcano.

"Yes, what is it?" I asked.

"Is Alex with you? Can he hear me?"

"Yeah, he's here." I looked over at him.

"Alex, Mitch just called. He said your sister just phoned the motel with an urgent message for you. Your dad has been rushed to the hospital. They think he's had a heart attack. They want you to fly out of Alpine and back home as soon as you can. Your assistant has a private plane waiting at the airport for you now. She said you can leave as soon as you get there."

Alex's face paled. "Let them know he got the message. I'll drive him into town okay, Flex?"

"Okay." There was talking in the background as I watched Alex climb off his horse and double over. "Emma Jean said she'd get the boys off the bus for you."

"Thank her for me, Flex," I said. I climbed off Red and went over to Alex and pulled him into my arms. "It's okay, Alex. I'm sure he's okay." The man clung to me like I was a life buoy in the middle of a vast ocean.

It took several minutes for him to catch his breath. "I'm sorry," he said. "It's just my biggest fear being away from home."

"Shh, I'm sure he's fine. Can you ride? I need to get you to the airport, but do you need to go to the motel first to get your things?"

He thought for a moment. "No, I can do without my stuff there, and if he's fine, he'll be yelling at me for leaving my post without a contract." He chuckled, but I could hear the tears behind it.

"Then Flex or Mitch will put your stuff in their house until you get back, but for now, let's get you out of here, okay?"

I jumped back onto Red and not trusting if he was okay enough to ride alone, I pulled him onto Red behind me, luckily without resistance. There was no masculine stupidity about resisting support when he needed it.

I rushed us back to the barn, and Jimmy was there waiting for us. He said he'd cool the horses down while I got Alex to the airport. Concern was dripping from the man's face.

I drove like a bat out of hell toward Alpine, hoping that neither the sheriff nor his deputies were camped out around the various favorite ticket spots along the way. We made it into Alpine in record time. I was able to pull into the airport and drop him off at the gate less than an hour after Flex had given him the terrifying message.

I got out, came around the car, and to my surprise, the man hugged me. "Thank you, Eddie, for getting me here so fast. I'm in your debt."

"Hardly," I replied. "Now go home to your papa. I know this is stupid, but would you ring one of us and let us know that he's okay?"

He smiled. "Yes," he said, then he hugged me again. "You really are a dad, aren't you?"

I shrugged. "Guilty."

He turned then and rushed into the airport. I said a little prayer, asking that his father be okay, and if not, that he would be okay long enough for his son to get home to him. My father was a no-good piece of crap, but I could see the love Alex had for his, and I wanted nothing more than for the two to reconnect before any tragedy happened.

11

Alex

My head spun as we rode back toward the barn. I was surprised when Eddie pulled me up on the horse behind him, and the emotions that spun through me made me want to bury my head on the broad shoulders of the man in front of me, and weep like an infant.

He rushed me toward the airport, and I had to resist putting my hand out for him to hold. *God, get ahold of yourself,* I kept saying to myself. When we got out of his truck, I couldn't hold back any longer and pulled him into a hug. For a moment, I took comfort in being held in those strong arms. My father was a strong man and would've told me to get it together, be the strength for others, not be a pushover. Oh, lots of other thoughts he'd said to me swirled through my mind. He was a hard man, but he was a great father, and the thought of losing him made me hyperventilate.

As we took off in the private plane, I thought, for my sister's sake, he'd better really be sick. My father hated nothing more than pretension. If he found out my sister had rented, or God forbid called in a favor to use a private plane, he'd hit the ceiling.

We'd watched the movie *Steel Magnolias* years ago when my sister thought we should get the rights to do a similar version of the film in Mexico. The part where the father was attributed to saying, "An ounce of pretension's worth a pound of manure," really spoke to my father, and he quoted it over and over when he thought we were being *too big for our britches*, another saying he'd adopted from our Southern United States brothers and sisters.

I, on the other hand, couldn't have been more thankful for the plane. We landed in El Paso in what felt like moments after leaving Alpine. My assistant had a car waiting at the airport for me, and I was rushed to the hospital in record time.

When I walked in, my sister, Ellen, was sitting next to my mother, and both women were crying. My other sister, Francesca, always the cool and collected one, was pacing the room, grabbing me into a hug the second I entered.

"How is he?" I asked.

"We don't know," Francesca said. "He's in surgery, but besides that? We're still waiting."

I sat down on the other side of Mama and rubbed her back. "What happened?" I asked.

"Your father is so stubborn," Mama said. "We had another gardener quit, and you know he didn't want to hire them anyway, saying he could do the work as well as any other man. He was out trying to mow with a push mower, refusing to use the tractor. He got too hot and passed out. I was watching, thank the lord, from the window and we called the ambulance immediately. When we got here, they said he'd had a heart attack."

I shook my head. My father was probably the most self-determined, stubborn, and lovable man to walk the earth. He'd grown up in money, but he'd worked hard all his life, telling us all that a man who didn't work with his hands couldn't respect himself.

I'd spent a lot of days working in our hacienda's gardens, mowing, weeding, not to mention mucking stalls, cleaning and brushing down horses. I had only been allowed to enjoy the fruits of other people's labors after leaving my father's home and working for the company, but I had no doubt my expense account was watched like a hawk. My father wouldn't be having a lazy son messing around on his dime. Not that running our production company was easy, and I did the job of at least three other people.

"We'll hire more help when we need it," my father would say.

Luckily it took less than an hour before a doctor came out and told us the surgery went well, and Papa would be fine. He had several blockages, but his heart was strong, and we'd got him into surgery before there was much damage.

All of us drew a breath of relief at the news.

My sister, Francesca, broke away from the group and followed the doctor, until they stood outside the door. I assumed they were talking about legal crap, or something only her analytical mind would want to know. When she bumped heads with the woman, I knew immediately there was more to the relationship than I'd assumed.

When she came back over, I noticed the woman watch her walk away, and if there had been any doubt before, there was none now.

Francesca gave me an *I dare you* look, and I smiled, but hid it under my hand. As we waited for them to move Papa to a room, I had a moment alone with Francesca.

"So," I whispered. "You're gonna have to be more discreet if you don't want our hawkeyed mother to catch you," I said.

Francesca just shrugged. "I don't know what you're talking about." I'd known this woman all my life and I knew when she was squirming inside. She could've beaten anyone at poker, and I was probably the only one who knew her that well, except Ellen, maybe, who knew when she was bluffing.

"Don't you mean you plead the Fifth?" I asked, causing her to chuckle.

She punched me not so lightly on the arm, and said, "Not another word. You hear me? I can still kick your butt."

"Butch much?" I asked, and winked at her.

She shook her head and walked away from me, sitting next to Ellen and Mama. Our other sister had caught onto the fact that we were up to something, but always the dutiful one of the three of us, she'd bide her time and get to the bottom of our story later.

Francesca may have been the one who controlled her emotions the best, and God, she was a powerful attorney as a result, but Ellen had the probing capabilities of an investigator. Francesca must have hoped Ellen had missed our exchange, but her face told me she knew the game was about up.

We were taken into Papa's room shortly after. He had tubes going everywhere. Francesca's doctor, as I thought of her now, came in and assured us this was normal, and as he recovered, they'd be removed.

Mama was working hard to be strong, but the tears slipped silently down her cheeks. My parents' love for one another was legendary. Papa drove her mad at times, but she melted when he touched her. Even when we were young, we'd hear Papa whispering to her and see her blushing in his arms. Often, we'd walk into the room and the two would be dancing to music only they could hear. The memory caused me to remember Flex and Mitch at the motel, and for the first time, the thought that I could find someone to love like that wormed itself into my thoughts.

My parents argued as anyone does, but they were respectful to one another, even when they were spitting mad. Once my papa pulled me aside after he and Mama had been at each other's throats. He was about to go to the bedroom to find Mama when he turned and winked at me. "Never go to bed angry with the one you love, hijo." Over the years, my father would repeat this advice to me time and time again. "You want to know your loved one knows you love them every night, no matter how angry she is."

Of course, at the time, he had no idea I was gay, but I doubted that would've changed anything. He wasn't speaking to me really, mostly he was reminding himself.

Papa lay asleep in the hospital bed. Our worries, at least slightly relaxed, flowed over us as we watched him breathing. Believing he was going to be okay, Ellen looked at me. "You had better fill us in on your progress before he wakes up. He'll be on the warpath when he finds out you came all this way for nothing," she said. Of course, we all knew it wasn't nothing, but she was right, he'd think it was.

"I did make a lot more progress than you think. When you called, I was on a large ranch that borders the Big Bend National Park, the Texas Wildlife Reserve, the Rio Grande, and therefore Mexico's Canon de Santa Elena."

"Wow," Ellen replied. "How did you manage that?"

"Pure luck," I told her. "The owner of the little motel I'm staying at is dating the owner of the ranch. They showed me the property after I asked if they knew anyone who might have what I was looking for. It's almost like providence, since they also have a new lodge and an RV park for guests."

"How much are they charging?" she asked.

"That's the part that didn't get negotiated. We were literally on our way back from touring the property when you called."

"We're lucky he's asleep," Francesca said. "Or he'd scalp all three of us for letting you come back without those contracts in your hand."

My father started moving his hand, hitting Ellen's knee. We all three froze, and Mama laughed. "You always think you can get things past your papa, but he's always listening," she said as she moved up to him. "Hola, mi corazon," she said as she kissed his cheek. "You scared us all to death."

My father's hand moved again, and Francesca walked out of the room to find a nurse.

There was a flurry of activity then as they extubated my father. "He's going to feel groggy," the nurse said as he worked on getting our father situated after removing the tubes. "He's going to be sedated for a while, so he won't remember much of the conversation."

"That's a relief," Ellen said, earning an instant glare from our mother.

"Don't try to make him talk," the nurse cautioned as he stepped toward the door. "He'll be in and out of consciousness and may even fall asleep during the conversation." Then he smiled. "Your dad is really strong, he did well in surgery. Dr. Rameriz was pleased with the outcome."

I noticed Francesca blushed slightly at the name of our father's surgeon. This would be something I'd be getting to the bottom of, sooner rather than later.

"Go home, hijos," my mother said. "You'll all be kicked out soon enough anyway."

We kissed Papa, who had passed out again, and then Mama. Francesca and Ellen had ridden together to the hospital, so I climbed into the backseat of the car.

"So," I began, and Francesca turned around in her seat and pointed at me.

"Don't you start," she said, then looked at Ellen. "You neither."

"You know you're gonna tell us, so you might as well spit it out," I said, trying not to smile.

Francesca gave me her best attorney look, which caused me to lose the battle, and laugh out loud.

"God, you're both such pains in my ass," she said, and Ellen backhanded her as she drove.

"Hey, watch the girls," Francesca said after Ellen's arm bounced off her boobs.

"Please, those girls bounce like a soccer ball." Then, Ellen bumped them with the back of her hand again. This time all three of us laughed.

"Yours are bigger than mine," Francesca laughed, but when she went to pay her sister back, Ellen pointed her finger, and said, "Leave mine alone. They are sensitive."

"Why?" Francesca asked.

"You first, then I'll share my news," Ellen said.

Francesca sighed. "Okay, okay. I'm seeing the Medica okay, happy now?" she asked.

We both knew Francesca swung both ways, but we'd never met any of her female relationships, and truth was we didn't know until now if she'd ever dated a woman.

"Wow," Ellen said. "The one who worked on Papa?"

Francesca nodded. "Neither one of us knew she was working on him until she came out to tell us he was out of surgery. It was sort of a shock to see her."

"I bet it was," I said. "So, how serious is it?" I asked.

"Well, it's been going on for several months. You have to admit she is so beautiful and talented. Now add to that she saved our papa."

"Wow," Ellen said. "I've never seen you this over the moon."

Francesca shrugged. "I'm not saying anything else, or it'll jinx it. You know how bad I am at relationships. With my work and lack of downtime, it's best not to put much pressure on it, not yet at least."

"You'd better not tell the parents, then," Ellen said.

Francesca sat up and looked at us both. "You can't tell them, not yet, especially now, they'd drive her insane!"

Both Ellen and I laughed. "You are right, you can't tell them, not until you've decided if she's the one or not," I said.

Francesca sighed. "I'm glad you two know, though. She is special. I wanted to tell someone, but I was so afraid it'd spoil things."

Ellen reached over and patted Francesca's hand. "She is beautiful, hermana."

"Now, buckle your seat belts 'cause I'm going to blow you both away."

Francesca and I focused on Ellen as she turned onto the little back road that led to the hacienda.

"Ernesto and I are expecting. We are turning you two into tios!"

Francesca screamed, and I jumped up and grabbed my sister in a backseat hug.

"Oh, my God!" Francesca said. "No wonder the girls are sensitive. You've got a baby in there!"

"I'm working on it," Ellen sighed and grabbed her sister's hand.

By the time we pulled up in front of the hacienda, all three of us were crying with the news.

We all got out and were in a big sibling hug as soon as we could get to each other.

"Have you told Mom and Dad yet?" I asked.

Ellen shook her head. "No, not yet. I just found out, and I was going to wait until you came home, Alexandro, then tell everyone at the same time. Then Papa..."

The tears streamed down her face. "All I could think about was that he wasn't going to get to meet his grandbaby, and that I hadn't told him he was going to be an abuelo."

Of course, that caused Francesca and me to cry as well. "Let's make it a thing," I said. "Papa will be livid, but I'll not leave until he comes home, then we'll have a huge party, and you and Ernesto can announce your news."

"I should have Ernesto's parents over too," Ellen said. "That way it'll be the entire family."

We embraced again. I couldn't believe it. I was going to be a tio. My sisters and I were close, I was surprised I didn't sense it, but Ellen was the most secretive of the three of us. Heck, we didn't even realize she'd fallen in love with Ernesto, our gardener's eldest grandson, until after it had happened.

"I have an idea." I told my siblings. "Let's play up the getting-old concept, and Papa will think it's because he had a heart attack. He'll be so mad that we are harassing him about it. We can all play innocent when he gets angry, then when he blows his top, we can say it isn't about the heart attack, but because he's going to be a grandfather."

"You must want to die young," Ellen said, but laughed.

"You know we'll rat you out when he asks whose idea this was, right?" Francesca said.

"Of course, you will," I said. "But, I'll be going back to the job site, so I won't have to deal with his wrath. Besides, if I close that deal for the ranch, I'll be instantly off his shit list anyway."

We spent the next few hours planning the, *you're getting too old* party. "It's too bad we can't decorate the place for Dias de la Muertos," I said.

"Why can't we?" Francesca chimed in. "It's not that far away, and you'll be working away from home. We can just say we're celebrating early."

We giggled as we used to when we were kids setting our parents up. We were always brats like that, playing practical jokes on them, which always earned us a ton of laughter and usually mutual grounding. But the punishments often included having to make homemade ice cream by hand, or if we were really in trouble, helping señor Apodaca, Ernesto's grandfather, in the gardens.

Papa came home four days after his surgery, and we had our family party the following Sunday. Of course, he was grumpy that I wasn't at the site working out the details, and was predictably upset that I hadn't secured any contracts for the ranch. Mama put an end to any complaints when she said it was her wish that I should come home and be with family when he was so sick, otherwise, I was sure he'd have dispatched me right away.

We knew Papa didn't have much energy to attend the party. We got everything set up before we brought him out. Our guests, mostly family and a few friends as well as Ernesto's family, crowded around the long harvest table we used for such occasions. It was decked out with black tablecloths and Dia de las Muertos décor.

Papa was already suspicious and threatened not to come down if we were going to make a big deal about his heart attack, but Mama insisted, and as usual, that did the trick.

He threw up his hands and winced at the pain when he saw the décor, and of course, looked right at me. How did he know I was the one behind it? "What?" I asked.

As we'd guessed, he complained. "I'm not dead. I just had a little episode. Why does everyone act like I died?" he asked.

"You are getting older, Papa," Francesca bravely said, earning her the same glare he'd given me moments before. I had to hold back my laugh, knowing all three of us were skating on thin ice.

As soon as Papa was seated at the front of the table, the place he preferred, I stood up as we'd practiced. Ringing my glass, as they did in the movies when they wanted to get everyone's attention, I began my speech, "As you know, this family has had a recent scare, and this has shown us how precious life is." I waited for my father's predictable sneer and eye roll. "For this reason, we've called you together in celebration of those who've gone before us. Please, raise your glasses as we celebrate our forefathers and the gifts they've given us."

Even my father couldn't refuse to toast that, but he glared at me anyway.

Francesca stood up after I sat down and raised her glass for a toast. "Let us also celebrate those who sit around this table now. Friends and family, loved ones all of you. We are all better people because of the ones who join us here today." Francesca got a little emotional when she looked at our father, then over to Ellen, but kept it together as she raised her glass, and everyone, especially Papa, raised his glass in salute.

Finally, Ellen stood up, and tears flowed down her cheeks. "I raise this glass of water in salute to the past and the present, but especially to the future. Ernesto stood up next to her and put his arm around my sister. She was overcome with emotion, so he said, "Here is to the next generation," and put his hand over Ellen's stomach. The entire group leaped from their seats, talking a mile a minute.

"Everyone calm down," Ellen said. When they did, she turned to Papa and Mama, who were both weeping uncontrollably. "Papa, you scared us half to death. I was so afraid we'd lose you before we could share this news, but by the grace of God, you are here with us still, to celebrate a new generation of Zitlal Apodacas!"

The entire group raised their glasses in salute, and Ellen went up and hugged our parents.

Papa only lasted until the food was eaten, before he had to go and rest. I volunteered to push his chair back to his room.

"You and your sisters surprised me, hijo," he said. "I thought you were going to give me grief for having the heart attack. I was fully prepared to punish the three of you."

I laughed. "Trust me, Papa, we knew the risk when we planned this."

He chuckled. "You would, considering you three seemed to be scheming ways to get in trouble your entire lives."

When I got him into his bed and pulled the covers up around him, he grabbed my hand. "Hijo, I was afraid," he admitted. "I thought I would die, but death wasn't what scared me. While I lay on that bed, I kept asking myself when the last time was I'd told my son how proud I was of him."

I couldn't help the tear that slipped from my eye. Papa reached up and wiped it from my cheek. "You bring me so much pride, my son. You work so hard and care so much for those who work with and for you. All that shows me the man you are. I am so sorry it took so long to tell you."

I bent down and kissed my papa. "You are my rock, my foundation. As a boy, I wanted to be just like you, and now, I want that more than ever."

That mollified him, and he patted my hand. "I love you, son," he said, as he rolled over toward the wall.

I checked the baby monitor Francesca had bought, so we could hear him if he needed us. When I confirmed it was on, I left the room, closing the door behind me.

I was scheduled to leave the following day, and still needed to contact the ranch owners to set up an appointment to visit them again, but I couldn't find it in me to work today. Instead, I went back outside to the party and to the people I loved most in this world.

12

Eddie

FTER DROPPING ALEX OFF, I drove back to the ranch, my heart heavy, thinking about all the man stood to lose. Of course, I'd be lying if I wasn't also mourning the fact that if anyone in my family died today, it'd be weeks, if not months, before anyone would tell me. With the exception of my boys, Flex and his mom, my Aunt Katherine, my birth family had all but abandoned me.

Alex's assistant contacted us the following day to tell us Alex's father was okay. Alex was going to spend a couple weeks in El Paso, but he was very interested in discussing using us as the location for the crew during filming.

Flex was beside himself with excitement. Mitch's attorney friend Lisa, had agreed to do research for us. She was investigating what we needed to negotiate regarding insurance, liability issues, and even what was a reasonable fee for using the property during filming.

Flex, Emma Jean, and Jimmy all confronted me the night I came back from dropping Alex off regarding why I'd had a change of heart. I told them about the dream and how this time, I'd seen Diamondback Jack in the dream as well as in person that morning, and that he'd instructed me to trust the one who was coming.

I didn't put it together that the guy must be an ancestor of Alex's until he told me his ancestor had been from this area. I didn't think he bought it when I told him we had a similar legend.

"Did you tell him about your dream?" Emma Jean asked.

"No, I was about to when we got the call about his father."

Flex shook his head. "Of course, you know we believe you, but I think it's probably best if you don't share your dream with him just yet. Let things mellow a bit before you do."

I sighed. "I think Alex should be kept fully abreast of the situation, especially if his crew were going to be at risk being on the property. If the serpent is back, everyone is at risk."

Flex thought for a moment. "Let's do this. We'll tell him we have reason to believe my shooter is coming back. We don't have to give him details, but we're being honest with him, nonethe-less. We'll recommend that because of the potential danger, he should have security on staff to ensure no one is hurt inadver-tently."

I thought that was fair. If I'd been in the man's shoes and someone told me they were being haunted by my great-great, so-far-back ancestor, I'd think they were certifiable and avoid them like the plague.

"It sounds like a plan. Now, what do we do about the warning?" I asked.

"Well, we need to install some security," Flex said. "The cameras we have around the house aren't adequate, since they didn't pick up the perp's face the night he shot me. We'll need to get a better system now that guests are staying anyway."

"Do ya think Eddie is the one in danger now that he's havin the dreams?" Jimmy asked.

I turned to Flex. "Yeah, about that, I thought only the owner of the ranch was supposed to be the one having dreams."

Flex shrugged. "I think it's a mutual thing. You're an equal partner, and my heir if I die."

I looked up at Flex, shocked by what he'd just said. "What do you mean I'm your heir?"

"Effie, *of course* you're my heir. Who else would it be? The next one in line would be one of your sons, since I don't have kids of my own."

The shock settled hard in my stomach. "When did you make that decision?" I asked.

"Right after I got out of the hospital. I called our attorney and had him draw up the paperwork, and I signed it as soon as he could send it to me."

"Why didn't you tell me?" I asked.

Flex laughed. "Because, I knew you'd react like this," he said.

I flipped him off. "You should've told me. I don't…"

Flex stood up and came over to where I was standing. "Dude, you didn't ask, but besides my mom, you're the closest thing I have to a next of kin. My mother wouldn't set foot on the property again if her life depended on it. Your mom and brothers can kiss my lily-white ass. I'd rather give the property to the devil than to them."

"Same here," I said, shaking my head.

"Exactly. You belong here, probably more than I do. That night, I felt my life flowing out of me, and I woke up surprised I was still alive. I'll tell you right now, it wasn't the ownership of this property I thought about as I lay on the ground dying. It was you, the boys and my mother, Emma Jean and Jimmy," he said, looking over at them. "And Eric and Mitch, if you can believe it. You all went through my mind. The fact that I was dying having been loved. So, I don't give a fuck about this once everything is said and done, family, specifically you, Effie, that's what matters to me."

I was struggling with the emotion of it all. I'd been feeling sorry for myself, because I had shit for family, all the time forgetting that my real family were the people right here on this ranch with me. That realization sent a wave of peace through me. It didn't really matter about my mom or brothers, or even my father, who cared more about his wife's kids than he did us. What mattered was this group of people and my boys.

"If you get married, won't you want to leave all this to him?" I asked.

"Nope, I've already talked to Mitch about it. *When* we get married, he understands that the ranch belongs to you and the kids if something happens to me. Of course, if he moves out here with me, he'll have the rights to the house until he no longer needs it, but the ranch stays in the family it originated from."

"What if you have kids?" I asked.

"Then we'll have a pow-wow with your boys to determine how to work it out. There's not gonna be another situation with your mom and me. From now on, we'll work it all out as a family, and everyone will be in agreement before we make any decisions. Agreed?"

I nodded, but was still too overwhelmed to speak.

Luckily, my two boys burst into the house tackling me. Luke was wound up as he usually was coming home from school. "Dad, today we went on a field trip behind the school and found a Leopard Lizard, and it was eating another lizard. Our teacher told us not to bother them. They aren't poisonous like the Gila monsters, but they'll bite you if they are scared."

I laughed at how excited my son was, considering we had the lizards all over the ranch. I guessed seeing it at school made it special.

Drake had begun taking on some of the moody qualities of a preteen. He was still young enough not to mind hugging his dad when he got home from school, but he quickly sought out his personal space away from the rest of us.

I looked over at Flex and winked. "Still think you made the right decision?" I asked.

Flex just chuckled. "No doubt in my mind," and just like that, everything was cool again.

We'd installed satellite internet shortly after moving to the duplexes, but it was still pretty spotty, and everything from high winds to clouds could block our coverage. Despite that, we researched several surveillance systems that would do well monitoring all the new buildings, including the duplex, the lodge, and the RV park.

Several thousand dollars later, we'd ordered the system and it was scheduled to be delivered within the week.

"I'll admit, just ordering that makes me feel better," I said.

Flex nodded. "Now, we need to have a conversation about getting a dog, or maybe several dogs. Had Emma Jean not been clever when this all started and borrowed dogs from the neighbor, this house would've likely been burned to the ground along with the barn," he said.

"With us in it," Emma Jean replied.

A couple weeks before Flex had been shot, someone had snuck onto the property and burned down the barn and tried to burn the house down too. Emma Jean had borrowed the neighbor's dogs for a few weeks, and they'd driven off the arsonist before the house caught on fire.

"So, let's talk about what kind of dog to get."

Luke homed in on our conversation like a ballistic missile, and was bouncing like Ace, Flex's Jack Russell, after hearing we were looking at getting another dog.

I had to settle him down, so we could actually talk about it. I let him sit in my lap and contribute to the discussion.

"What about Ace?" I asked.

Flex humphed. "The little traitor has taken up with Mitch and basically follows him wherever he goes. He's useless out here, and besides, I'm terrified he'll be eaten by the first Coyote he comes across. The dog is stupid fearless."

We all laughed at the truth of that statement.

"Wasn't it some of Lucille's dogs you kept last time?" Flex asked Emma Jean.

"Yeah, they did a good job too," she said.

"What kind of dogs does she have?" Flex asked.

Jimmy laughed. "That'll be run-a-the-mill mutts. I think they're part cow dog, part border collie. Frank, her husband, calls them Mexican dogs since they got them from *Boquillas* originally."

"Emma Jean, do you mind finding out if she has any puppies. I doubt their old dogs have ever been spayed or neutered."

Jimmy almost choked. "Not likely," he agreed.

As fate would have it, within a week, we received three little fuzz balls and their mama, since puppies weren't gonna do much to keep the place guarded. Frank said we just saved them, because otherwise, he would have had to either dispose of them, or give them to the shelter in Marfa.

Jimmy said he doubted they'd ever be lucky enough to get to a shelter. "You never know these days though, things are a changing."

We had agreed to take the mama dog back to their farm when we were done, but the look Frank gave Lucille told me we might as well accept the fact we owned her too. The puppies were already weaned, and I figured if we didn't act fast, we'd end up with a hundred dogs on the ranch, so when we took the group to the vet, I asked him to have her spayed as soon as possible. Even if Lucille and Frank took her back, I was sure they wouldn't miss any new puppies.

Alex showed back up a few weeks later, and the negotiations were worked out a lot faster than I'd thought they would be.

Since Flex had agreed to let Alex use the main home, he, Mitch and I collected the personal belongings from the house and moved them into the storage shed that was now empty after Emma Jean and Jimmy had moved all their stuff into the duplex.

It was sad to see the old place so empty of our grandparents' things.

When I said something to Alex about moving in, Emma Jean chastised me saying to let him be. "He'll move in when he's ready," she said. "Don't push, I'm guessing this has to do with him missing your grandparents as much as it is about all of us."

Emma Jean scrubbed the place to the point that it shone, and although we were several months out from when production would begin, Alex made his first installment on the contract and moved in.

One evening while sitting on the little shared porch of our duplex, I told Emma Jean my thoughts. "It feels funny that someone is living in my grandparents' house," I said on a heavy sigh.

Emma Jean shrugged, "If you ask me, it's the best thing that could've happened. Now, when Alex and his crew are done with it, it'll not by your grandparents' home any longer."

I looked at her shocked, causing her to chuckle. "Listen, Eddie, as long as that's your grandparents' house, Flex will never make it his own. Just too many memories, not unlike what you're feeling right now. Trust me, this is the best possible situation. You'll see."

I sat silently then, pondering what she'd said. There was sense to it. I guess if he'd done a full renovation of the property, I'd have felt upset about it. Now at least, we were getting a break from what the property had been.

Feeling better, I went inside to do my final check on the boys before turning in myself. I kissed Emma Jean on the cheek. "Tell Jimmy night for me," I said, and headed in.

I thought of Alex that night as I lay in bed staring up at my ceiling. For the most part, he'd negotiated the entire deal and moved in without treating me any differently than he would've if I hadn't kissed him.

That moment had been a profound one for me, though. So much so, that I'd contacted my wife and set up a time to meet her in Houston.

Not unlike letting go of the way the old house had been all my life, I'd decided it was time to let go of my fractured marriage as well.

I doubted Alex would ever give me more than a fleeting thought with his big business attitude, but he did help me realize it was time to make the divorce final, and to my surprise, that no longer upset me the way it had a few weeks before.

13

Alex

THE NEGOTIATIONS FOR THE Big Bend ranch were easier than I'd anticipated. They'd done their due diligence, which, believe it or not, was always a relief. When my location owners were savvy, it helped form a bond and avoid emotional pitfalls that seemed to always plague a deal. Not the least of which was the owners feeling like we were trying to take advantage of them.

Luckily, Flex and Eddie accepted my offer without argument. I was surprised when Flex offered the house as a base. That wasn't originally in the deal. We had fully intended to rent an RV for me and to put up a big tent. Being able to use the house changed everything, however. Not only did it provide comfort, but it allowed me to house our higher paid actors while shooting. Of course, they wouldn't want to stay on location all the time, but they'd prefer the house to a camper or worse, the lodge.

I would be spending a serious amount of time in the area before we were ready to shoot, getting permissions from the parks, local authorities, the university, so when Flex vacated the premises, I readily moved in.

It must have been a win-win, because Flex smiled ear to ear when I gave him the check. He continued to maintain a camper next to the house, however. Luckily, he said he'd either move it or if we needed it, he'd move out while we were filming. That meant, at least during the most crucial times, we'd be able to dedicate all our time to the property without having the family underfoot.

Over the next few weeks, I'd have various assistants, consultants, evaluators and other people who worked for us needing a place to stay. Luckily, the house had room for me to accommodate them as well. Truly, I couldn't have asked for a better situation.

I'd done everything in my power to ignore the tasty cowboy who'd kissed me while we were touring the property. He was married, had kids, not to mention he was part owner of the property, or at least I assumed he was. It was best to leave him alone, and keep my distance, but that didn't mean I couldn't fantasize about him.

It seemed like he was just as happy to avoid me, so we danced around each other, at least until I moved into the house.

The first full day I was at the ranch, Emma Jean, the woman whose husband I assumed was the property's official caretaker, knocked on my door and announced dinner would be ready around six. She smiled and said, "You don't have to dress for dinner." And she turned to leave.

I noticed it wasn't a question of *if* I wanted to come for dinner, or did I want to join them? It was an announcement, and having grown up with a strong mother, I understood it for the nonnegotiable command that it was.

When I arrived at the little duplex, I could tell she was struggling for space and prepping meals for everyone in the tiny kitchen.

"Did you used to cook in the main house?" I asked, after she bumped into her husband and let out a curse word that would've been more appropriate coming out of one of the ranch hands than the woman.

"I did," she said. "This'll take some getting used to, but don't you worry, I'm a resilient old bat."

I laughed. "You mean beautiful falcon," I said, earning myself an eye roll.

"Why don't you use the space to cook. I won't use it. I never cook, and when staff come in, they usually bring their own stash of junk food and garbage they like to eat."

The woman thought for a moment. "Well, it'll need to be cleared with Flex and Eddie, but if they agree, I'll cook for your crew and mine, but you're in charge of getting me supplies," she said. "My policy is if I have to shop, cook, *and* clean, you're all eating beans."

I laughed. "Mrs. Emma Jean, I wouldn't ask you to cook for all of us, we are a ragtag bunch, and you have enough to do already."

"Psst, I used to cook for anywhere between twenty to forty men, and sometimes as many as a hundred. Your little crew ain't gonna disturb me," she said. "Besides, after you taste my cooking, you'll see I'm up to the challenge. Flex said most of your crew were from Mexico, and I've had some mighty good Mexican cooks help me through the years. They've taught me a few skills in the kitchen. Your crew can pretty-much tell me what part of the country they're from, and I can whip up at least a couple dishes they'd be familiar with."

I hadn't thought about hiring the housekeeper as our cook, and still wasn't sure it was a good idea, so I put the thought to the back of my mind and just smiled. "I'm looking forward to sampling your cuisine, señora," I said.

She winked at me then, and returned to her tiny kitchen and her bad attitude at being forced to work in a small space she was clearly still unfamiliar with.

Eddie walked in with his boys, and I heard them before seeing them. Apparently, they shared a wall with Emma Jean and Jimmy. The boys immediately ran into the living room, and began playing games on what appeared to be a couple of Gameboys from the '90s.

I looked at their dad and smiled. "You punishing them with your old toys?" I asked, pointing at one of the old games.

He looked confused for a moment, then at the device I was pointing to, and laughed. "No, I challenged them to a game and won, so now they're determined to beat me. We found those at the thrift store in Marfa last week. Besides, their phones don't really work out here, so there's limits on what they can play anyway."

I smiled again. "Well, it's good for the new generations to learn their history."

I could see the wariness in Eddie every time I ran across him. It was the same today, but talking about his kids mellowed him. It warmed my heart to see a father who loved his kids. Unfortunately, in my travels around the more poverty-stricken parts of Mexico, I'd seen a lot of kids whose parents didn't give a damn. Some kids the age of these two lived on the streets and were forced to be fully independent. I was a sucker when I saw any parent show affection for their children, a loving father, even more so, probably because I was attracted to men, and I found any type of human kindness in men attractive.

"I see Emma Jean informed you of the required attendance at evening meals," Eddie said, and winked at me.

That wink sent a thrill up my spine. Damn, this dinner was going to be more difficult than I expected.

"She pretty-much just told me dinner was at six and left it at that. I've been well trained not to question my elders."

Eddie snickered as Emma Jean came up behind me and patted my back, while squeezing around me to put something on the table. "It's good to see a young man who's had good raising," she said, before she slid back around and toward her kitchen.

"Yeah, I see this situation isn't really going to work. Your cousin should've consulted with her before agreeing to give me the house," I said. "She'll be shooting all of you within the week if she has to keep cooking in here."

Eddie shrugged. "That's all down to Flex. Seemed like he was happy to hand the house over. We're all betting it's because he doesn't want to move in by himself."

"I thought he had a boyfriend."

"He does," Eddie replied. "But, Mitch has to spend most of his time at the motel, and whether or not he does much work, Flex does have to pretend like he's helping out here."

"Hey," Flex said as he walked in the back door. "I heard that, Effie!"

Eddie laughed. "Well, it's true. Lately, all you seem to have time for is that man of yours."

Mitch came in the same back door with Jimmy and replied to Eddie himself, "You're just jealous," he said, patting him on the shoulder as he walked past and into the living room, where the kids were still playing. The youngest one immediately showed him the Gameboy, and asked if Mitch wanted to play. "I have had a lot more practice than you, so don't get mad if I kick your butt," he said, causing both boys to start smack talking him."

I laughed at their banter. It was clear this little crew was close, but way too close in these confined quarters to breathe.

We sat at the table, and even though they'd added an extra leaf, we were all shoulder to shoulder.

"Listen, from now on, this place is too small. I asked Emma Jean to use the house kitchen while it's just me or my skeleton crew. She said she had to talk to you, but you need to take me up on my offer. I highly recommend you let her use it," I said, and everyone laughed.

"We're close," Flex said. "But maybe this is a little too close. Are you sure that wouldn't be an imposition? We were already talking about creating a summer kitchen for all of us to use while you were in the house."

"No, it really won't. The house is divided up well enough that my crew and I will have all the privacy we require. You can tell the house was built so business could be done separately from food prep.

"I am curious, however, where did everyone eat back then?" I asked. "The dining room isn't big enough for all those men."

She laughed. "Back when I first got here, almost every meal was eaten on that front porch, or when we had a lot of men working, we'd stretch out makeshift tables under the cotton-woods."

"That's good to know," I said. "When we're filming, I'll have over a hundred people here and we'll need a place to feed all of them."

"Summer's the rainy season here, so you're probably safe at the time you say you'll be filming to use the shade of the Cottonwoods like we used to," she said.

She turned toward the meal. "There isn't enough room to do the buffet style like we usually do," she added, and pointed to the food that was sitting out on a makeshift buffet between us and the kitchen. "Y'all pass me your plates and I'll fill 'em up."

To my surprise she served cochanita pibil with soft tortillas as well as stuffed pepper burritos. I wondered if this was in honor of me, or if she cooked traditional Mexican food often. No one seemed to blink an eye, though, at least until she brought out sweet empanadas filled with apples for dessert.

"What's the occasion," Flex asked.

"You hush," Emma Jean told him. "I'm trying to impress Mr. Zitlal," she said, and flashed a bright smile toward me.

I laughed out loud. "You've succeeded. I've seldom had such a delicious meal, even on the Mexican side of the Chihuahua Desert."

She beamed with the compliment, and Jimmy, who was sitting next to me, leaned over and said, "You need to come to dinner more often. She usually don't serve us dessert these days, says we're all getting too fat."

When the meal was over, we all took our dishes into the kitchen, and Flex stayed back to help while the rest of us quickly left the tiny space. "I have a nice bottle of tequila I brought back from Los Altos de Jalisco if you'd like to join me for a nightcap over at the house. No offense, señor," I said, looking at Jimmy. "But this space is a little suffocating."

Jimmy laughed. "I sure agree, son, and count me in. I'll get Emma Jean and Flex and we'll head on over."

"Does Flex always help her with the dishes?" I asked, when Jimmy walked into the house.

"Hardly," Eddie laughed. "We all take turns helping her clean. She used to try to chase us out of the house, but we all told her it wasn't proper for her to do all the cooking and cleaning, so now she lets one of us take turns helping her clean the kitchen after the meal."

I laughed. "She lets you? That's funny, I was forced to help clean up every night in our house."

"Well, Emma Jean says we make more work helping, but I think that's just because all these years, that's how it's been for her. She makes it fun and you end up laughing the entire time you're helping, so I think secretly she likes us being there."

"Do the boys help?"

Eddie laughed. "She makes them help with everything, including cooking. When they get home, they have to report to her first thing, and she either uses them in the kitchen, or sends them out with Jimmy or me to do work on the ranch."

"Wow, your Emma Jean and my dad would get along perfectly," I said dryly.

"Oh, don't feel bad. My boys love the work and the attention from her. They've blossomed under her care," he said. "It's like for the first time in their lives, they have purpose. Not only that, but their grades have improved as well. I used to ride them to get their homework done, but now, no one even has to ask. It's part of their daily routine."

I smiled again. You could see how proud this man was of his kids, and the love for their housekeeper was there as well. My family had always treated the staff like family. I'd been punished or praised, whichever the occasion required, just as quick by the housekeeper, gardener, or cook as I was by my parents. The saying, *it takes a village*, really did apply to me and my sisters, as well as a host of other kids that came in and out of the hacienda. I'd grow up respecting adults no matter what station they held. Again, it was one of my father's strongest principles.

It seemed so natural when the family were all seated on the great porch, me pouring shots of tequila for the adults, and seltzer water for the boys. They pretended to enjoy it, but I knew they didn't. I'd have to remember to grab some soda or something for when they were over here.

As we all sat around, a gentle buzz settling in, Jimmy told stories of his days on the ranch. More often than not, he had us all in stitches laughing at the antics of the farmhands of the past.

As Jimmy finished his last tale, Eddie's oldest boy asked Jimmy to tell the legend of Diamondback Jack. The entire group seemed to freeze, and furtive glances were sent my way by more than one person, but Jimmy drew a deep breath, looked at me one last time, shrugged, and began the story.

I listened to the story, so similar to the way my family used to share the same legend, but from the property owner's perspective. Jimmy's telling of it started with how a man, unusually tall for his Mexican heritage, but whose height came from his Aztec ancestors, dared to challenge the property owner, who also happened to be his brother's father-in-law. He talked about the bandits, how the feud started between them, and how Diamondback Jack had been challenged to find the gold mine. "If you do, you're hired," was the message he was given.

Jimmy hesitated after he got to the point where Diamondback Jack had called his son to join him, and I jumped into the story.

"Jack was shot by the bandits, but not until he'd mortally wounded one of the bad men. He died in his son's arms, but not before he'd told him where he'd stored the gold the rancher had allowed him to mine as payment for providing protection. That son, Rodrigo Zitlal, moved back to El Paso, where his mother and sister lived, and sold the gold his father had mined. With his new wealth, he purchased a large parcel of land divided by the Rio Grande River that, unlike today, still ran with water. A third of the land was in Mexico and the other two thirds in the US. At the time, of course, no one noticed such things. Juarez and El Paso had been the same city long before Texas even existed."

I looked around the group, and everyone was focused on my story. Clearly realizing this was a part of the tale they'd never heard, I continued, evoking the storytelling skills my abuela used to use when telling the same tale.

"Rodrigo had been impressed by the large ranch his father had worked on, so he replicated the place as close as he could. Unfortunately, we aren't really designed to be ranchers," I chuckled. "My great-grandfather, Rodrigo's grandson, was the first to disappoint his abuelo when he announced he would never be a rancher. Instead, he wanted to be an actor, like the ones on the talkies he saw at the Wigwam theater in downtown El Paso." Before continuing, I looked at the two boys and explained that long ago, when movies first came out, people called them talkies.

"In a huff, Don Antonio, as he became known later in life, left the ranch and went to Hollywood to find his place in cinema. Unfortunately, there were no roles for him in Hollywood at the time, so he returned to the ranch with his tail between his legs."

I looked around the group to see if they'd grown tired of the story, but when it looked like I was going to stop, the youngest boy asked, "So what happened to Don Antonio?"

"Do you all really wanna hear this?" I asked.

Heads nodded all around, so I laughed, and continued, "Fate must have intervened, because his mama somehow got the family to attend the first movie in Juarez. It was a bilingual event, where interpreters yelled out the lines in English. The male lead fell sick, so in a total panic, the stricken theater owner rushed into the crowd, asking if there were any actors there who could interpret Spanish. Two men raised their hands, Antonio, and the famous Salvador Toscano Barragan, the father of Mexican filmography, who was there with his daughter Carmen.

An esteemed man such as Salvador Toscano would never stoop to interpreting for the crowd," I began to feel the joy I always felt when hearing or sharing this story, "...but this was a big opportunity for Don Antonio. He agreed to read the lines for the audience. Luckily, he was able to read through the script and rehearse briefly with the other English-speaking actors."

I almost chuckled at the rapt attention I had from the group. I wasn't the storyteller my abuela was, nor was I as good as Jimmy. I just assumed it was because of Diamondback Jack. I took a breath and hid my smile, before continuing, "That night would change Antonio's and the Zitlal's lives forever. Salvador and his daughter Carmen took a liking to the young man, and just like that, he was introduced to the world of Mexican filmmaking.

"The second life-changing event that took place as a result of meeting the Toscano family was when Salvador invited him to visit his home in Mexico City. Antonio was working there at the time, and they were celebrating the arrival of a distant relative, Lucia, who was visiting from Guadalajara.

"According to family legend, Lucia and Antonio fell in love the moment they laid eyes on each other. They were married three months after they met, in El Paso's Ysleta Mission. Antonio and Lucia agreed they'd like to film their wedding and much of the preparations for it. The wedding was the first film my ancestor produced on his own, and because it featured the history of the old mission, the oldest church in the United States, several smaller theaters showed the film. That catapulted Antonio into a business that lasts to this day in my family."

I leaned back in my chair and downed another shot of Tequila, and sighed contentedly. "Now, it appears, I'm back where this entire thing started."

"We even have our own bandit," Drake, the oldest boy exclaimed. "Maybe you can take him down like your ancestor did in the story." He ran around the room, pretending he was shooting with his fingers.

I laughed. "I only make stories and movies. I don't actually act them out, hijo," I said, then realized I'd responded to the little man like my father did me. I decided it was best to let that little slip go, hoping this mostly Anglo family wouldn't catch it.

I seemed to be in the clear, except for Emma Jean, who beamed at me. I shrugged inwardly and smiled, I doubted much got past that one anyway.

"It does seem strange, maybe a little spooky, that we all appear to have come full circle," Eddie replied.

"It's all coincidence, I'm sure. Both our families have a long history in West Texas, it isn't that out of the ordinary."

Eddie shrugged, and I could tell from his expression he was holding something back. I suddenly remembered the day out on the mountain when Eddie seemed to be about to tell me something about Jack.

"You were going to tell me about something regarding my ancestor when the call about my father interrupted us."

Eddie's face blushed, but he smiled to cover it up. "Let's just say, he's still influencing us today," he said.

I was about to push for more when Emma Jean stood up. "Well, the boys have school tomorrow, and it is almost nine o'clock. I have an early morning too, so I'm going to turn in as well," she said.

The boys, Eddie, and Jimmy stood to follow her out, when she patted Eddie's hand. "If you don't mind, I'll tuck the boys in tonight. I've been missing them since y'all moved into the other side of the duplex, and I promised to tell them a story."

Both boys snickered, and Eddie looked at the older woman through squinted eyes. "What story are you telling?" he asked.

"Oh, nothing much," she said. "Just about that time you, Flex, and Eric got caught skinny-dipping in the river by the girls from the convent school who were canoeing to check out the newly christened Canon de Elaina."

"Emma Jean!" he exclaimed, but she'd already pushed the kids down the steps and toward the little duplex across the way.

Jimmy and I laughed out loud, but both Eddie and Flex were blushing bright red. Flex shook his head and said he was going to the camper to bury his face in shame. Mitch laughed as he followed him out.

Jimmy followed behind his wife and the kids, leaving Eddie and me alone on the porch.

He sat back down and handed his empty glass back over to me. "I'll need a couple more of these before I can go back and face my children after *that* story," he said.

I chuckled as I filled his glass then mine.

"Tell me about living here as a kid," I said.

Eddie leaned back with a smile, and began telling me adventures of his childhood, his love for this place becoming more and more evident. When he talked about his grandmother he waxed nostalgic, causing me to smile.

"Tell me about her," I said, wanting to continue the easy conversation we'd started.

He chuckled. "She was only five foot tall, a full foot shorter than my grandpa. She loved what was thought of then as men's work, and she dressed the part. She could ride a horse better than any man on the ranch, and was the first person out the door and riding the fences. I remember her saying that was when she got her thinking done. Occasionally, she'd take one of us with her even when we were little, throwing us up in front of her on the horse. God, I loved her. Flex wasn't much for the day-to-day work and would've preferred to sleep in, but I wanted to ride with her every chance I got."

He sat for a moment, deep in memory. "I guess that's why I volunteer to ride the fences now. It just reminds me of her."

"Are you all going to build up your cattle again?" I asked.

"No, not to the level it was then," Eddie said sadly. "Unfortunately, raising cattle isn't what it used to be."

I sighed. "Yeah, things have changed since we were kids. Our ranch was turned into a wildlife preserve, and we even expanded our Mexican side of the Rio Grande, making both sides of the line a nature preserve. Of course, there's a wall between the two countries now, but even that's become something of an important component since scientists are studying the impact the wall has on the wildlife in our region."

We sat in companionable silence then for several long minutes before I turned to him, and asked, "What were you really going to tell me that day?" I asked.

Eddie looked at me for a long moment. I could tell he was reeling from the abrupt change of topic, and hadn't been prepared for me to ask that question.

"It's too strange," he said. "There's a lot going on with Flex being shot and all. We still don't know who wanted to hurt him, or why."

"What's that got to do with my ancestor?"

Eddie shrugged. "Not sure, but something."

I opened my mouth to ask another question. Eddie stopped me, and said, "Just trust me and leave it there. I have no doubt when or if you need to know more about all that's been happening, or did happen, you will." He stood up to go then, but before he did, he looked at me and, waving his hands in the air, he said, "Trust the spirits of the ranch! Wooooooo." And walked off the porch, headed toward the duplex.

I chuckled to myself, thinking they were all up to something. I assumed they were probably trying to set up another movie about Diamondback Jack. If that were the case, they didn't need to try too hard, the thought had already occurred to me. The legend was just perfect for a movie, and the border elements made it that much more appealing.

I wondered if my family would be down with us doing a movie about our ancestors. I sat down on the sofa to try to get some work done, but unfortunately, the internet was out. *Note to self, ask your assistant to research reliable networks in the region.* Could we somehow boost the coverage?

Without the internet and access to the cloud where all my files were stored, I couldn't do much work. I'd probably have to drive to the university tomorrow and use their Wi-Fi or something. It might be a good idea to just get an office there, since I doubted we'd solve the internet needs here.

I closed my computer and decided I'd turn in as well. I usually didn't go to bed until the wee hours of the morning, but, *when in Rome, do as the Romans, right?* Apparently, that applied to West Texas ranches as well.

My mind raced when I lay down, I thought of all the preparations I still needed to do and began to count them off in my head.

Before I knew it, I was asleep but not asleep, at the same time.

I figured I was dreaming, because dreams just had a certain feel to them, like I could manipulate the outcome, but not necessarily the events.

I looked around me. I was sitting on a barrel inside what looked to be a cave. No, a mine. I could see the chisel marks on the walls, and if I looked further along the shaft I could see wooden beams.

I got up and walked toward the shaft, but immediately knew it wasn't safe. Something ominous was watching me from within the cave's interior, like the Eye of Sauron from the Lord of the Rings.

I backed away from the entrance and immediately bumped into someone. I jumped and twisted around, ready to fight if I had to, but the figure whose face was hidden by the shadows chuckled at me. "So, you'd fight your own granddad, I see."

This was really getting weird, I thought to myself, and the old man in my dream seemed to be able to hear my thoughts, and laughed.

"It lurks in the shaft. It knows the mine is here. I tried to drive him back, but his mind is too far gone to be afraid of ghosts," he said, and turned to me. "You must protect them. It's your destiny, son," he said. "My promise is your destiny."

The man turned and walked out of the mine. I followed him, but when I got to the entrance, he was nowhere to be seen. It was dark out, but I could tell the mine opened into a clearing surrounded by brush.

I was about to turn back around when the hairs on the back of my neck stood up. Something was behind me, stalking me. I slowly turned around, and when I did, a huge black shadow lunged at me.

I woke up screaming, covered in sweat. "Damn," I said out loud, "No more bedtime stories for me."

It was still early, around one in the morning. I usually didn't even go to bed until now. I got up and stretched. After that nightmare, I wouldn't be going back to sleep anytime soon, so I went downstairs and rummaged through the refrigerator that was, for the most part, empty. How I wished I'd snagged some of Emma Jean's empanadas. Just the thought of one of them made my mouth water.

I went back into the living room and opened my laptop, not hoping for much luck with the internet, but to my surprise, there was indeed a little coverage.

I quickly pulled up a few documents I was working on, including the script, which frankly was still a mess.

The love story was still dull and predictable, and there was little intrigue. It was like my writers had lost all inspiration. Was I working them too hard? Maybe, I'd need to give them time off *after* this movie was done, but they couldn't fall apart on me now. This was happening, and we were too far in to back off now.

I kicked my feet up on the sofa and opened the script, reading through the opening scene. It sucked... like *really* sucked.

The male character was a stereotypical rough and tough dude, shooting at everything that moved, and the female character was one-dimensional as well.

I'd had the writers rewrite this scene at least half a dozen times, but it still didn't set the right tone.

I lay back and imagined the scene, and of course, my ancestor's story came to mind. Would it be possible to integrate that story? To build something that would complement both nationalities? Show that this area was once a place where collaboration could be had?

I sat up, pulling the laptop on my lap and began typing.

I changed the scene entirely, using the story of how Diamondback Jack had arrived on the property. The opening scene needed to be of men harassing the ranch owner, a stout, strong-willed, middle-aged veteran, who was able to fend them off, but barely. Then the handsome, Latino man walked in while the family was cleaning up the mess created the night before. I should change the story slightly, so it was his daughter who came to help. That would catch the millennials, showing a woman defending her father, and then falling in love with a ranch hand. I could use the rancher who had initially hired the man, or maybe his son or nephew. That would need ironing out, but the writers could probably do that without me.

I saved my text and emailed it to my father and sister Ellen, asking if they would be okay with me taking our family history and manipulating it a bit, so this movie had a better plot.

I sat staring at the wall, allowing my mind to wander about how the plot could flow with the new storyline. The love affair was real enough, although not that common. Mexicans and Anglos did mix back in the day. Hell, look at the family who owned this ranch. A civil war vet married an Apache woman, then their descendants married Mexican Americans up until Flex and Eddie's grandmother.

"Where did Eddie get that blond hair?" I asked out loud, then laughed. Clearly, from his dad's side, but he maintained the high cheekbones of his native ancestors.

Why was I thinking about Eddie? Didn't I swear I was done with all that? *Seriously, get a grip*, I chastised myself, but I knew it did no good. I was already attracted to him. Add to how sweet he'd been when I got that dreadful call about my father, then watching him tonight with his sons.

It was going to be difficult to keep my hands off him. The kiss, that one hot kiss was enough to keep me enthralled.

I sort of regretted my strict policy of no married men. I hated a liar, and a cheater was one of the worst liars—at least in my opinion.

Sleep, take two. I was growing tired again, so I went back upstairs to try again. "Abuelo Diamond, I'd appreciate you letting me sleep this time," I said to the room. Luckily, there was no reply, and before I knew it, I was out and enjoying a dream-free sleep.

14

Eddie

I THINK THE GREATEST surprise for all of us was how much we enjoyed Alex's company. The kids especially had taken a liking to him, even little Luke, who was usually wary of strangers seemed to accept him as one of our own.

I was happy when Alex's cast and crew began showing up at the house. They started as a trickle, then there were weeks when the house and lodge were full of them. Several of the kids from the university in Alpine would spend the night in the lodge as well, when he had them working on different projects.

Alex hired security almost immediately, which was a relief, especially after that last dream. Luckily, that had been a while ago. Maybe the lack of dreams was an indication that things were calming down.

Alex surprised me while I was out riding the fences. Shortly after he officially moved into the house, I found him riding the same mare I'd given him the first time we rode out. This was usually my quiet time, and although the fences seldom needed mending, I loved the morning rides. It was my time to meditate and prepare myself for the day.

When I came up behind Alex, I surprised him as well, and we laughed at each other's startled responses.

"What are you doing out this early?" he asked.

I laughed again. "You haven't been on a ranch in a while, have you? I'm riding the fences to make sure the cattle don't get out."

"Oh, that makes sense," he said, and pulled his horse in behind mine without asking.

"You do this every day?" he asked.

"Yep, it's a daily chore. Why, you gonna volunteer a few shifts?" I asked, trying to be snarky enough to drive him away and get back to my morning.

"Sure, if you want me to. Just show me what to do," he responded, to my surprise.

I turned around and looked at him. "You serious?" I asked

"I like to ride, and lately, I'm in bed at such an early hour. I wake up early, so I figured I'd be doing some morning riding anyway."

I looked forward and gestured for him to ride up next to me. When his horse pulled up next to mine, I pointed toward the fence. "Sometimes the javelinas will run through the fences. It's worse when they have babies." I pointed at a wash that was right in front of us. "Washes tend to be the places we have the most trouble. We've tried putting the wire up, but then the cattle get out, so we just have to fix the problems when they occur."

We rode companionably for several minutes. This was usually my alone time, but having Alex riding next to me felt... well, it felt right and connected. I pondered on how surprising that was. Hell, I'd basically told Flex he was off the hook, except when I needed to run into town, or wasn't able to because of the kids, but there was something about Alex. He was clearly from a well-to-do family. I could see it in the way he dressed. The way he addressed people was also... well, not arrogant per se as much as authoritative, but he was also great company, not to mention he was insanely good-looking, and every day he spent on the ranch, I was feeling more and more attracted to him.

"I've been meaning to talk to you again," he said, and I could feel the butterflies begin to swarm in my stomach. I nodded for him to proceed.

"Well, you and I had a moment that day you were showing me the ranch. I think about it, and you, a lot."

I nodded, but didn't reply. I didn't trust myself to.

"It's just that you're married, and I... well, I don't think it's right to get involved with married men. If you weren't, though, I would want to date you."

When I turned toward him, his face was bright red, and I laughed. "You aren't used to wooing a man, are you?" I asked.

He blew out a half sigh, half laugh. "No, to be honest I'm usually the one being pursued, or it's a mutual hookup."

"I am married, and as I told you, I'm not on the market at least until the divorce is final."

"You filed for divorce?" he asked, surprised.

"She wants it, and..." I rode on a bit, aware that I was in very rocky territory with this conversation. "Well, after that day, I realized I wanted it too, but I have kids. Even when the divorce is final, they are my priority. I won't lie to you, Alex, you've caused a fire to burn inside me, one that hasn't burned in a long time. I thought maybe it never would again, but it isn't like I can just throw caution to the wind. My kids are already attached to you. If I were to get emotionally involved, well, there could be consequences for them."

Alex nodded his agreement, and we continued the trail ride, both of us deep in thought.

"I need to go back to El Paso for a few days, then I have a meeting in St. Augustine, Florida about a potential new film that'll be set there and in Cuba. Why don't you go with me?"

I sighed. "Because, I'm still married, and I have obligations here."

He smiled. "I bet if you asked Flex, he'd say yes. Emma Jean has a strong grasp on your boys too. I'm sure she'd take kid duty."

"Presumptuous much?" I asked laughing, before I finally turned him down. "I'm sorry, maybe some other time."

He didn't really respond, but when we could see the barn in the distance, he said, "I think I'll ride a bit longer. I'll see you this evening for dinner?"

When I nodded, he smiled that beautiful rich-boy smile, and turned his horse toward the backcountry.

What would it be like to have just said yes and spent time with him in El Paso and then Florida? I'd never been to Florida. My dad actually lived in southern Georgia, and my brothers and I always threatened to show up at his house one day. We'd never done it, and my mother hated to travel, so we never did. I became a dad when I was still a kid myself, so there was no money or time for travel. It would sure be nice to get out, and when you added the thoughts of loving up on that sexy man.

Unintentional visions of our two naked bodies entwined doing god only knew what to each other caused me to get hard, and a hard on in the saddle was never a good idea. Time to wipe all those thoughts from my mind. Time to let all that go.

I'd just gotten Red settled and was about to comb her down, when I got a call from Emma Jean. "Eddie, you better come home pronto," she said, in a bit of a panic.

"Shit, why, what's going on, Emma Jean?"

"You have a visitor," she said.

"Who?"

"It's your wife, honey, she's here with her... well, she's not alone and they're with the kids. Jimmy is with them. I came over to get the radio."

I was already running before she finished speaking. I ran across the yard and took the trail behind the house that went directly to the duplex. When I got there, I saw a brand-new F-Type Jaguar convertible in the driveway. "Fuck, she brought the drug dealer to my house?" I said under my breath.

When I got to the front door, it was standing open, and I could see my wife in the living room. Drake and Luke looked like they were seeing a ghost, and behind my kids was the fucking asshole.

"Theresa, wow, it's good to see you." I had to work hard not to sound like I was angry. It would alarm the kids and possibly send the hopped-up asshat she was hooked up with into a dangerous rage.

"Why don't you come out and talk. John, good to see you again," I said to the man behind my kids.

Emma Jean came up behind me then and said, "Boys, y'all need to finish getting ready, the bus will be here any moment."

The boys turned automatically toward their bedrooms. Emma Jean walked through the door like a boss between Theresa and her crook boyfriend and headed toward the kids' rooms.

I walked out of the house and toward the Jag. I knew two things were in my favor. Theresa was here for me. She didn't give a fuck about the kids, and John would be worried what I was going to do to his new car, so I was fairly confident I'd get them to follow me if I went in that direction.

Luckily, I guessed right, and they followed me to the car.

The second I turned around, Theresa handed me a folder. "It's done," she said. "I brought the paperwork to you, so you'd know we are no longer married. John and I are headed to Las Vegas to get married, but we both wanted to see the look on your face when I told you I was no longer yours to control."

I never did understand how she thought I was controlling her. Transference from her childhood and hatred of her parents onto me, a therapist I'd hired to try to save our marriage once told me. I took the paperwork from her and smiled. Emotions stirred inside me, but the one I was most concerned about was what the man she'd brought here might do to my kids or me. I internally shook off all the warring emotions and nodded. "Then that's it. Have a great life, and congratulations on your wedding. May we never see each other again."

I started to walk away when I felt Theresa push me. "Fuck you, you arrogant asshole!" she said.

I just kept walking. I knew she'd want a showdown. Had I known she was coming, I'd have gotten the kids out of the house and away from the inevitable drama. I thought things would've blown up and probably gotten violent if John's history was any indication of how things went, but just as Theresa was getting wound up, two security men walked around the house, and asked me if everything was okay.

I turned back to see a very angry Theresa, and could see that John was reaching behind his back for what I assumed was a gun.

"Hi, guys, I think it's all good. This is my *ex*-wife Theresa and her fiancé. They were just stopping by to say goodbye to the boys. They're getting married in Vegas," I said, as I continued to walk toward the front door.

The security men stepped in behind me as I walked away. I continued until I was in the house with the door closed. When the lock clicked, I leaned back against it and let out my pent-up breath. Luckily, the boys were in their bedrooms, and hopefully had missed the drama.

I heard the Jag start up and gravel spray as it took off. God help me, I hoped that was the last I'd see of her, for all our sakes. Had Alex's security not been there, I was not sure how it would've played out. I was guessing Theresa and John had come for a showdown, and my getting an ass whooping was probably also in the plans. John had threatened as much when I'd gone to Houston last time to check up on her.

She didn't want the kids, never did really, but if she'd thought it would hurt me, she'd have gladly taken them. It wouldn't have been a pretty picture.

The boys came out of their rooms, and when they saw me, they ran into my arms. "Is she gone, Daddy?" Luke asked.

"Yeah, baby, she's gone," I replied.

Drake had tears flowing down his cheeks. It had always been harder on him. Luke was so young when she started leaving that he didn't have the same attachment. Drake, on the other hand, had seen the good, well, what good there was, and the bad. Too often, I'd watched the love and the fear of her war across his face.

Today, I couldn't read which emotion was winning. "Do you guys feel up to school today?" I asked.

Both boys nodded. Luckily, they loved their little country school, and they'd both made good friends. Unlike me and Flex, who were always looking for an excuse to play hooky, both boys liked going to school. "I'll drive you in, okay?" I asked.

They nodded again. "Hey, since you're both being so brave, I'll pick you up from school this afternoon, and we can go for some ice cream."

That cheered them both up, and as they ran to my truck, book packs on, I heard them talking about what they were going to order.

"How did it go in their room?" I asked Emma Jean.

She shrugged. "They were terrified. Neither one of them trusts her, and that man scared Luke to death."

Did they hear any of the chaos outside?" I asked.

"No, they just finished getting ready."

"Good," I said. "At least that's good."

She nodded. Before I went out the door, I said, "If they show back up, you call the security guards back over, and then the sheriff. I'm going to stop by his office after I drop the boys off and explain the situation. He'll need to know the infamous John Princeton is lurking in these parts anyway. If you and Jimmy can explain the situation to Alex and his security, I'd appreciate it."

Emma Jean nodded, and as I walked out toward the two security men that were still standing outside the duplex. "Emma Jean and Jimmy are going to explain what that was about, but…" I looked over at the truck to make sure there were no ears listening to me. I lowered my voice and said, "My ex-wife's boyfriend is a bad dude. He's a drug dealer in Houston, and although I don't think they'll come back, they might. I'd stay on high alert if I were you."

The biggest guy nodded. "We'll keep an eye out," he said.

I got in the truck and let the boys lead the conversation. Neither one asked about Theresa, and it seemed neither one of them wanted to talk about her. I parked the truck when we got to the little schoolhouse and went in to talk to the principal.

I'd already given them a heads-up about the boy's mother, and told them it was unlikely she'd ever show up, but if she ever did, I'd let them know. Seeing John Princeton with her kicked the concern level up several notches. The man was trouble, and he was slick as Vaseline when it came to getting out of trouble with the law. I had a friend on the police force in Houston, and when Theresa first disappeared, he told me she was seen hanging with John's gang of thugs. "I know you two are having troubles, but you might let her know Princeton tends to leave a bloody mess in his wake," he'd told me.

When I found her, shortly after the last time she'd left, she was shacked up with him, and I decided it was probably best to leave her and him alone. Luckily, she ignored me, for the most part.

Well, at least she did until my mother stuck her fucking nose in the middle of it. That was when Theresa and this Princeton fella got riled up, and Theresa started harassing me for a divorce.

The principal walked over to his desk and called the secretary into the room, so I could explain the situation to both of them. They both swore they'd ensure the kids wouldn't be allowed to go with them if they showed up. Luckily, the school wasn't far from the sheriff's office, so unlike the ranch, if something went down, the school would have fast backup.

I went to the sheriff's office next, and when the older man saw me, he smiled. "I hear you and that movie man made up," he said, before I was even in the room."

I laughed. "Well, it was a case of mistaken identity. I know how to grovel when the situation calls for it."

The sheriff laughed out loud. "I'm sure their pocketbooks helped grease your pride a bit."

"Sheriff, you've known my people all these years. If I didn't think I was mistaken, there ain't enough money on this planet to make me change my mind."

He smiled. "That's for damned sure, son. Your grandpa was as good as anyone could get, but once his mind was set, nothing short of an atomic bomb would change it."

"Then you know his money isn't what changed my mind. But, now that they've pretty much taken the ranch over, it sure is nice not to have to worry about how to pay this year's taxes and the other expenses of running that huge tract."

He nodded, the smile never leaving his face. "So, what brings you in this morning?"

"Well, that's a sticky situation. My wife...well, ex-wife as of just an hour ago, stopped by the ranch this morning. You ever heard of John Princeton?" I asked.

The sheriff's face melted, and the smile was instantly replaced with concern.

He nodded. "We think he may be connected with a cartel that runs drugs through the parks occasionally."

"Well, that son of a bitch, is my ex's fiancé. I've never had reason to believe he'd ever step foot on the ranch, but since he did this morning, I figured you needed to know."

"You're right about that," he said, and went to get some paperwork to take my statement.

We went through all his questions, including why they had come and what they said.

"I'll contact the Vegas police and let them know he's coming their way. I'm not going to beat around the bush, if Princeton is involved and he wanted to kick your ass this morning, I doubt he'll stop until he does. I recommend you take a vacation for the next few days, and I'd take those boys with you."

I sighed. "Damn, I thought the same thing, but I was hoping I was overreacting."

"You weren't, not if Princeton is involved. I doubt I have to tell you he's been credited with murders on both sides of the border. You may not want to hear this, but he don't care if he kills adults or kids. He's a real monster, that one."

"Yeah, I've heard that too." I sighed and waited a moment for my stomach to settle. "Okay, well, it wouldn't hurt for y'all to keep your eyes on the school. I'm gonna go plan a vacation. I doubt they'll come for the kids. Theresa never showed any interest. Even this morning, she was standing further away from the kids than John was. She hates them and thinks they were my way of controlling her. Me, on the other hand, she'd love to watch someone beat me to a pulp. I'd be willing to bet if those security guys hadn't intervened, that's exactly what would've happened."

He nodded. Truth was truth, and luckily, nobody was pretending otherwise.

I left the office sick to my stomach. Well, fuck, at least the end was here. I was divorced, and instead of regret, I felt... well, I felt relief that was strongly mixed with fear for my boys.

I'd luckily saved up enough cash between the good season we'd had with our guests along with the payments that Alex's company had paid. So, for the first time, I could actually afford to take my boys on vacation. *Where to go?* That was the real question.

When I arrived at the ranch, I was confronted immediately by the entire group, including Alex, which seemed weird.

Flex seemed to be the designated person to ask questions. I explained all I knew, and even mentioned the sheriff wanted me to take the boys away for a while, at least until they knew Princeton was back in Houston.

"Do they think the boys are at risk?" Emma Jean asked nervously.

"Well, no one knows what to think. It may all be a false alarm, but it's better safe than sorry. Anyway, Flex, Jimmy, I'm going to have to be away for a bit. You think you can run this place without me?" I asked.

"We'll survive," Jimmy said dryly, then winked at me. "It'll do Flex good to do some real work for a change," he said, then laughed as Flex gave him the eye. Poor Flex had been given so much grief since he'd moved in with Mitch. There really wasn't much hard labor to do, but since we'd signed onto this project together, Flex had shown he preferred the indoor work. It was all fine, but that didn't mean he shouldn't get a good teasing about it.

"Where do you plan to go?" Alex asked.

I shrugged. "I don't know yet. Probably won't spend much time in Texas, since Princeton has a lot of connections in this area. We haven't been many places, so anywhere will be a treat. Besides, I doubt I should tell you where we are, just in case. It might be best that you don't know."

Flex shrugged. "You've been watching too much TV. I doubt anyone's going to tie us up and question us about where you've gone."

I agreed. "You're probably right. Well, I'm gonna go see where I can plan a quick vacation." Emma Jean patted my back and then headed to the house to get the meal on for the crew. The woman had come into her own cooking for large numbers. She really was a pro at it, and her food had actually improved with the added numbers... if that was even possible.

Alex followed me up to my door. "You know my offer still stands, you could come to El Paso with me, and even though I might get my ass kicked by my dad, we could borrow my colleague's private jet to fly out to Saint Augustine."

"I have kids, Alex. That's the point in leaving, to keep them safe, but thanks anyway."

"I know you've got kids, Eddie. I meant bring them along, they'd enjoy it. My parents would love them and spoil them horribly. I have a couple meetings in Saint Augustine, then we could take the boys to Disney World. It could be fun."

I looked at him and thought for a moment. It would be more fun to travel with someone who knew where they were going. Besides, it'd be fun to take a look at where Diamondback Jack's son had gone after leaving here. Like a history lesson.

"If you're serious, sure. It's not like I had a lot of warning about this. Where do you live? I'll set up a hotel close to your home."

Alex laughed. "You think my parents would let you stay in a hotel? No, man, they would be beyond offended if you didn't stay with us. The hacienda is way too big anyway, it was built to house all the domestic workers and ranch hands. My parents block off sections of the property, except for special occasions, so it's like staying in a hotel anyway."

"It seems like an imposition," I said. "I'd feel like I was invading their personal space. It'd be better if we stayed somewhere else."

Alex laughed again. "I'll tell you what, stand here while I call my parents, if after I let them know you're coming you think you can still stay in a hotel without offending them, then I'll be happy to help you book a room."

I nodded. It seemed like a fair way to deal with this.

He used the landline since mobile phones tended not to work out here consistently. When it started ringing, Alex turned the speakerphone on. Within seconds his mother answered.

"Alexandro," she answered. "¿Qué te hace llamar a tu mamá cuando no es su cumpleaños?"

I didn't speak much Spanish, but I knew a mother's guilt trip when I heard one, and I chuckled in spite of myself.

Alex gave me a look but continued with the conversation. "Mama, I've got Eddie here, he's the man I told you about, the co-owner of the ranch. He is coming back with me to the hacienda with his boys. They need a vacation. I'm going to take them with me to Saint Augustine, and when I'm done with all the meetings, we're going to take the boys to Disney World. Do you mind if he comes to visit?"

"Oh, what an honor. Pedro has been wanting to meet him ever since you told us they were the owners of the ranch where our ancestor mined the gold. It's taken everything in me to keep your papa from flying down there and meeting them himself."

"How's he doing, Mama?" Alex asked, concern on his face.

"He's doing great. The doctors have given him the all-clear, and he's slowly getting back to his routine, but Ellen keeps him pretty well controlled, telling him he needs to take it easy and she bribes him with seeing his new grandbaby. I think that's the only thing that would work on him."

"Is Ellen still doing okay?" he asked.

"Hijo, she glows with that baby. I haven't seen her so happy since she was a child. It's like watching her bloom right in front of us."

Alex laughed. "Mama, you're so dramatic."

Alex looked at me then and smiled. "Oh, Mama, Eddie said he and the boys will stay in a local hotel, he doesn't want to be an imposition. Is that hotel they just built close to you good?"

Spanish began ringing out of her mouth so quick I couldn't follow it at all. "¿Por qué no se quedará con nosotros? ¿Le dijiste cosas malas que lo harían querer quedarse en un hotel?"

"No, Mama, no, I didn't tell him anything about you, *or* the hacienda. He just said he didn't want to be an imposition."

"It's an imposition to have your guest staying at a hotel when we have all this room here. Besides, he is all but family with his connection to your ancestors."

"Si, Mama, I'll tell him what you said, but, he is a stubborn man. I may not be able to convince him…

Before he finished speaking the other line went dead, and Alex burst out laughing. "I told you," he said.

"You did," I laughed. "I guess we'll be staying with you after all."

"Well, you are welcome to explain to her why you didn't, but I think you'd be better off staying here and facing down that Princeton man."

"I agree, okay, so that's settled. I don't know anything about private jets. Do I need to set up a reservation before we fly to Saint Augustine?"

Alex laughed. "Private means you don't have to do anything other than show up. My assistant will get everything ready."

"You do realize I won't be able to manage my kids ever again after this. Their first flight is going to be on a private jet. They are going to have a warped view of what it means to fly."

"Well, they'll learn reality soon enough. I usually fly commercial myself, and my father will truly be pissed when he hears I'm using the plane. He thinks it's ridiculous and bad for the environment, which he's right about, but it's probably best to fly below the radar for the time being. He'll understand when I explain."

I sighed, "I hate being such a bother. Now I'm not just putting my family out, but I'm putting yours out as well. Wouldn't it just be better if I went in a different direction? I could take the boys to the Grand Canyon, or something like that."

"You could, but then it wouldn't be as much fun as hanging out with me. You'll enjoy the hacienda too. It's pretty there, they've turned the area around it into a garden, or at least my great-granny did, my family just maintain her gardens, but the rest of the property is protected for wildlife. The birds are beautiful, and we can go horseback riding along the old riverbed. Sometimes the border patrol ride over and you can talk to them. They are usually pretty decent, and the boys will be totally enamored with them. You can call it an educational visit, since they'll be missing school."

"Crap, that reminds me, I need to call the teacher and let her know I'm going to have the boys out of school. Okay, Alex, you win, but if at any point you grow tired of us, you have to promise to let me know. Two boys are a lot of work," I said, and chuckled to myself. If he spent time with kids, he'd get the picture soon enough.

We left late that night, wanting to give the boys some time to adjust to the idea of a spontaneous vacation. He'd told me to either bring a passport or birth certificate for the kids and me, since we might end up going over into Juarez. Luckily, I'd gotten all of us passports when we moved to the ranch, just in case we needed to cross into Mexico from here.

We agreed it was best for Alex to drive, since he'd need his car in town, and my old truck, although still a good one, needed fewer miles put on it.

It took four hours for us to get to Alex's place. He kept calling it the hacienda, and to be honest I thought he was just being snooty, but the moment he pulled into the desert oasis, I understood. The house looked like we'd arrived at some luxurious hacienda in Spain, or at least what those haciendas looked like in the movies.

It flowed across the landscape, both imposing and unobtrusive at the same time. The gardens were spectacular. Beautiful plants that normally didn't grow well in the desert bloomed all around the property. I wondered where they got the water to keep all the plants alive.

We climbed a great staircase onto an enormous porch that stretched the length of the home. It wasn't what I thought of as a porch in West Texas, it was built into the structure, with arching frames surrounding it. The second we walked onto it, a gentle breeze swept across us. Clearly, the architecture was designed to create a wind-tunnel effect. I stepped back off the porch where there was no breeze, then back on again and looked at Alex. "That's cool," I said.

Alex laughed. "You would be the only person I've ever brought here to notice the breeze on the porch."

"Hey, in my line of work, a breeze is a valuable commodity."

The boys were exhausted. The morning had been stressful, and then when I picked them up from school and they found out we were leaving town, both boys were excited. Drake must have realized why we were leaving, and since then he'd shut down both emotionally and physically. He slept most of the way, and not knowing what else to do, I let him.

The great door opened then, and there stood a stunning woman. She smiled at Alex and pulled him into a hug. "Mi hijo, welcome home."

"Mom, this is Edward Crawford and his two sons, Drake and Luke."

"What handsome men you've brought home with you," she exclaimed, and knelt down in front of Luke and Drake, extending her hands. "Welcome to the hacienda," she said to them, then looked up to me. "Come in and meet the family."

We followed her into the magnificent home. The boys and I looked around like we were watching a tennis match. Everywhere we looked was beautiful. The entry was surrounded by brightly colored tiles. I'd seen similar ones when I was a contractor, and knew these must come from the Mexican city of Puebla. Even with the differences in the two economies, I knew these tiles were worth their weight in gold. I searched my mind for what they were called, Talavera or something like that.

She escorted us into a great room to the left of the entrance and once again, the three of us stood in awe. The room was large, more like a banquet hall than a living room. The ceiling was tall, with a cathedral-style roofline. There were magnificent beams that ran the length of the room, slanting on all sides until they met in the middle of the ceiling. The effect was stunning.

In the middle of the room stood a large double-sided fireplace and impressive chimney. It was encased in the same Pueblo-style tiles, but a different design from the ones in the entry. These were more subtle, but colorful, nonetheless.

There was a massive leather couch with smaller, more modern furniture flanking it. The room had various different sitting areas like it'd been designed as a hotel lobby and not a private residence.

The woman led us around the fireplace to the other side of the room. We were greeted by an older man, who I assumed was Alex's father, and two women. One was pregnant with another man at her side. In this room, he looked like he could be a personal servant ready to run at a moment's notice to fetch her whatever it was she might want. Since people didn't tend to have personal servants any longer, I assumed this was her husband.

"Gentlemen," she said as we came upon the small group. "This is my family, Ellen and Francesca, my daughters and Alexandro's hermanas... sorry, his sisters. This is Ellen's husband, Ernesto. This man," she stopped introducing him and went to stand next to him. "Is señor Zitlas, and I am señora Zitlas, but..." she looked at the boys and smiled. "You may call us abuelo y abuela." She gestured to herself and her husband.

A hush fell across the room, and I could tell something significant had just happened. My boys had been accepted into this family. I wasn't sure why. We'd only just met them, but we were lacking family, so I wasn't going to say or do anything that would get in the way of a possible relationship for them.

I stepped up and said, "It is such a great honor that you've allowed us to stay here with you."

Alex smiled. "Everyone, this is Eddie and his sons, Drake and Luke."

"So, you will be staying with us then?" señora Zitlal asked me.

"Of course, ma'am," I said. "We would never be so rude as to refuse your hospitality." I looked at Alex and winked, which earned me a smug look in return.

The older woman smiled, then looked at her daughter. "Francesca, would you please show these gentlemen to their rooms? Alex, you can catch us up on things while they are getting settled."

"Will Eddie be staying in your room then, Alex?" Francesca said, causing my face to bloom red and Alex to look at her with wide eyes.

"My friends will require their own accommodations, sister. Now, shall we talk about a certain doctor?" he said.

Francesca's naughty smile froze on her face, and she quickly escorted us out of the room and down a corridor.

"We aren't dating," I told her after she'd shown the boys the room they'd be staying in, and escorted me into mine that was next door. "He was just kind enough to let us come visit while… well, while things settled down at home."

She blushed. "I shouldn't have asked that. It was rude of me, and I've got a tongue lashing coming when I go back in there," she replied.

"It's okay. I just got divorced… in fact, it was just finalized this morning. My ex is dating an unsavory man, the authorities believed we'd be better off on vacation for a while."

"I'm sorry, Mr… I'm sorry, I missed your last name. "

"Crawford. I'm Eddie Crawford," I said and shook her hand.

She quickly excused herself then. I laid my stuff on the bed and went to the window. The hacienda was set on a cliff overlooking the riverbed. My room faced south, so I could see where the riverbed was and the great wall that separated the two nations on the other side of it. The wall was the only ugly thing in view. I could only imagine how frustrated the family must have been when the US government built it.

I turned back to the room, noticing for the first time how luxurious it was. I put my stuff away and went to check on the boys.

"Why did that woman want to know if you were going to sleep in Alex's room?" Drake asked the second I walked in.

I laughed. "She was picking on her brother. I think she was trying to get Alex kicked out of his room so we could stay in there. It probably has a swimming pool in it or something." I knew I was lying, but it was okay. I'd rather they thought that than have to deal with their dad dating someone when they'd just dealt with their insane, drugged-out, worthless... *Okay, time to get off that... their mother,* I thought.

Luke laughed. "You think Alex will let us go swimming in his pool?" he asked.

"Maybe, but I don't know if he has a pool or not. Remember, the woman is Alex's sister, just like you and Drake are brothers. Sometimes you like to pick on each other for no reason. So, don't make too much of that, okay?"

We walked over to the window that looked out over the Rio Grande dry riverbed. "That used to be a big river," I said.

"It doesn't look like a river now, though," Drake said, sort of put out by the conversation.

"Yeah, it's been diverted. I think two cities share the water, but you'll have to let Alex tell you."

"Tell you what?" Alex asked as he came through the open door.

"What happened to all the water that used to be in the river?" Drake asked.

"Good question. We live in a really dry area like you two do, but there are a lot of people here, so the river water is collected into two lakes called reservoirs. Sometimes they release the water into the old river again, but usually only when there's been too much rain for the reservoirs to hold."

"Can we go see the lake?" Luke asked.

"It's a long way away," Alex said. "It would be a long drive like the one we just did from the ranch to here. Maybe you can come back another time, and we could go see it, though."

That seemed to mollify Luke, and he jumped off his bed where he'd been sitting. "Do you have a swimming pool in your room?"

Alex laughed. "No, why do you ask?"

"Dad said, your sister was trying to get you kicked out of your room, because you probably had a really nice room with a swimming pool in it."

Alex looked at me, and I shrugged. He chuckled.

"My room is almost exactly like this one, except it looks out over the courtyard instead of the river. My papa wanted to be able to keep an eye on us when we were younger, so he and Mama moved us all into the inner rooms. Why don't you all come with me and I'll give you a tour. Mama said they held off eating dinner, so we are all supposed to meet back in the kitchen in about thirty minutes.

"I'm hungry," Drake said.

Alex smiled. "Good, cause my mama is a good cook," he said.

The rest of the hacienda was just as magnificent as what we'd already seen. The corridors were wide, with low ceilings, but the rooms themselves were large and airy.

We came out into a courtyard that looked like we were in the middle of Mexico. There was a large pool on one side of the courtyard, but there were plenty of comfortable sitting areas that lined what was obviously where the family lived. There was a large table in the middle of the courtyard, and two French doors that led into what I assumed was the kitchen.

"Mama, we've completed the tour," Alex called out.

"Un momento," was her reply, then she said, "Bring them into the kitchen while we finish up."

We walked into a beautiful, antique kitchen. The same tiles as before lined the area, and the floor tiles were terracotta. It just looked right to see the family working together in the space. The father was sitting at the table, cutting up what looked to me to be cilantro.

The three women were bustling around the stove as well as the rest of the kitchen. Alex pointed toward chairs next to where señor Zitlal sat. Both of my boys stared at the cilantro with twisted faces, but luckily, Emma Jean's work was paying off and they hadn't said anything offensive.

Señor Zitlal chuckled when he looked at them. "So, you don't like cilantro, I see. I didn't used to either, but I learned to after a while."

Neither boy responded. "Señor Zitlal, you have a beautiful home. Are the tiles Talavera, from Puebla?" I asked.

He nodded. "I'm impressed you know them. They were installed in the early 1920s when the majority of the house was built, or I should say finished. How do you know about Puebla pottery?"

I smiled at him. "I used to be in construction, and the customers our company worked for swooned over Talavera tiles. Most of them couldn't afford them, though."

"Puebla has become very popular lately. I'm glad, it's quite an artisan trade."

"Have you been to Puebla?" I asked. "Ever since I learned about them, I've wanted to go."

"We have all been," the man said, pointing to his family. "Mi esposa hermosa is from that region. Her brother still lives in Puebla."

Señora Zitlal came over and kissed her husband on the head. "You should ask Alex about the movie he did there a few years back. It's even won a few awards."

Alex smiled. "The Talavera tile story tells itself, I just had to put the tile makers on the screen telling about how they did the work and what they loved about it. Also, most of them have been making these tiles for generations."

Señor Zitlal looked at the boys and asked them, "So, tell me about living on a working ranch. I always thought it'd be fun."

Luke, the kid who had been the shyest since we arrived, stood up, and said, "You get to be a real cowboy!"

The older man leaned back and laughed. "I always wanted to be a cowboy, just like my ancestor, Diamondback Jack."

Both boys sat to attention at the mention of the man. Ever since they'd heard that story, they'd been fascinated with it. "He still haunts our ranch," Drake said.

I looked at him, surprised he knew that.

"Is that so?" the man said, and his eyes twinkled. "I used to ride around out here pretending I was Diamond Jack, fighting off the bad guys."

Luke immediately said, "Maybe we can go play Diamond Jack while we're here."

Señor Zitlal laughed as his wife came over. "Abuelo is still recovering from surgery. He can't ride a horse yet, but Francesca might take you out."

The boys looked at her warily. I could almost hear the words, *'But she's a girl'* swirling in their minds, but again, thanks to Emma Jean, they kept their mouths shut and just nodded.

The entire room erupted in laughter. Francesca came over and knelt between the boy's seats and whispered, "I used to beat Alexandro at rope throwing all the time. I'm out of practice, but I could teach you how, in case you ever need to hogtie a bad guy at your ranch."

Both boy's eyes lit up and she was immediately forgiven for being a girl. They loved everything to do with ranching, almost like living on the ranch had transformed them from being stuck in an endless rut, which was probably true, when you compared the life we led now to the one we had in Houston.

"If I weren't so pregnant, I'd show you how to ride the barrels," Ellen said. "You'll have to come back once the baby is born, and I'll make you both stars at the rodeo. Have you been to a rodeo before?" Ellen asked.

The boys shook their heads, and I inwardly groaned. They'd been desperate to go to the rodeo since they heard about it at school this year. We'd missed it the first year, because Flex had been shot and I forgot about it. This year, I would've taken them, but the kids didn't bring home the flyer until the last day. I promised to take them next year.

Ellen smiled. "Well, if your dad doesn't mind, the rodeo in El Paso is happening *this* week. I was going to make Ernesto take me." She looked up and smiled toward her husband, who was talking to someone on his phone outside the kitchen. "Even though I can't perform this year, I wanted to watch my friends. Mr. Crawford, would you mind if I took these two handsome gentlemen as my date?"

First, I was surprised that this family were so friendly. Second, I couldn't imagine why anyone would volunteer for kid duty who wasn't related, or loved them by proxy like Emma Jean and Jimmy.

"We'll see," I said, knowing I was going to be hounded for the rest of the night. I would probably say yes, but I needed to know more about these people before I gave them my kids.

The meal was served outside on the big table we'd passed on the way in. The kids pretty much owned the conversation throughout dinner. They had a hundred questions for Francesca and Ellen about the rodeo. We'd almost finished eating when Francesca outed Alex as a former rodeo clown. The boys were dumbfounded. We'd watched some *YouTube* videos of the clowns running to keep the riders safe once they fell off the bulls. I accidentally clicked on a video that had shown a clown who'd been gored. I was afraid that would upset the kids, but instead, they became obsessed with them.

Boys and danger seemed to be an ongoing trend, no matter what generation.

The conversation became all about rodeo clowns and how dangerous it was, and, well... poor Alex was now their biggest hero. Now that they knew, they would hound him for weeks.

"Why don't we all go to the rodeo?" señora Zitlal asked. "I haven't been since the kids were in school."

Alex smiled, leaned over and whispered as the entire table cheered. "Seems you're going to the rodeo."

I smiled at him. "It's meant to be, I guess."

15

Alex

H AVING EDDIE AND THE kids at the hacienda was more fun than I'd anticipated. My family seemed to absorb them into our daily routines, and they had fun riding, hiking along the old riverbed, and helping Papa work in the garden beds while I was stuck in meetings.

Eddie and Francesca hit it off a lot better than I'd expected, and before long, I felt myself getting jealous. Francesca was bisexual, and as far as I could tell, so was Eddie. He was recently divorced, and to be honest, I'd hoped this would be a time when he and I could grow closer. Damn, if I hadn't underestimated how long my meetings here would take.

Ellen also spent time with the kids. Of course, she was involved with the same meetings I was, so her time was limited, but she especially enjoyed hanging with the boys. I thought seeing them play and interacting with them helped her see what it was going to be like to have kids of her own. Ernesto had younger siblings, but they were terrors on legs according to both Ernesto and her, so they didn't tend to take them out much.

Drake and Luke were incredibly well behaved. I assumed that was because Emma Jean spent so much time with them. The woman was formidable.

I had all my old games stored in our media room, and with Eddie's permission, I showed them how to play a couple of the less violent ones. Mom must have gone in after I'd shown them the room and put all the games rated T or higher away, because the next day when I went in to play with them, they were gone, even though I'd planned to do the same thing.

I was surprised at how fast my family had integrated Eddie and the boys. I knew they'd like them, and with the link to Diamondback Jack, I figured there'd be a connection, but it seemed like they'd been a part of our family for years. I guessed the fact that my parents were about to become new grandparents had a lot to do with that.

I could tell the boys and my papa were getting close. I seldom came home when he wasn't snuggled up with them, similar to how he used to be with us, reading a book to them, or even once or twice trying to play one of the games with them. Although, from my own childhood, I knew he really sucked at those. Anything other than Pacman or Mrs. Pacman, and he was toast.

Regardless, they all seemed to be about as happy as they could be together.

I noticed a sadness in Eddie, however, as he watched my parents' interaction with the kids. I had a bit of a break between meetings, and I asked him if I could take him out to dinner. The parents were planning to watch a movie with the boys, one of the *Kung Fu Pandas*, but I hadn't paid attention to which.

I'd asked them beforehand if they could watch the boys, and they'd agreed. My mom, always the observant one, had also caught the sadness on Eddie's face, and said this might be a good time to get to the bottom of that. I kissed her and told her we were on the same page.

Eddie hesitated when I asked, saying he didn't want to burden my parents with the kids. I couldn't help but laugh at him. I pulled him over to where the kids were helping in the kitchen, preparing something together, and asked him if he'd had a moment alone with the boys since he'd arrived?

He chuckled. "You do have a point."

"My parents are desperate for grandkids. They have one coming, but clearly, yours are ready to be played with. Would you deny them that pleasure?"

Eddie looked at me and shook his head. "Dude, you don't play fair, do you?" he asked.

"Hell no, not when I have a chance to have a handsome man on my arm for the evening."

Eddie surprised me when he smiled. "Yes, I'd love to go on a date with you, but only if you are absolutely sure this won't be an imposition on your parents."

The guy's concern for others both frustrated me and touched my heart. I could tell he'd spent his entire life worrying about other people's reactions, and that saddened me.

"You know, it's okay to rely on other people from time to time," I said, before I realized I was saying it out loud. It was one thing to think these things, and another to voice them. I was afraid I'd offended him when he laughed.

"Okay, okay, I get the point. When do we leave?"

I smiled. "Let's go in about an hour. I want to stop and show you something along the way."

He went directly to the boys and asked if they thought they'd be okay if he went out with Alex for the evening.

Luke looked a little concerned, and Drake asked, "Will you have your phone on you?"

"I will, you can text or call me anytime."

"I'll give you my number as well," I added. "That way, if you can't reach your dad, you can call or text me."

This seemed to mollify the boys as they looked between my parents and their dad.

"Abuela is going to teach us how to make sopapillas tonight," Luke said.

"Oh, that's Papa's favorite," I added, getting a smile from both my parents.

"I expect you both to be very good for señores Zitlal," he said

Then he turned to my parents. "If you have any trouble, you call me right away."

My mama chuckled. "We've raised three of the most hard-headed children to walk the earth, I think we'll be fine."

Eddie looked at me and smiled. "I believe you, señora."

My family had a tendency to keep every car we've ever owned. Much of that came from the intense care that was taken of our vehicles. My great uncle owned a beautiful blue 1971 Ford Mustang Convertible that I'd been obsessed with since... well, as long as I could remember.

I'd come out to my father when I was eighteen. I remembered my dad told me about my great-uncle, who was out and gay while he was growing up. He'd moved to Los Angeles, because El Paso was less-than accepting of gays at the time, and he worked in the film industry out there.

He bought the Ford with the money he'd inherited after my great-grandfather died, so the car meant a lot to my family. Despite all that, my dad handed me the keys to the car on my birthday, and told me his uncle would've approved.

I seldom drove it. As the years passed, and cars of this quality seemed to become fewer and fewer, I was terrified something would happen to it, but tonight I wanted to do something special for Eddie. I knew he liked cars from past conversations, so I figured my Mustang might impress him.

I knew I was acting like a lovesick teenager over this guy. I wasn't quite sure why I was so attracted to him. I wasn't one to pursue guys who weren't fully out. If I was going to invest in someone, he damned well better be able to return my affection, but something about Eddie made me want to gather him in my arms and hold him... well, okay, maybe there were other things I'd enjoy doing with and to him, but we could start with holding.

When Eddie saw the Mustang, his mouth fell open. "Damn," he said. "That is one fine car!"

I laughed. "He's a beauty, that's for sure."

"When did you get this?" he asked.

"Oh, it belonged to my uncle. He used it to pick up guys in the '70s."

Eddie burst out laughing. "And he lets you drive it?"

"Well, he's no longer with us, so it's mine now, but from what I've heard about him, he'd have been happy that I'm using it to impress you."

Eddie smiled and looked at me warily, then opened the door and climbed in. "Oh, it feels like heaven."

I climbed into the driver's seat and pulled it out toward the road. "I want to show you a place El Paso is famous for. We'll need the convertible for that."

I drove up toward the Franklin Mountains and got onto the scenic outlook road. I lowered the top and handed Eddie a pair of sunglasses I kept in the car for passengers. Eddie looked at them and then over at me. "You just keep a pair of Ray-Bans in your car for passengers to use?"

I laughed. "Well, those belonged to my uncle as well. Notice they are square? Vintage..."

He put them on and looked over at me. "They are a little Fight Clubish," he said, and I laughed at the accuracy of his statement.

I could tell he was enjoying the ride. The wind made talking impossible, so we rode in silence as the sights of El Paso and Juarez came in and out of view. This had always been one of my favorite places. I'd always dreamed of bringing a guy up here and necking on one of the trails that led up and around the panorama.

We got to the main lookout, and I could tell I'd made a good choice. Eddie looked more relaxed since I'd met him. We walked down the staircase and I was able to point out the different places you could see from the vista. I showed him where our studio in Juarez was, then I pointed out the different mountain ranges in Mexico and where the line was. El Paso looked small from up here, and the truth was it really was. You could see the low-rise buildings lining this side of the Rio Grande, but the lights were brighter, and the buildings bigger on the other side. Being up here really did show how different the two cities were from one another, even though they were right next to each other.

"If you follow the border, you can see where the ranch is." I pointed in the right direction. When he turned toward me, we were standing face to face. He smiled and blushed a bit. Damn, he was so fucking cute.

To my dismay, he stepped back and looked toward the ranch. "I should probably text the boys," he said, and raised his phone to take a picture of where the ranch was and sent it to them with a description.

I wasn't sure if I was impressed that he'd think of his kids when we had just had a moment, or if it killed the mood. Regardless, I wanted to see if I could get more of those moments before we were done with the night.

We stood there looking out over the vista for about half an hour before we both naturally started walking back up the steps. "What are all these locks here for?" he asked.

I looked down and smiled. "They are an expression of love," I said. "The tradition started in Paris. Lovers would put a lock on the bridge, then they throw the key away as a symbol of their unbreakable love."

Eddie knelt down to get a better look at the locks. "I like that tradition," he said. "I doubt it would've helped my last relationship, but it's a really cool concept."

We walked up to the car and climbed back in. Before I pulled away, I asked him, "Do you prefer steak or Mexican?"

"I like both," he said. "What's popular for El Paso?"

"Well, have you ever been to Mexico?"

"No, not really. We meant to go, but never did."

"Let's go to Juarez. I have a friend that owns a restaurant that has real authentic Mexican food, and they have a show as well. We can just catch the show if we go now."

He looked skeptical, but okay with the idea, so I took that as a yes.

I tended to take clients there, so I had the number saved in my phone. I could text letting them know and they'd usually get me in. Although it was popular enough, if you didn't make reservations, you were usually out of luck.

I got the confirmation back that they could get us in, and we headed to the border.

"Do you have your passport?" I asked, kicking myself for not asking him before we left.

He pulled out his wallet and confirmed he had it.

"Then let's go!"

The drive down from the scenic outlook was just as beautiful as the way up, and I kept the top down until we were off the mountain.

As soon as the top was up, Eddie asked, "What kind of place are you taking me? I'm not really dressed for fancy dining."

"It's casual. There are a couple of nicer places in Juarez, but they can be stuffy, and the food isn't always reliable. This place is perfect if you want a laid-back atmosphere and a little history as well."

"Is it in English or Spanish?"

"Spanish, but the show is interpreted in English, and I'll help translate for you. Remember, that's how my ancestor got his start in show business. We are experts."

He laughed at me and leaned back, enjoying the ride.

I went through the border crossing so often I knew most of the agents who worked in the area. "Señor Zitlal," the female agent I knew as Maria said as I pulled up. "You going to work?" she asked as she leaned out of the small building that sat between the lanes of traffic.

"No, going to eat tonight. This is my friend Edward Crawford," I said, knowing it was best to give formal names. "He's never been to Mexico before."

"Do you have your passport, señor?" she asked.

Eddie handed it to her, and she looked it over and gave it back.

"You two have fun and stay out of trouble," she said, making me laugh.

"¿Cómo es eso, divertido, Maria?" I asked, and she chuckled as she waved us along.

"What did you ask her?" Eddie asked.

"Oh, I said, where's the fun in not getting into trouble?"

"Do you know all the border guards?"

"No, but I know most of them. I do drive through here a lot. They change them every few months, but I've been around to see most of them at least once."

Eddie stared out the window. There were significant differences between El Paso and Juarez. I could tell he was getting a bit nervous by the quick changes between the two.

"The cities are really different, no?"

He nodded.

"Juarez is more than double the population of El Paso," I told him. "It was the original city. When the US acquired El Paso, Juarez actually held that name. What's now known as El

Paso was just a small outcrop of the original city. This city was established in 1659 by the Spanish, so, Juarez has a bit more wear and tear on her than El Paso."

"You said Juarez used to be called El Paso too?"

I nodded. "El Paso del Norte, actually, but it was so confusing after the Texas rebellion that in 1888 they renamed it Juarez."

"How do you know so much about the history?" he asked as we pulled up to the restaurant.

"It's my job to know the history of an area, especially one so dear to my heart as Juarez and El Paso, but we also did a documentary here when I was a teenager. It was the first show I was allowed to help on, so I learned as much as I could."

I was curious how well Eddie would handle a real authentic Mexican restaurant. Everything was a bit different here than in the states, even though they were just a stone's throw from each other. When we pulled up to the restaurant, Eddie looked at it, then over at me, and I had to bite my tongue not to laugh out loud.

The building looked like it could fall in. It was long overdue for a paint job, and the roof had a definite sway to it. To his credit he didn't respond, but got out and followed me to the front door.

The interior immediately made up for the first impression. They had renovated about five years ago, making the inside bright and cheery, getting rid of the old 1960s décor that had been the place's theme before Julianne, a woman I had become friends with long ago, inherited the place and immediately began work on it. The result was stunning.

Eddie's mouth dropped open when we walked in, and Julianne sauntered over. After seeing Eddie, she spoke in English. "How many do you have tonight, Alexandro?"

It's just my friend Eddie and myself tonight," I told her, and she winked at me. Julianne had been trying to fix me up with every gay man in her family since we were young. There were a lot of gay men in Julianne's family, but they were all ugly as homespun sin. How Julianne turned into such a beautiful woman, I'd never understand.

When we were seated, Julianne asked what kind of drinks we'd like. Eddie shrugged. "About anything," he said. I smiled and looked at my friend. "Why don't you bring us your special?"

She winked at me. "If you trust me, we've been working on something different. It's potent, but it's so yummy."

I looked at Eddie, who was smiling at our hostess and nodded. "Sounds good."

When she was gone, Eddie asked me, "How the hell did you find this place? Did you just drive by and say, *Hey, I bet there's a beautiful restaurant inside the rickety old building?*"

I literally laughed out loud. "Not quite. This restaurant has been around for a long time. They've been doing the same play for decades, and my grandfather was bringing his associates to this place in the early '70s. It's like our business, it sort of got passed down."

"The inside is amazing, it looks like something you'd find in Europe. The hostess is a beauty also. What's her name?"

I immediately felt a pang of jealousy and quickly tamped it down. "That is Julianne, she's the owner and a good friend of mine."

"Wow, she seems young to be the owner."

"She's my age. We used to have birthday parties together actually. Her birthday is a month before mine. She inherited the place a few years ago and has been updating it ever since."

"Too bad she hasn't gotten to the outside," he said, and I chuckled.

"That's partly by choice, I imagine. She enjoys flying under the radar. The place has a great reputation, but with the local clientele, there's another restaurant closer to downtown that has a better reputation with tourists, and as a result, they get harassed by both the police as well as the drug cartels. By flying low and quiet, Julianne is able to keep all the sharks at bay."

Eddie shook his head. "Politics always plays a role. The players may be a little different here, but the game is the same."

Julianne showed up then with our drinks. She waited while we tasted them, and when I did, a burst of alcoholic flavor hit me. "That's delicious," I told her, and Eddie nodded.

"What is it?" he asked.

"It's several drinks mixed together, sort of like a Long Island Iced Tea, but with a few different ingredients. Go slow, she packs a punch," Julianne said as she scurried away toward the front.

The food was delivered shortly after we ordered, which surprised Eddie as well. Julianne looked like a petite pushover, but she ran this restaurant with an iron fist, so I wasn't as surprised as he was. The service was perfect, along with the taste of the food and the historical production that was about to start.

We'd finished our meal, the plates were taken away, and two small containers of flan had been placed in front of us, just as the curtain came up and the performance began. I always laughed when the interpreters yelled lines out in English. They'd turned it into a comedy routine, although the historical elements of the play were accurate, and, well... serious.

Eddie laughed at the interpreter's antics and the cast's continual annoyance with their interruptions. I was always impressed at how everyone, both Spanish and English speakers, left the production well entertained, and educated on Mexican history since the revolution.

We were in a great mood as we drove back across the border. The American side had several of the same people I'd met before. We chatted the same as when we crossed into Mexico, me introducing my friend Eddie as we handed them our passports.

"Where'd you go?" the border guard asked.

"To Casa del Banquete. Hey, did you ever make it there after we last talked?" I asked the guard.

"No, we've been pulling double shifts."

"Well, you need to go, it's fun, and the new owner has done a great job improving the performance."

The guard looked up at the woman across from him. I already knew she was his wife. "We'll see if we can get time off. It sounds fun."

We were waved through, and I drove us straight to the hacienda. The boys were already in bed when we arrived. I'd only drunk a little of my drink since it was pure alcohol and I knew I had to drive back. Eddie, however, had finished his and proceeded to drink most of mine. He'd been in a nice buzz since leaving the restaurant.

When we came into the house, however, he sobered up fast. He went to the boys' room to check on them, and came back to report two snoring bodies. "How'd you get them to bed so early?" he asked my parents.

Mama laughed. "I let them swim after we ate, then we watched some TV. They were drifting off before the movie was over."

"If it puts them out like that, I need to install a pool," Eddie said, and laughed.

We sat with my parents for a few moments before they too turned in, leaving the two of us sitting alone in the great room.

We were sitting in chairs that were adjacent to one another. The way they met in the corner caused our two hands to meet. Eddie reached over and laid his hand on mine, curling our fingers together. "I had fun tonight. More fun than I've had in many years," he said. "Thanks for that."

I knew he was still buzzing, so I ignored my deep desire to kiss his luscious-looking lips. Alcohol seemed to mellow him, and the little blush on his cheeks make him look vulnerable and sexy. I wanted more than anything to pull him into my arms and hold him.

I brought his hand up to my mouth and kissed it. "You are one of the most handsome men I've ever met, Eddie."

He looked at me from the corner of his eye. "You aren't seeing very many men then," he replied, and laughed.

"You aren't looking very closely in the mirror if you don't already know what I said is true," I replied.

Eddie sighed. "You are so dignified and well put together, I'm sure you have men falling over themselves for you. I'm a country bumpkin, half redneck, half backwoods, awkward hick."

I chuckled. "You aren't either of those things. Now when we first met, you could've convinced me of that, but you've shown me something different since then. I can't quite keep my eyes off you, and it's taken everything in my willpower to keep my hands to myself."

Eddie looked at me, and there was hunger in his eyes. "I want you to touch me, but I think it'd be a bad idea. Too much is going on right now. Hell, you're a tenant or whatever you call it of mine."

To my great disappointment, Eddie stood up, but held my hand a moment later. "Let things play out. If I know my kids are safe, and my ex-wife and her boyfriend are out of the picture, ask me again, then we can see where this leads."

It took a lot out of me to let go of his hand, but I sort of understood. He had a lot on his plate, and not a small part of that was those two boys of his. He loved them, and I understood he'd protect them with his life if need be. I appreciated and respected that, even if I did wish he was a bit more available.

16

Eddie

LEX'S FAMILY WAS A trip. He was right, they were hungry for grandchildren. We all went to the rodeo and took the boys around to meet the different performers. Alex introduced them to the head rodeo clown, who was on break at the time. I heard the man talking to the boys about tricks of the trade… "You have to make sure you have an exit plan before you distract the bulls," he said, and I chuckled at how serious the kids were taking in the man's advice.

When we got home, they told the Zitlals all about him and reiterated his advice, like at any moment they were both going to become rodeo clowns.

Everyone enjoyed the rodeo so much that Alex's father announced the entire family, who were all on his payroll, were going to Orlando and Disney World. "We've been needing a family vacation, and I was already going to force everyone to take time off before Ellen gives birth, so this is a perfect time to do it," señor Zitlal said. "Besides, Alexandro has to go to Saint Augustine and finish up his work and then he can meet us at Disney World. That way the boys have plenty time to enjoy it."

They rented hotel rooms right on the grounds. I wasn't a savvy traveler, but the rooms were huge, and luxurious. The service was excellent and reminiscent of swanky hotels you saw on television. I could only guess this all cost a pretty penny. I struggled with my pride during the trip, because they pretty-much refused to let me pay for anything. I felt like I was taking advantage, and when Alex got back from Saint Augustine, I told him it was too much.

"My father is one of the tightest penny-pinchers to walk the Earth," he told me. "If he is spending money on you, it's because they're all enjoying you and the kids. They need this, Eddie. My dad had his heart attack, and now they are about to become grandparents.

"We usually do a family vacation, every year about this time too, and so I'm sure Mama and Papa just figured this was the perfect time. Besides, Ellen, Francesca and I have all talked about it. The parents need some downtime to adjust. I know it's uncomfortable, and I apologize, but if you can just let them do this, I promise it is doing more for them than you realize. Besides, they can afford it, trust me."

"It doesn't take the sting out of it, though. I'm not a rich man, Alex, but I'm not someone who takes advantage of my friends either."

"That matters, and I'll share a secret with you, if my parents thought you were someone who'd ride their good intentions for your own self-interest, they wouldn't have offered to bring you here."

With a sigh, I gave in. "Tell me something your parents appreciate or need. Anything that I can do to repay them."

Alex thought for a moment. "I'll tell you what, I'll ask my sisters and see what they say. If there's something they need or want, Ellen or Francesca will probably know."

That was enough to satisfy me for now, at least, and so I pushed my pride down and enjoyed this incredible family.

Alex's father was still dealing with the consequences of his heart attack, and sometimes had to stay back at the hotel. I noticed he was really hurting one day after we'd had a particularly eventful day at Animal Kingdom, I volunteered to stay with him. Francesca and señora Zitlal told the boys they wanted to take them to Epcot, while Ellen and Ernesto were visiting friends. I was confident the kids were in good hands, and I was also pretty sure they'd all like to have the kids without their father, who was seriously getting in the way of their spoiling.

Since we'd arrived, I kept trying to enforce the same rules on not spending too much money. The Zitlals were not crazy spendthrifts, far from it, but they were constantly looking at buying the boys stuff. I'd pretty much prevented that as much as I could. Alex had told me to back off a bit after the first day, but seriously, it was hard to watch my kids showered with crap they really didn't need.

No one complained when I said I'd stay home with their papa.

Señor Zitlal spent most of the day sleeping in his room. I watched a movie, went down for a swim in the pool, relaxed in the sauna, and when I came to check on him, Mr. Zitlal told me he'd book me a massage.

"Okay," I said. "This'll be a first for me."

He chuckled. "It's good for you, and I'm almost sure it won't be your last."

"What about you?" I asked.

"No, I have a woman that comes to the hacienda who specializes in helping people recover from surgery like I've had."

I sat down next to him and watched some TV while I waited for my massage.

"I've noticed you're recovering well. It's only been a few months since your surgery, right?" I asked.

"Yes, four months last week," he said. "I still get tired too fast, though. I'm working on getting my stamina back."

"My cousin was shot by some crazed man. It took him months to recover, so if you're this good after having your chest torn open, I think you are doing pretty well."

"Have they caught the man who shot your cousin?" he asked.

"No, they have a person of interest, well, a couple if you count my mom, but the main one has been missing since the day my cousin was shot."

He shook his head. "Life is short, young man. Things like this remind us of that."

We sat companionably for several minutes when señor Zitlal turned the TV volume down and turned to me. "My son is very taken with you, have you thought about how you feel about him?" he asked.

I smiled. "I wondered when one of you was going to ask me that. If some strange man and his kids had popped up in one of my boys' lives, I'd have been wanting to know more about them."

The older man chuckled. "When you're a father, you worry about these things, and it's taken every ounce of willpower for his mother not to intervene."

I chuckled. "I'm sure that's true. It's been refreshing to see how much you all love each other. Even Alex's sisters, who love to harass him, love each other unconditionally. Not everyone has that, you know."

He nodded, but I could tell he was waiting for me to answer the question.

"What you've asked is complicated. Until right before we came out here, I was married to the only person I've ever been with. Now, I have two boys that depend on me for everything in their lives, and those boys mean more to me than anything in the world."

"But you have feelings for Alex?" he asked.

I looked at him for a long moment, trying to figure out how to answer the father of the man I wanted to rip the clothes off of.

"I can only say this, Alex is the only other person I've seriously wanted to go out with since I was in high school, but I've been honest with him, and I'll be honest with you as well. I won't do anything to jeopardize my children, no matter how badly I'd like to."

The older man chuckled. "Your children adore my son. I can see it in the way they talk to him and call him their uncle. Francesca has even got them using the Spanish version of the word. Tio Alexandro."

"That's part of the problem, isn't it?" I asked. "They do like Alex, a lot. They like y'all too. So if Alex and I try this, and it doesn't work out, my kids could lose someone else they care about. They've lost so many people in their lives, I can't be the reason they lose any more."

The older man reached over and patted my hand. "You can't protect them from being hurt, you can only be there to help them pick up the pieces. I'm going to tell you something I heard a long time ago. Loving others is meant to be a difficult process, sometimes even painful. When we grow, we have growing pains. It hurts to be born, and it hurts to give birth, so why would we think learning to love another would be without pain? My son is already..."

The man thought for a moment. "I've been watching the two of you, and I can tell my son is already more attached to you than any other man I've seen him with before. You should know he cares about you and your children a great deal. I know that can be scary, but I see you and he are the same in that regard. When you care about someone, you are committed to them. Not everyone is that way. Don't be too quick to let that go. Besides, Alexandro won't hurt your boys, even if you try and it doesn't work out."

I sighed. "What happens if I let myself try again, and it fails as badly as the last one did?"

I hadn't meant to be quite so candid. In fact, I wasn't sure I realized until that moment that, although I did worry about my boys, I worried about my own heart as well.

"Ah, well, son," the man said. "That's a whole different can of worms, but the flower that's kept hidden under a pail will wither and die, whereas the flower left out to withstand the elements grows strong and makes beautiful blooms. You'll have to decide if you're strong enough to let yourself try again. Now, hijo," the man said. "Go on down to the spa, don't keep your massage therapist waiting."

I would've been concerned about the massage and having to strip in front of a stranger had I not had señor Zitlal's and my conversation on my mind. The massage was amazing. My therapist was truly gifted with his hands. I'd never been so relaxed physically, although mentally, it was a different story.

Could I trust Alex enough to give this a try? What if I fell in love with him and he dumped me? I knew the whole, *to love and lose, is better than never to have loved at all* shit, but that must have been written by someone who didn't have an ex-wife that wanted to see him beaten to a pulp.

By the time I'd gotten back to my room and had a nap, I'd decided I wasn't someone who could take that chance again. I needed to be honest with Alex. This wasn't going any further. I might try hooking up using the app I'd heard about, the one for men that didn't want a relationship, but were looking for sex. I knew for damned sure, now that my wife was no longer my wife, I wanted to have sex again with someone other than my hand, but my heart? That I wasn't willing to sacrifice again. I might be a coward, but after growing up with a mom and dad who'd tossed me aside like unwanted trash, and then giving myself to a woman who'd done the same thing, I was sure I'd rather be a coward who was intact than the suffering mass of loss I would be if I tried to love someone again and was once again rejected.

17

Alex

WE HAD SO MUCH fun at Epcot. I hadn't been there in years, and the place had changed significantly. The boys didn't give a damn about all the different cultural elements, but they loved the rides. It was so much fun to watch them play and have fun. I'd never really understood what it meant to enjoy something through another's enjoyment. The whole parenting thing began to make more sense to me now. When Luke clung to me because he was afraid, it made me automatically pull him close, letting him feel secure enough to be brave and face his fear. Although Drake was putting on a brave face, he too turned to me when he was afraid. The fact that they trusted me made me feel stronger.

When Mama took the boys for ice cream, Francesca hung back with me. "So, the boys seem pretty attached to you."

"Yeah, they're pretty great, huh?" I asked, trying to put her off the scent.

"Yep, they're great. How does that make you feel, Papa Alex?"

"Stop that, Francesca, they have a papa and he's a really good one."

"Defensive much?" she asked, and chuckled.

"Hey, seriously, Eddie and I aren't dating, we're friends, that's all. Yeah, I like his kids, but who wouldn't? They are well put together, especially when you consider how fucking awful their mom is."

"Seems to me, the one who gets credit for that is Eddie," she said.

I nodded in agreement.

"So, you aren't pushing Eddie, why? It isn't like you not to chase something you want, and before you deny it, I can see how much you want him. Is he not interested?" she asked.

"I don't know, Francesca, I think he's scared."

"Is he a closet case?" she asked, looking at me in an alarmed way.

I laughed at her expression. "You should see your face. No, I don't think he's a closet case. His cousin is fully out, and they are close as brothers. I think he's scared of getting hurt, and he's terrified of hurting his kids."

"He's hot as fuck too," Francesca said, causing me to give her a look. "Don't worry, don't worry," she laughed, and put her hands up. "I'm not gonna tread on your territory, but you do need to be prepared, though. He isn't a hook-up kind of guy. If you convince him to let you in, he'll be looking for a lifetime commitment. That hasn't really been your forte, brother. Even if you get him, are you completely sure you want what you'll be getting?"

Before I could respond, Luke ran up to me and grabbed me in a hug. He was covered in melted ice cream and when he pulled back, I was covered as well.

"Wow, that looks good, did you bring some back to me?" I asked, ignoring the goo that was now plastered to my neck.

"No, do you want me to go back and get you some?" he asked as Drake came up behind him.

"I'm good," I said, and pulled him into a side hug. "Drake, what kind did you get?" I asked.

"Butter Pecan and Chocolate," he replied, but clearly, he was too cool to show the level of excitement his brother had.

When we stood up and the boys ran ahead, Francesca pulled a wet wipe out of her purse, and handed it to me. "You have it bad, brother." She laughed as she walked away.

I did, that was the fucking truth. I liked this little family. I liked the boys and enjoyed hanging out with them. I liked Flex and Mitch, Emma Jean and Jimmy, and I *really* liked Edward Crawford. I just needed to figure out how to convince him to give me a chance, so I could show him just how *much* I liked him.

When we got back to the hotel, the boys went to my parents' room to see Papa and tell him about their day's adventures. I went to Eddie's room to find him and let him know we were all meeting down at the hotel restaurant for dinner.

I knocked on his door, but he didn't answer. His room door was ajar, though, so I pushed it open and yelled his name. He still didn't answer, so I went in, assuming he was in the shower or something. When I opened his bedroom door, I saw him lying on his bed, stripped down to only his boxers.

I salivated. The man was so fucking gorgeous. I acted before thinking and slipped onto the bed next to him. He smelled like lavender and mint, and on him, that was the sexiest smell I'd ever encountered. I leaned back on the bed, resisting the urge to lie right next to him and pull him against me. I was convinced he'd fit there perfectly.

I shook my head and turned the TV on. "Hey," he said as he woke up. "What're you doing here?" he asked.

I chuckled. "Mama told me to get you and let you know we're going down to the restaurant for dinner, but I didn't really wanna disturb you, so I decided to watch TV while I waited for you to wake up."

He looked at me, his eyes sleepy and guarded, but amused nonetheless. "So, you couldn't just holler at me?"

"Nope, if I didn't obey my mama, she'd make my life hell, and I'd have felt guilty if I'd just woken you when you looked so peaceful, so I only really had one option."

He rolled over and leaned on his elbow. God, he was so sexy. I leaned down and kissed him. "I'm guessing from the smell of you, you've had a massage."

He nodded, then he shocked me when he took the remote and turned the TV off. He pulled me down on the bed, and half lying on me, kissed me back.

"You know what I was dreaming of before you came in?" he asked.

I couldn't really talk, not with his muscular chest lying on top of mine. I shook my head instead.

"I was dreaming of you, but you didn't have clothes on," he let his hand slide up under my shirt.

"I'd convinced myself before I fell asleep, I wasn't going to do this." His hand slipped down my chest and caught under the band of my pants. "But then, I dreamed of you and all the things we could do to each other, then when I woke up, here you were in my bed, looking like the sexiest thing I've ever laid eyes on."

I gulped, the front of my pants just below where his fingers rested became significantly more interested.

Before we could do any more, the door to the room opened, and two loud voices came toward us. Eddie removed his hand from my pants and tuned over so his beautiful bulge wouldn't show as the boys rushed into the room.

"Dad, Dad," they said. "Wake up, we're going to dinner. Abuela says we have to dress fancy to eat here. Wake up, Papa!"

Luke was shaking his dad, who was pretending to be asleep, and I couldn't help but laugh.

"I tried already, boys," I said. "He's dead asleep. Hey, I know what, let's tickle him."

Eddie jumped up. "No… no tickling!" he said, and the boys chased him as he rushed toward the bathroom and locked the door, before they could follow him in.

I was laughing when Francesca came into the room. When she looked at me, she laughed out loud. Without saying a word she winked at me, then left the way she had come.

I got up and said, "Okay, guys, y'all need to clean up too. Go wash up like Emma Jean has taught you, and change into your nice clothes. I gotta go clean up too. Can you get ready yourself, or do you need me to pick out your clothes?"

Drake looked at me oddly. "We're not kids, tio," he said, and I had to force myself not to laugh. "Okay then, I'll see you *men* back in here in a few minutes."

The moment I stepped out of the room, I saw my sister leaning back on the wall just outside the door. "So, *that* was interesting," she said.

I stuck my tongue out at her and walked toward the room I was sharing with my parents.

She laughed as I walked by. "Go get ready," I said behind me, and disappeared as quickly as I could into my hotel room, ignoring my sister and her sneer.

18

Eddie

I'D CONVINCED MYSELF I didn't want Alex. That was until I fell asleep. But, my dream betrayed my real desires where he was concerned. Before the TV woke me up, I was doing some pretty specific things with his cock. When I turned over and saw him sitting next to me on my bed with that sexy smirk of his, I was still reeling from the sexual heat of the dream.

When he kissed me, even though it was chaste on his part, it certainly wasn't for me. If the kids hadn't walked in, I'm sure I'd have done to him in real life what I'd been doing to him in my dream.

After meeting Alex, I'd begun watching gay porn again, just to get an idea of what it would be like to be with a man.

I was a gay virgin, and knowing someone like Alex was anything but, I didn't want to go too far down that rabbit hole, until I knew I wanted this, or at least I was fairly sure I did.

Watching porn. Well, I knew pretty quickly it was exactly what I wanted to do with Alex. When he'd kissed me, it sent shivers throughout my body. Yeah, it was different, *very* different than it felt kissing a woman. Alex's body was hard, unyielding, and damn if that didn't feel right.

I locked the bathroom door, turned the shower on hot, and with the thought of Alex fresh in my mind, I jacked off, letting my soapy finger probe my ass. What would it be like to have his tongue or cock there? Just the thought of it almost made me come. I leaned back against the tiles, continuing to probe my hole and jack off. I thought of Alex's beautiful body pressed against me, maybe his cock in my mouth, like it'd been in the dream. Thrusting aggressively into me until he came.

Just at the thought of Alex emptying himself in my mouth, I spewed into the shower.

"*Fuck!*" I said out loud. I was sure before this trip was over, I was going to try that with Alex, and consequences be damned. "This is a bad idea," I said to myself, letting the words echo around the shower. In my mind I thought, *Even if I'm lost after all this is done, please God, don't let it hurt my kids.*

I let the warm water wash over me, willing the feeling of hunger that plagued me over Alex to wash away. By the time I finally got ready, I was at least partially presentable to be in the company of other people.

The restaurant Alex's parents took us to was nicer than the ones we'd been to before. The boys had been taken on a shopping spree with Alex's sisters before we left, and they'd even come back with a suit for me. Which I fully intended to never wear. God, I hated suits!

Unfortunately for me, I was currently wearing the stupid thing. I felt like I was headed to a fucking funeral. Despite that, when I walked into Alex's parents' room, the entire group turned to look at me. The look on Alex's face was enough for me to bear the discomfort of the suit. Pure lust swam in his eyes, and I couldn't for the life of me look away from them.

Drake broke the spell, however, when he whistled. "Dad, you look *fancy*," he said, and Alex's mom laughed.

"I take it, Eddie, that you don't dress in a suit very often."

I smiled at her. "No, in fact, I intended to find every excuse not to wear this one."

"I'm glad you did," Alex said, causing me to blush. I didn't dare look at him again.

"Well, are we ready?" I asked, hoping to cut some of the tension I was feeling being this close to Alex with him looking at me in that way.

We walked to the elevator, the boys talking a mile a minute. I was embarrassed that I hadn't noticed how good my boys looked in their little suits. I thanked the stars Emma Jean had taken them into town before we left and had their hair cut. I didn't think their usual wild unkempt hair would've really gone well with their dressed-up looks. I had to admit, my kids looked like fine gentlemen as we got off the elevator and walked into the fancy restaurant.

Alex sat next to me at the table, and as soon as he sat down, he reached over and took my hand. The second he did, electricity sparked inside my heart. *God,* I had it bad for this man.

We were all enjoying ourselves. My kids' manners were impeccable, and they were laughing along with the stories Alex and his sisters were telling. I had to make sure I bought a special gift for Emma Jean, since she'd really brought my kids up to standard.

I felt so proud of my kids as Ellen finished telling a particularly embarrassing story about their mom and Francesca coming back from shopping and finding Alex skinny-dipping in the pool.

Drake looked at me, and I could tell the internal conflict about a story he wanted to tell. I gave him the meanest *you'd better not* look I could muster, which did nothing to deter him.

As he told the story of the Catholic school girls catching Flex, Eric, and me as we skinny-dipped in the Rio Grande, the table guffawed with laughter. "Remind me to dock your allowance when we get home," I told Drake, causing the table to go into another fit of laughter.

We were having so much fun that when the meal was served, I didn't think any of us had thought about it. Luckily, the Zitlals had preordered before we got here.

As we ate, the conversation drifted onto business, and the family spoke about the film and how things were going. They had several questions about the ranch, which either I or the boys answered for them. I was surprised at how even Luke contributed to the mature conversation at the table, offering valid points and helpful suggestions about where certain scenes and locations would be most appropriate for the story.

I was shocked to find out that much of the storyline had been modified to mimic the Diamondback Jack story. The love affair had been a mix of his story, and his brother who'd married my ancestor's sister. They even had the main character as a prostitute, although that was implied instead of stated. All the adults looked at the boys to ensure they weren't being inappropriate with their discussion.

"I think it's great you're using that story as part of the film. It's been a legend in my family for generations. Although, I didn't really know the whole story until recently." I paused for a moment, trying to figure out how to tell the story without disclosing that Flex and I had both been visited by our ancestors.

"After Alex visited the ranch, I decided to learn what I could about Diamondback Jack. I began digging through the old newspapers at the library in town. I found an article that said there were three brothers, though, not two. Diamond was the baby, and his mother was from Puebla, just like you, señora Zitlal. His older brothers had a different mom who'd died shortly after they moved to West Texas."

"We knew about the older brothers, Sampson and Levy, the lawman who'd been killed and of course Jack. Do you know what happened to Sampson?" señor Zitlal asked.

"No, we don't know anything about him really. After his brothers died, he seems to have disappeared. My best guess is he moved away from the area.

"Wow," Francesca said. "That's sad."

Alex looked back at me. "Do you happen to have a copy of that article?" he asked.

"I did, we put it in the family archives up in the attic before you moved in. We were all intrigued by Diamondback Jack's story after you came to visit us. The boys even went with me to the library to help me research it."

"Did they have anything in the papers about Diamond?" señor Zitlal asked.

I shook my head and looked at my boys. "We looked through all the papers at the time and found information about the first brother's death. It's interesting, because my cousin is dating his descendant, Mitch. Mitch owns the motel you stayed at initially, Alex," I said, and he nodded. "That being said, I never found anything about Diamondback Jack. I doubt it'd be news that a bandit had attacked someone back then. It's my understanding that it was pretty common for the time."

"That's too bad," Alex's father said, then turned to Alex. "I think you need to have the writers include all this in their story, but make all the brothers from Mexico and the women they fall in love with from the American side. This is the best way to make the story include both sides of the international line, and it keeps everyone on an equal standing.

"I wonder if we can find any information about the other brother," he said, pondering.

"We are using creative license with the entire story anyway," Alex said. "But, when we're mimicking real life, we do make an effort to get the story correct, or at least, as close as possible."

I smiled. "Well, it's a great story, and when the press ask about it, I'm sure that being able to say the story was based on both your family and that of the people who owned the ranch where you filmed it, will go a long way in helping you promote the piece. People love when there are personal connections."

Señora Zitlal smiled. "You are smart to say that," she said. "Maybe Alex needs to hire you in our public relations department."

I laughed. "More like Alex should hire me to manage the horses and other animals used in the film. I prefer to get my hands dirty. You can see, I'm not much of a suit person."

Francesca quickly responded, "I would disagree with that assessment, señor Crawford," and she let her eyes drift downward, then over at her brother with a wink.

Alex slanted his eyes at her, making me want to chuckle, and then turning to his father, asked, "Papa, when was the last time you saw your surgeon? What was her name? Dr. Rameriz, wasn't it?"

Alex's father looked suspicious at his son's question, then over to his daughter, and it seemed as if a lightbulb came on. "Well, she checked the wound before I came home and gave it her blessing. The nurse did tell me..." he looked at Francesca. "That it was very unusual for a surgeon to come back and check a wound. Usually, they let the nurses do that."

He looked at his younger daughter, and winked. "I spoke with Dr. Ramirez about you, Francesca, during the visit. She said you and she were friends. It's nice when we have *friends...*" he emphasized the word, "...in the medical field."

Francesca's face was blushing bright red, and I could tell she wanted to kill her brother. I glanced over at Ellen, who was working very hard not to laugh, and I realized a secret had just been revealed. So, figuring out for myself that Francesca was dating this Dr. Ramirez, I instantly felt sorry for her. I knew, growing up with Flex, if he'd had a secret like this on me, it would've burned a hole in him until he told someone what my secret was.

I changed the subject, bringing it back to the ranch. "If you'd like, I could have Flex take a picture of the article and send it to me. That way you could print it out and see all the details.

"That would be very nice," Francesca said. "If you'll excuse me, I need to use the restroom." Then, she got up and walked away.

"Oops," Alex said, and his sister Ellen kicked him under the table. "Ouch," he said, but we all knew he had it coming.

We talked about how the story could be integrated with all three brothers, and when Francesca rejoined us there was no more talk about her doctor friend. That didn't mean she wasn't going to kill Alex the moment she had him alone. Luckily, I thought I'd earned a couple brownie points by taking her out of the hot seat. At least, I hoped I had. I had no doubt the attorney in Francesca could rip and destroy if need be. Revenge was undoubtedly on the horizon.

The last two days were spent in the actual Disney World park. The boys ran around like they'd lost their heads, and because the entire theme park was designed for kids who'd lost their heads, it was totally cool.

By the end of the second day, we were all done in, and even the kids barely showed any concern that we were leaving the next day. In fact, as we flew home, the kids both laid their seats back, and slept the entire trip. I'd honestly never seen them so exhausted.

When we got back to the hacienda, I called the sheriff in Alpine and asked if they'd had any other issues. When he informed me that Princeton and my ex had been seen in Las Vegas, I figured we were good to go home.

I informed the group while the boys were swimming, preferring to let them know when we were alone. I figured there'd be some separation anxiety associated with this departure.

"Can you stay a couple more days?" Francesca asked. "I've got a surprise for the family tomorrow night, and I'd like for you to be here."

I was perplexed by the invitation. I wasn't really part of the family. *But, sure, why not. What could a couple more days hurt?*

"Sure, I guess, but aren't y'all tired of us yet?" The entire room said no at the same time, causing me to laugh. "Y'all are just being nice, but thank you. I do have to get back soon, though. I'm sure my poor cousin is chomping at the bit with having to actually do some work."

"If you're staying, then why don't we take you out. Ellen, do you think you'll feel up to it?" Alex asked.

"No, my pregnant ass isn't going clubbing, but you three should go," she said, waving at Francesca, Alex and me.

"You up for it?" Alex asked me, and I shrugged. "I've never been clubbing, so I don't know. Am I?"

All three siblings looked at me like I'd grown horns. "What, I was married with kids while most people were out clubbing, so it wasn't really an option for me."

"You are really deprived," Francesca said. "We're totally taking your virgin ass out for a night on the town."

I chuckled at the virgin part. "You missed the part about me having kids, but I get your point."

It was late when we left, so I was able to tuck the boys in and let them know to find abuelo or abuela if they needed anything.

They truly didn't care this time that I was going out. That was a testament to how much they'd come to trust this family.

19

Alex

T HE MINUTE HE'D AGREED to go out, I was ecstatic. My sisters and I had a favorite dance bar that we always went to in Juarez, but I decided to take it easy on him and start in El Paso at a gay bar that was, well, tamer.

Francesca's girlfriend met us at the bar. "Hi, I'm Lia Rameriz," she said as she extended an elegant hand toward me.

I smiled. "We met at the hospital, I'm Alexandro, Francesca's brother, and this is Edward Crawford, my date," I said. Eddie cocked an eyebrow, but didn't correct me.

"Hello, Dr. Ramirez," he said. "I've heard good things about you."

"Is that so," she replied. "We'll have to get together later and compare notes."

I cleared my throat, and simultaneously, Francesca and I separated the two.

God, we had fun. We danced and laughed. This bar was way calmer than the one in Juarez, so we could talk and just hang out. Juarez's bar didn't start kicking until midnight, so we spent some time here. I decided to forgo drinking, because I'd have to drive, and Francesca's girlfriend, I noticed, only nursed one before switching to something nonalcoholic. When Francesca and Eddie got up to dance, I leaned over, "It sucks to have to be the responsible ones, huh?"

She chuckled. "I usually don't, but I'm on call starting tomorrow, and I can't start my week off with a hangover.

"So, how long have you two been dating?" she asked.

I laughed. "Not dating, wanting to date, but haven't made anything official yet."

"Francesca mentioned he has a couple kids. It's my understanding your family have gotten fairly attached to them over the past couple of weeks."

I nodded. "They seem to fit perfectly."

She patted my back. "It's tough when you have a family. It took several weeks for me to let your sister in."

I looked back at her inquisitively, making her smile. "Yes, I too have two rambunctious boys, Frank and Evan."

"Wow, how old are they?" I asked.

"They are both five," she said.

"How is Francesca doing as a step-girlfriend?" I asked, and Lia almost spat her soda out. "I like that, step-girlfriend. They only just met. Your sweet sister gave me an ultimatum. Either I include her in all my life, or she steps out of it, so, just before you all ran off to Disney World, I introduced her to my kids."

"Did it go well?" I asked.

"Like a charm, the three hit it off instantly. I've dated a lot of women since I decided to become a single mom, but I've never introduced my kids to any of them."

"Wow, you two *are* serious, then?"

"I think that's something to ask your sister," she said as Francesca and Eddie came back, smiling from ear to ear.

"That's my favorite song," Eddie laughed. "Both jazzy and insane all at the same time."

"You have the moves there, Eddie Crawford. Where'd you learn to move like that?"

He laughed. "You wouldn't believe me if I told you."

"Try us," I said.

"I took ballet until I was in high school. I only stopped because my mom said it wasn't manly enough once a boy hit puberty to be dancing in tights.

"Really? So, why did she let you before?" I asked.

Eddie chuckled. "Probably because mom had a crush on a guy who had a daughter in my ballet class. I never asked. I enjoyed it well enough, but I loved the fact that my brothers were forced to sit and watch while I was practicing."

"Did they tease you?" Francesca asked.

I laughed out loud.

"Never, my mom threatened their lives if they did. Besides, I'd gotten pretty tough helping out on the ranch during the summer before, and even though I wasn't much older than Drake, my oldest son," he clarified to Lia. "I could totally kick their butts. I doubt my mom really cared about my reputation, anyway. If she and my dad hadn't been trying to reconnect, I think I could've continued until I graduated. Regardless, I now have an odd love of ballet, which may seem a bit strange when you consider I'm a construction worker turned rancher."

Lia looked at him and winked. "If I weren't a lesbian and totally captivated by the beautiful woman right here," she leaned over and kissed Francesca on the lips. "I'd be trying to tease you away from this one," she said, pointing at Alex.

Eddie shocked me when he turned toward me all happy and sexy, and said, "Oh, I think this one will keep me busy for a while." Then, he laid a hot, mind-blowing kiss on me that almost had me seeing stars.

When he pulled back, I said, "Well, girls, this has been fun, but we'll see y'all later."

They laughed as I tried to pull Eddie up and toward the door. "Hold your horses. You promised me a night of clubbing, and a night of clubbing it'll be!"

I sat back down pouting. "I never get any loving."

Eddie pulled me back over. "That's all about to change, just be patient," he said, and kissed me again. The intensity of the promise caused my heart to pound heavily in the middle of my chest.

When he leaned back, I looked at Lia, and said, "If he does that again, I may need a cardiologist on hand."

Eddie smiled, and said, "Let's see if we can force her to use her skills then."

"Wait, not here. Y'all have to do that on your own time," Francesca said, and pushed Eddie back into his seat. "Besides, this is my baby's day off. I don't want her to have to revive my brother 'cause you've caused his heart to stop," she said to Eddie, making him laugh.

I loved buzzed Eddie, I decided. I needed to make sure I had spirits on hand all the time when he was around.

We left the bar and crossed into Juarez, to the nightclub we used to frequent when we were younger. The place was as nice as anything you'd find in New York or LA. It was bustling with lights and loud music, and hot men danced shirtless all around us. This particular club always rocked after midnight, no matter what day of the week it was, and damn, if I hadn't had some of the best times of my youth dancing on these floors.

By the third drink, Eddie was minus his shirt, dancing with all the men in the room. I wasn't the kind of guy to share my man, but seeing his beautiful body swaying with all the other sexy bodies on the dance floor steered my thoughts toward one thing, and one thing only. Raw, hungry sex.

If I'd been concerned about Eddie's sexuality, I wasn't now. He liked being touched by men, and the way he moved in the crowd showed it. The thought that I was going to be the first man to touch him that way excited me. Yes, I knew it made me a caveman, but I couldn't help it. I liked the thought of being the first, his first, and god help me, I was going to be his first sooner rather than later.

We danced until the early hours of the morning, and were about to leave the bar when the DJ announced the border had been closed, due to a drug raid. "The wait is supposed to be at least two hours."

"Don't worry," I told Eddie, who was looking concerned. "I'll text my parents and let them know you won't be home until tomorrow. They'll manage the kids fine."

Francesca asked Lia about her boys, and she shrugged. "No, they're with my parents. They're spending the night anyway."

"What are we gonna do?" Eddie asked. "They've already called last call here."

I chuckled. "You forgot we have our studio over here. We have several rooms there that we stay in when we're working on a project. We'll crash there."

He looked at me strangely, but his look quickly turned to lust. "Then let's go crash," he said, and leaned over to give me a passionate kiss.

"Yeah, let's go," I squeaked, and Lia and Francesca laughed.

We actually had six apartments attached to the studio. The original studio was located next to a beautiful eighteenth-century hacienda that had been converted to a hotel. When it fell into disrepair in the nineteen fifties, my grandfather bought it, expanded the studio and attached the hotel. The lower part of the hacienda was converted to offices, while the upstairs was converted to rooms where people could stay when they were visiting or when we were filming.

Eventually, only our family were using it, so he had it renovated into official apartments. My parents even lived there for a time before they took over the El Paso hacienda. Of course, that was before I was born.

We walked into the studio and up the stairs. Eddie wanted to look around, but I wasn't interested in playing host. I wanted him in bed and under me.

He laughed as I pulled him toward the apartment I'd taken over and made my own. As soon as we were inside the door, I pushed him back and took his mouth with mine. "God, Eddie, I want you so bad it hurts. If you want me to back off, you'd better tell me now, because if I get started, I'm not going to be able to stop."

He shook his head. "I don't want you to stop. I want to feel you, touch you..." He grinned. "I want to taste you." The look he gave me made it clear what part he wanted to taste.

I pulled back and looked at him. "You've never had sex with a guy before?"

He shook his head. "But I've been doing some..." he shook his head and looked shy, "...some research."

I laughed out loud. "Have you now. Well, by all means, let's see what you've learned."

I pulled him toward the shower. No way was I gonna let his first time be with a sweaty man. I wanted it to be perfect, so he'd let me do it again... and again... and as often as possible.

We stripped as we went, clothes flying across the room. Once in the shower, I used the soap to lather his skin, starting at his shoulders and letting my cock slip into his crack as I lathered him there as well. He moaned deliciously as my cock nestled into him, and as my hand rubbed the soap into his muscles, then onto his cock.

When I turned him around, something switched on inside him, and he pushed me against the tiles and took my mouth forcefully, while he ground his cock into mine. "God, I want you so bad," he said, catching my nipple between his teeth. When I caught my breath, he let his tongue soothe where he'd taken a love bite.

Before I knew what was happening, Eddie slid down to his knees and took my cock into his mouth. "Are you sure?" I asked, and when he looked up at me, the tip of my cock resting on his tongue, I knew he was fucking sure.

I thought he'd be shy, that he'd have to be taken care of, but I was wrong. He took my cock in his mouth, too deep at first, and he gagged. Had I not been so carried away, I might have laughed at his eagerness. He pulled back, regained his composure and went straight back to sucking me.

"Fuck, Eddie, careful you're gonna make me come too soon," I said, and he chuckled.

"You only got one time in you?" he asked.

I thumped him on the head. "Take your time, greenhorn," I said, making him laugh again, but this time while my cock rested in his mouth.

He sucked my cock, still being ruthless, until I couldn't hold back any longer. I pushed his head back as I said, "I'm coming." To my surprise, Eddie opened his mouth and let the white cum spew onto his face, some of which landed in his mouth.

I shuddered. That was so fucking hot, especially when Eddie licked his lips and used his finger to push the rest of my cum into his mouth.

When I looked at him, he smiled. "I've been really wanting to try that."

"Have you? What else have you wanted to try?" I asked.

Eddie stood up then, kissed me, and flipped me toward the tiles. He got some soap, lathered my ass up along with his cock, and slipped it into my crack, letting it slide up and down, teasing my hole.

"This," he said. "Can I fuck you?" he asked.

"Oh, fuck yeah!" I said, and would've let him fuck me bareback had he not asked for a condom.

I used the showerhead to rinse us off, handed him a towel, and when we were dry, I led him into the bedroom and pushed him down on my bed. "You can fuck me, but I get to play a little first," I said.

I lay on top of him, kissing his neck and licking that delicious Adam's apple I'd noticed and fantasized about since the day he first kissed me out on the ranch.

I moved my body down, teasing his nipples, as I ran my hands up and down his sides. When I got to his cock, I looked up, wanting to see his expression when I took him into my mouth.

He was staring at me, eyes clouded with desire, and I could see he wanted me. When I pulled his head into my mouth, he arched against me. The blood pounded in my cock as I watched him receiving the pleasure I was giving him.

When I sucked him down into my throat and swallowed, he moaned loudly. "Fuck, now *I'm* gonna come."

"Not yet," I said, and began edging him.

When he was begging me to let him come, I pulled off him, and with a mean laugh, said, "Oh, you're gonna come..." I grabbed his cock with my hand, "...but not until this is inside me."

I pulled the lube and condom out that I kept in my side table for an occasion like this. I lubed my hole, stretching it and prepping myself as I continued to suck on his cock, edging him closer and closer.

When I was loose enough, I slipped the condom onto his throbbing cock, lubed him, and straddling him, began to ease his cock into me.

"Fuck," he moaned as I slowly pushed him inside, riding it more and more as my hole stretched around his fully erect cock.

"Wanna try a different position?" I asked.

Before I knew it, Eddie had slipped out from under me and climbed up behind me doggie-style onto the bed. He kissed my back as he pushed his cock back up to my hole.

"Fuck yeah," I said, and began to push up against him. He rode me slowly and I could tell he was trying to be gentle. "Is this okay?" he asked.

"Mm-mmm," I moaned and shoved myself back onto him.

"Oh, shit, Alex... fuck!" he said, when my ass engulfed him.

20

Eddie

I'D FANTASIZED ABOUT FUCKING another guy. I'd thought about it since Theresa had left, and I'd jacked off to the thought while in the shower, but nothing had prepared me for Alex's tight hole.

My cock slipped into him, and he pulled me in. My hips began to move with him, and before I knew what was happening, I was pounding his ass like a caveman.

I pushed down on his hips, causing him to arch against me, forcing my cock further inside him. Instinct had taken over, any fear I'd had that I might not know what I was doing was gone, and I rode Alex hard. Each moan, each curse, or cry to God, pushing me to fuck harder and faster.

Before I knew it, Alex's moans increased. "Eddie, I'm coming again, fuck me. Goddamn, pound my ass!" he demanded, and I complied.

Just as he came, he squeezed my cock, plunging me into ecstasy and forcing me to come myself. I swore I saw stars as I emptied into the condom.

Alex collapsed under me, and I ended up lying over him with my cock still in his ass, leaking into the condom.

I leaned up, kissing his muscular back, and felt guilty, because all I could think about was when I could do this again. I rolled over onto my back in a blissful, euphoric afterglow.

As soon as I lay back down, Alex crawled into my arms and snuggled.

We fell asleep like that. The feeling of having this beautiful man in my arms was pure heaven. He was taller than me, and I wondered briefly before we dozed off if he was hanging off the bed, but it must not have mattered, because both of us were quickly asleep.

When I finally woke, about thirty minutes later, Alex was breathing heavily into my chest. I rolled him over, waking him and leaning over him. I kissed him gently on the lips.

When he stirred, I said, "That was amazing. Like I could never have imagined."

He chuckled. "It gets even better than that," he said, and I immediately wanted to try again and find out.

When I nuzzled his neck again, he laughed. "You gotta give a man a moment, though."

"Do I gotta?" I asked.

"Just a moment," he said. "You hungry?"

"Just for you."

"Mmm, good answer," he said, and rolled over and went into the bathroom.

He came back in with a washcloth and began wiping me down. He also had a wastebasket he tossed the condom in. He threw the washcloth into the bathroom and jumped on top of me. "Okay, I'm ready again," he said, and I laughed out loud.

"I'm game," I said, and was immediately hard again.

By the time the sun came up the following morning, I was fully broken in with gay sex. I'd come so often that night, my balls hurt, and when I told Alex, he just laughed and said the feeling was mutual. "Maybe we can just cuddle now?" he asked, and I agreed.

"I should probably get back to the kids," I said to Alex, and he shook his head. "No, my parents are already up and texted, saying they were going to take the boys out for breakfast, and might catch a matinee at the theater. We don't have to be back until tonight for whatever Francesca has planned."

I yawned. "Then I wanna sleep," I said.

"Good idea," Alex agreed, and before I knew it, we were snuggled into the bed again. This time when we fell asleep in each other's arms, we didn't wake up until just before noon.

I stretched long and hard, letting Alex's head rise on my chest as I did. When he finally stirred, he looked up at me and all but purred in my arms. "You're sexy as fuck when you wake up, señor Zitlal," I said.

"Blah, don't call me that," he said, and I laughed when he said that was his father's name.

He crawled off me then and went toward the bathroom to pee, something I needed to do myself. I waited a moment, letting myself doze in the bed, enjoying the fact that I hadn't slept this late in the day in… well, I wasn't sure when the last time I slept this late in the day had been.

Alex came back out and asked if I wanted breakfast or lunch. "No, I'm not hungry yet. I do have to pee, though, then maybe you can join me for a shower," I wiggled my eyebrows at him.

"Mmm," he said as he crawled toward me, and lay naked on top of my covered form.

The way he lay on top of me put pressure on my bladder, and I chuckled. "If you don't let me up, I'm gonna wet the bed for the first time since I was little."

"Not a golden showers, man," he said. "Sorry."

"Dude, me neither!" I pushed him off and rushed toward the bathroom.

He was still laughing when I came out.

I jumped on the bed, pinned him down, then kissed him.

"Morning breath kisses, nothing better, huh?" I asked, and kissed him again.

"I'll take a kiss from you any way you wanna give it," he said. "But I've had fresher, that's for sure."

Being intimate with Alex was fun and light. It had never been that way with Theresa. She was intense all the time. I knew I shouldn't be comparing the two, but since I'd only ever been with two people, it seemed inevitable.

Alex certainly fit me better. His body molded into me, all hard edges that seemed to fit into all my soft ones.

Alex flipped me back onto the bed and straddled me. "So, how was last night, your first time with a guy? Any regrets?"

I shook my head. "Only that I'm not eighteen and have limits on how many times I can do it in one night."

He laughed. "We can work on getting your stamina up."

"Oh, is that so? Should I ask what secrets you possess for that?"

"Practice... practice makes perfect," he said, grinding his fine ass into my crotch. I immediately felt myself getting hard.

"God, you are so hot," he said. "I can't believe how long it took me to get you in my bed."

"Good things come to those who wait," I said, tongue in cheek.

"Hardly. Good things are usually lost by those who wait." Alex got serious. "I know this is different, and I'm not going to make it weird when we are around your boys or your family, okay?"

"Fuck that, we aren't going to hide this, Alex," I said, and took a deep breath.

"Listen, I don't play the secrets game. My life, my choice, and I'm not going to hide and pretend I don't like you. That being said, when this comes out, no one, not my family nor yours, should be putting on too much pressure. I'll handle mine, and good luck with yours," I said, laughing.

"You are an observant man," Alex said, rolling over and lying on the bed next to me. "My parents aren't slow when it comes to relationships. The way they've already adopted your boys, even before they met them, that's just how they do things. I'm afraid we'll just have to ignore them when they ask us when we're gonna have the ceremony."

I laughed. "Well, the boys will start calling you Daddy Warbucks once they know this is happening, especially after how you and your family have spoiled them. I swear if Drake or Luke break into the song, *Tomorrow*, I may have to dump you."

"So, just so I'm clear, we aren't going to pretend this isn't what it was?" he asked.

"No, no pretense. I'm not good at that anyway. We're dating and..." I leaned over and kissed him deeply and passionately. "We're doing it while we're at it," I finished.

"God, I hope so," he said, and came back up for another kiss.

21

Alex

Making love with Eddie all night long meant that our shower sex, take two, was sweet and affectionate. Eddie lathered me up, washing my hair while his engorged cock slid in and out of my lathered crotch. Our height difference meant that my cock rubbed up against him right below his navel, and the sensation of his pubic hair against my head felt wonderful.

As we washed and rinsed, kissing, nibbling, licking, and sucking, until we were both so worked up, either of us could explode at any moment.

I could tell Eddie was about to drop to his knees, when I stopped him, and pulled him out of the shower. "Let's take this to the bed," I said.

"We'll just end up back in the shower again. I think I'm seeing a pattern. You intend to keep me here forever."

"I wouldn't mind that, but no, let me show you the joys of sixty-nine with a guy."

"Oh," he said, his eyes lighting up. "I hadn't thought about that."

He hurriedly dried off, and all but pushed me out of the bathroom and onto the bed. I straddled his head, but instead of taking his cock into my mouth, I lifted his legs and bent his body up toward me. I let my tongue find his hole and began to explore it.

"Oh, fucking Christ!" he said. "That feels amazing, nasty as fuck, but amazing!"

I chuckled in spite of myself. "Hush and suck," I demanded, and he laughed. "Bossy, much?"

I pulled back and asked, "You want me to continue?"

"Dear God, I really do!"

I couldn't help but chuckle again. "Okay, get on all fours. Let me show you how this is done."

Eddie quickly complied and seeing the sexy cowboy on all fours on my bed sent my libido into overdrive.

I spread his butt cheeks and let my tongue find his hole again, driving it into him as deep as I could, then pulling out. Each time I fucked him with my tongue, Eddie moaned that low bass moan, forcing me further and further.

Finally, I rolled over and slipping my head between his legs, I took his cock into my mouth and began sucking him off.

He pulled out of my mouth, though, and sat back on my chest.

"I-I think I'd like for you to try to fuck me," he said.

I looked up into his face. "You sure, that's something that takes a lot of practice, and I'd prefer you to be ready if this is going to be your first time."

"I'm sure I want to try, no promises," he said. "But if your tongue feels that good, what's your cock gonna feel like?"

I laid him on his back and got the lube. "I'm gonna try to stretch you out, but if this doesn't feel good, you tell me, okay? It's not like you have to do it, and we've fucked a lot the past few hours. You may need to wait 'til you're more rested." I knew when I said it, he was going to take offense.

"Buddy, I am rested. What are you two years younger? Please, it's not like I'm an old man."

I laughed. "I meant you've come like a million times in the past twenty-four hours. The intensity often makes it easier to take it," I said.

"Let's try, I'll tell you if I wanna stop."

I lubed up my fingers and began playing with his hole, similar to how I'd used my tongue earlier. Eddie moaned with pleasure as I played with him. When he began bucking against my hands, I slowly slipped a finger in, telling him to push down on me.

As my finger entered him, I watched as he forced himself to relax while my finger stayed inside him. He finally started jacking off, and then slowly he began to ride my finger. When

I could tell he was enjoying the sensation, I gently began to slip my other finger in. I made it past the guardian muscle before he reacted. "Wow, that's a lot," he said, and once again he visibly relaxed before he began jacking off again. By the time I had my third finger moving into him, he was riding them like a pro. I began scissoring and stretching him, and all the while, the gay virgin seemed to be enjoying the sensation more and more.

I left my fingers inside him as I reached over for another condom. Tearing the wrapper with my teeth, I pulled the condom out and began to try to slip it on with one hand.

As soon as I had the condom started, I pulled my fingers out and rolled the condom the rest of the way up, lubed his ass and my cock up as much as I could and asked, "You ready?"

He nodded, his eyes hooded with ecstasy.

I let my cock find the hole I'd just vacated with my fingers and let the head slowly slip into him, looking for any discomfort.

"Mmm, oh fuck, yeah," he said, and I knew he was going to be able to handle this.

"Push down on me when you're ready," I said, and he did so right away. I was surprised how quick he took me in, moaning and squirming as my cock, thicker than my three fingers had been, found its way into his ass.

When I was fully inside him, he looked at me and smiled. "Fuck me," he demanded.

He didn't need to ask me twice. I began to move in and out, sending him into fits of sexual bliss. His moans got louder and louder, me watching for discomfort, and seeing none.

My moans began to match his, then my body took over.

"Oh, shit, Eddie, you're so tight, so hot." My cock pounded into him as I lost my mind to the sensation of being inside him.

His face registered only bliss as I continued to pound him harder and harder, lifting his ass so I could go deeper into him.

I was pounding him so hard at this point, I could hear our bodies slapping together above the sounds of our moans.

"Goddamn, your body is perfect," I moaned.

I shifted, and the next thing I knew, I hit his prostate. Eddie's eyes grew large and it looked like he'd swallowed his tongue for a moment.

"What the fuck, shit, oh, god... don't stop," he said, and I kept the position so I could continue fucking into his prostate.

He came like crazy, spurting so hard it hit the wall behind the bed. He clamped down so hard on my cock when he did that I came on the next thrust. "Fuck, oh fuck!" I yelled. My cum filling the condom.

We both shuddered simultaneously as we finished.

I pulled out, tugged the filled condom off, and tossed it into the trash can.

I grabbed a towel I'd left next to the bed for convenience last night, and began wiping him off. I'd have to clean the wall later.

When I'd finished, I collapsed next to him, his arm under me.

"God, that was amazing," he said. "Who knew that would be so amazing?"

"Well, that's a lot of people," I said, still out of breath.

"Let's do it again," he said, and I laughed. "You're gonna be sore for a bit. Might wanna wait, at least a few hours.

"God, it's worth it. Totally worth it."

"Have I turned you into a bottom then?" I asked with a chuckle.

"Mmm, no, I like fucking you too, but damn, that felt amazing!"

As we drove back to the hacienda, the weather was perfect, so I opened the convertible top, and the wind whisked around us blowing us back to reality.

I loved men, had been with a lot of them, but Eddie was different. I wasn't exactly sure why, and fuck if I cared at the moment. I was just enjoying the happy sensation he brought to me.

I reached over after we'd gone through the border, and took his hand.

When he winked at me, I felt my heart do a weird flipping sensation like you'd get right before you went headlong down a roller coaster ride.

The sensation caused me to smile and wink at Eddie. I'd always loved roller coasters. This was certainly a ride I was going to enjoy.

22

Eddie

We didn't see Francesca or Lia before they left. Of course, we were a little busy. I was surprised when we got back to the hacienda, and they were both there with Lia's twins in tow.

Señora Zitlal had monopolized Lia, thanking her over and over for doing such a good job taking care of her husband. I could tell Lia was overwhelmed by it.

I took pity on her, and asked if Francesca and she could escort me and the boys down to the riverbed to collect rocks, to compare with the type we had at our part of the river.

Her sons, both younger than mine, were wired already with their new surroundings, and began bouncing up and down at the thought of an adventure.

Francesca thanked me for the distraction after we got outside.

"Lia, I'm surprised you brought the boys with you," I said. "But, as you can tell, Francesca's family are great with kids."

Lia blushed, but smiled. "Francesca basically gave me the same ultimatum again, saying if you were brave enough to visit with your kids, I should be too."

I laughed. "Yeah, but Alex and I weren't lovers when this all started."

Francesca beamed. "That changed last night?"

"I don't kiss and tell, Ms. Zitlal," I said, but winked at her nonetheless.

Francesca laughed. "You don't have to. We saw how the two of you were all over each other last night. I'd be more surprised if it hadn't gone that way."

I bumped companionably against her, and said, "Even though we weren't technically together, it was pretty intense. Add the fact that you're definitely dating Lia, and you brought the kids over." I shook my head in an exaggerated way.

"Tell me about it. If they shower me with much more attention, I might not make it through the night," Lia said with a sigh.

The boys had run ahead and were becoming impatient with our lagging behind. "Hey, if you two want to take some time for yourselves, I can walk the boys the rest of the way down to the river. I just made this up as an excuse to give Lia a moment to breathe."

Lia chuckled. "I appreciate it too. Yeah, I could use some time alone with Francesca if you don't mind."

I left them by one of the big cottonwoods that had a little gazebo under it. The boys were excited about finding rocks, providing testament to how easy it was to be intrigued by things when you were young. "Watch for snakes y'all, and, Drake, you and Luke show the twins how to watch out for them."

"Yes, sir," they called back, and I could hear Drake telling them to avoid the shrubs or any boulders where the serpents could hide.

Since moving to the ranch, Jimmy had shown them how to walk in the desert, listening for the tell-tale warning sounds of the snakes.

When we got to the riverbed, it only took a few minutes for each of the boys to find the rocks they wanted. As we walked back up to the hacienda, the boys examined their rocks and talked about fossils and things they'd learned at school.

Lia and Francesca were no longer in the little gazebo, so I assumed they were back in the hacienda as well. I took the boys into the utility room, so they could wash their rocks and clean up before dinner.

Dinner was soon after we got back, and before the food was served, Francesca stood pulling Lia up with her.

"I know things have been crazy with the filming and Papa's heart attack, not to mention that Ellen and Ernesto are about to become parents, but I have some news as well."

Lia smiled and blushed as Francesca put her arms around her. "Last night I proposed to Lia, and she has agreed to become my wife."

Señora Zitlal screamed and jumped up, pulling Lia into a hug. "¡Me voy a dar otra hija!" I didn't know exactly what she said, but *otra hija* means another daughter, so I guessed it meant good things for Lia.

The tears flowed freely from everyone around the table. I felt awkward being here for such an intimate family moment, so I let them all fawn over each other, while I tended to the four kids, who really didn't seem to care about the emotional moment in the least.

After dinner, I took the kids to the playroom, and set up a few games that all four could play together.

I sat in the corner and watched them play, enjoying the comradery the boys had developed in such a short time. I was always so introverted growing up that I didn't make friends easily. It warmed my heart that my boys weren't that way. I guessed, once again, a lot of that had to do with feeling secure about their home life.

Alex eventually came in and sat next to me. "That was awesome," he said. "I can't believe Francesca is going to settle down. She was the wild one of the three of us."

I looked at him and chuckled. "Then, she had to be out of control, 'cause from what I've heard, you're quite the player."

"Hey," he exclaimed. "I wasn't that bad. I just like men, that's all."

I smiled, but the thought that he could still be a player nagged at me a bit. I put it out of my mind, though, and enjoyed just sitting with him, while we watched the boys battle one another in *Super Mario 3D*.

That night, Alex agreed to stay in my bedroom, since I told him I wanted to stay close to the boys, in case they needed me.

Alex and I sat with Francesca and Lia on the big wide porch after the kids had been tucked in. The twins had taken a bedroom across the hall from Francesca's, and were asleep a good hour before mine had turned in.

They'd talked about how they had met, and how Francesca had pursued Lia relentlessly before she'd given in and gone out with her. Their discussion of how the relationship developed over time had made me ponder my own situation.

The conversation earlier about how Alex was a player was needling my thoughts. Was this just a game? I was trying to keep my thoughts light, since one night of sex didn't mean a relationship. I kicked myself as I lay awake, him snoring lightly next to me, wondering if I could just let this be casual. The truth was, I was sure that wasn't me, and I cursed myself for being so domesticated.

I'd need to have a conversation with Alex sooner than later. People like me didn't need to let their hearts get involved too fast with people like Alex. It was destined to end in disaster.

The next morning, I slipped out of the room before Alex woke up. After finding a pot of coffee, I assumed had been fixed by señora Zitlal, I poured a cup and sat in the courtyard, enjoying the sounds of birds as they played in the citrus trees.

"You look contemplative," Ellen said, from behind me.

"Oh, hi, I didn't know you'd spent the night."

"Yeah, after Francesca's news, Ernesto and I decided to stick around and continue the party. You know today will be all about celebrating."

I laughed. "No, I didn't, but I'm not surprised. Your family seems to enjoy celebrating."

"Wanna talk about what's got you stirring this early?" she asked.

I smiled. "I'm usually up earlier than this. Mornings are my favorite time of day. It's when I get most of my thinking done."

"Something tells me your thinking involves a certain pain-in-the-ass brother of mine."

I chuckled. "Well, I have to admit he's certainly in my thoughts."

"Was last night overwhelming?" she asked.

"The engagement? No," I said. "I can tell those two belong together."

We sat in silence as we both enjoyed our coffee.

"Do you think Alex is the settling down type?" I finally got the nerve up to ask.

Ellen thought for a moment. "It's always been on his radar. You can't grow up with parents like ours and not think about having a lifelong partner, but I don't know if he sees himself that way."

I let that sink in. "I can't think of myself any other way, which makes it unfair to anyone who wants to date me. I guess, because I've always been in a relationship, whether it was with my wife and now with kids, I've never thought about the casual thing."

Ellen sat quietly next to me, staring out at the pool, her hand resting on her rather large belly.

"I can't answer the question you really want to ask. Will Alex be able to handle being in a committed relationship? Really, Eddie, that'll depend entirely upon him, but if you want to know what I think, then yes. I believe, if he ever falls in love, it'll be forever." She reached over then and laid her hand over mine. "Be patient with him, and just have fun. It's hard for those of us who act through emotion to let things just happen, and I'm guessing that's even more exacerbated by your being a dad, but I believe that's the only way you can play this."

Luke came out then and crawled up in my lap. It'd been so long since he'd done it, I hardly knew how to act. I kissed the top of his head, and asked, "Are you ready to go back to the ranch?"

He nodded, but didn't respond.

"Yeah, me too. I miss Mrs. Emma Jean and Mr. Jimmy," I said. "I'll ask Alex if he's ready to get back today."

"I'm ready too," Alex said as he appeared, rubbing the sleep out of his eyes, not unlike Luke had done a few minutes earlier. The sight of him looking like the youngster caused me to smile.

"Let's have breakfast, then we'll pack up and head back, so we'll be back in time to eat supper."

"Why don't you wake Drake up and you guys can get packed before we eat."

Luke hopped off my lap and ran toward his bedroom.

"They've never been away from the ranch this long before," I admitted. "I'm surprised they haven't wanted to get back before now."

Ellen chuckled. "Children like consistency. I'm sure they're ready to get back to a routine, even though we're going to miss them something awful."

I smiled at her, and stood to go check on the boys. Before leaving, I kissed Alex, and whispered, "Good morning."

"Morning," he replied, and slapped me on the butt as I turned to go.

23

Alex

I PLOPPED INTO THE chair Eddie had just vacated. "So, what were you guys talking about?" I asked.

"Whether you'll ever be able to give up your playboy mentality."

I sighed. "He's worried I'm not the settling down kind?"

"He's got lots on his plate, so I think anyone in his situation would be the same."

She looked over at me then, and said, "I'll give you just a little sisterly advice, even though you didn't ask for it. If you want to see Eddie as a possible long-term lover, I'd give up the hooking up until you know for sure. I doubt he'll be very forgiving if he thinks you're still playing the market."

I sighed again. "See, that's the thing. I haven't played around in a long time. I've wanted to, don't get me wrong, but life's been so hectic, I've pretty much been celibate the past few months."

"Do you think that's long-term?" Ellen asked.

"No, definitely not. If I hadn't met Eddie, I'd have eventually ended the dry spell."

"And now that you've been with him, do you think you can give it up altogether?"

"Seriously, sis, it's way too early for this conversation. All I know is I like him, more than I've liked any other guy, this early in the relationship, but I'm nowhere near asking him to marry me."

Ellen chuckled. "I doubt he'd say yes if you did. He's too cautious to jump in the deep end, at least while he's got those two boys in tow."

I leaned back and closed my eyes. "It's hard to take it slow when we're living on the same property, and I'll be damned if I don't want him in my bed every chance I get, but I'm going to try my best to give him space."

"I'm not sure space is what he's wanting—probably more assurance that you're his, at least while you're together."

I thought about that for a moment. "You're probably right, and I think I know just how to demonstrate that to him."

While everyone was having breakfast, I drove over to the studio to talk with my assistant about a couple things I needed her to do before I got back to the ranch. On my way back, I stopped by a store that specialized in jewelry from different tribes around Mexico.

I saw the perfect ring the moment I walked in the door. It was a spinning ring, with Aztec designs around the center. It was simple, but perfect for what I had in mind.

We left right after I got back to the hacienda.

I'd hugged Francesca and told her again how proud I was she'd found someone as wonderful as Lia, then I teased her about being the wicked stepmom.

"Careful, I see you slipping down the same slope, brother."

I couldn't argue with her, so I just stuck my tongue out instead.

"You always have been so mature," she said, and she was still laughing when she gave the boys and Eddie a hug goodbye.

Mama actually cried when the boys hugged her for the last time. When everyone was out the door, she pulled me into a hug. "You take good care of them. We've grown so attached in such a short time."

"I know, Mama," I responded. "They're special kids."

"He is too," she said immediately. "Make sure you treat him right, hijo."

I kissed her forehead, and said goodbye.

Papa had walked with them out to the car, and before I climbed in, he hugged me and said basically the same thing Mama had. I had honestly never seen my parents so gaga over my friends before.

The ride home was mostly the kids talking about what the horses had been doing, and whether they could ride before bed tonight.

Eddie was contemplative, and when he was so distracted that he didn't answer them, I told them that if they didn't get to tonight, I'd be happy to take them for a ride tomorrow after they got back from school.

Eddie just smiled at me, but didn't really respond.

The kids were both asleep by the time we got back to the ranch. However, the moment the car stopped, both boys shot out the door and into the arms of Emma Jean.

"Oh, I missed you two stinkers," she said, and bent to kiss each of them on the top of the head.

"Go get your luggage and take it to your bedrooms. I'll have supper done in about an hour. You two have just enough time to get your stuff put away before you need to be at the big house."

The kids did as she asked, and she came over and hugged Eddie.

"No more visits from my ex then?" Eddie asked her, and she shook her head.

"No, it's been quiet since you left. Way too damned quiet if you ask me. I've been bored out of my head since those boys have been gone. Next time you vacation, I'm going with you!" she exclaimed, then kissed Eddie on the cheek.

She looked over at me and smiled. "You look rested, young man. Don't think you get out of giving an old woman a hug yourself," and she pulled me down into an embrace. "I've missed you too. It's no fun cooking just for me and Jimmy. Flex and Mitch have been splitting the chores here while you've been gone, and Alex's crew haven't wanted any formal meals since you left. I'd forgotten what it was like to live without all the hustle and bustle."

"Well, it's about to get crazy," I said. "My film crew will arrive within the week, and they'll want to go over all the different locations we're going to film. I'm afraid after that, it's going to be utter chaos."

The older woman smiled, patting my back. "Perfect, I like it better when things are happening."

"Let's take the horses out for a bit before we have to get back into the swing of things," I said, before Eddie began pulling his own luggage out of the car.

"You want me to yourself already?" he chuckled.

"That goes without saying, but yeah, I'd like to talk to you, alone."

Eddie looked worried. "Okay, just let me get this into the house. I swear I have more clothes than I've ever owned. Between your mom and Francesca, I thought they were going to buy out every clothing shop between here and Florida."

I laughed. "It would've been worse if you hadn't fussed the entire time about them overdoing it."

"I guess. I'm not sure I have enough closet space to fit all these clothes. Are they always this into dressing your friends?"

"No, this was special. Just for you."

He shook his head. "I honestly have no idea where I'm going to wear most of this stuff. Ain't much use for fancy clothes on a ranch."

I pulled him into an embrace. "Maybe we'll figure out something. Hell, you can just put them on and let me get more practice taking them off for all I care."

Eddie laughed and wiggled out of my embrace as I began undoing his shirt.

"Down, tiger. I need to get unpacked and check on the kids. Why don't I meet you over at the stables once I get everyone settled here?"

I kissed him, making it as deep as I could, and when I pulled back, Eddie's eyes were clouded over. "Don't take too long," I said, and patted his perfect ass, before I climbed into the car and drove away.

24

Eddie

I SADDLED RED, AND after Emma Jean took the kids over to the house to help her prepare dinner, I rode out toward the stable. Alex was already there saddling the horse he'd adopted, and we rode together toward the old volcano.

I took the lead, wanting to show him where the entrance to the mine was, especially after all the talk about Diamondback Jack. When we arrived, I hopped off Red, tied her to a branch, and waited for Alex to do the same.

"Hey, come on, I want to show you the entrance to Jack's notorious gold mine."

Alex's eyes lit up like fireworks. "Really? I wondered if you were going to show me."

"I shouldn't have to, aren't you supposed to have some special Spidey-sense when it comes to gold mines?"

Alex laughed. "I think it might've dissipated over the years."

"Maybe I should've had you try before showing you. Anyway, follow me."

It took a moment for me to find the entrance through the dense growth. When I finally did, Alex followed me through and into the clearing. "Wow, this is so cool. You'd never know this was here from the outside."

"It's pretty awesome, huh?" I asked.

I let him explore the area, and we both walked into the wide opening where Jack had spent his last days. I hadn't spent much time here myself, so we both walked around and explored. Jack's old bed was still in a far corner of the cave, along with several utensils he'd used.

"It looks like nothing has changed since he lived here," Alex said.

"I don't think it has. I don't think my grandparents even knew where it was. I know Diamondback Jack had become such a legend, but I don't think anyone would've had any need to come here unless one of the hands was looking for a lost cow or something."

We crawled into the small shaft opening to the actual mine, and both of us stopped before going too far. Something instinctually told us simultaneously, this wasn't a safe place.

Finally, we went back to the cave and sat down on a rock outcropping.

"This is cool," Alex said. "But, I think you'd still be better off not letting others know about this place. It could be a liability waiting to happen."

"Yeah, I agree, but since Jack was your ancestor, I thought you had a right to see it."

Alex leaned back on the rock and stared up at the ceiling.

"Oh, I almost forgot why I wanted to come out here."

He leaned up and reached into his pocket, pulling out a ring box and handed it to me.

"Dude, are you proposing to me already?" I asked, shocked.

He laughed. "No, but I heard you talking to Ellen this morning, and it made me think you might need something to help you feel better."

I opened the ring box and was surprised by the simple but beautiful spinner ring.

"It has Aztec designs, see," he said, pointing at the intricate design on the spinner.

I pulled it out and put it on, surprised it fit as well as it did. "So, this is a promise ring," Alex said. "You were right. I've been a player all my life, and although I'm far from willing to make a lifelong commitment to you right now, I can say that as long as we are together, I will not play the field, and I promise not to hurt you or the kids if I can help it."

I laughed, which caused him to look at me oddly.

I stood up and reached into my pocket and pulled out one of Luke's tin rings he'd gotten out of a vending machine and handed it over to him.

"Seems like you and I were on the same wavelength. After talking to Ellen, I wondered how to handle this thing between us, and the truth is, I know I'm too intense. I've only had one person I've even considered being intimate with, and when you combine that with my responsibility for the kids, it's easy for me to get too serious and not enjoy things. I talked Luke into giving this to me, so I could give it to you as a way for me to promise not to be too intense. I want to let this happen as it will and just enjoy it. Sorry, but I can tell yours cost a bit more than mine."

Alex chuckled. "No, it's perfect, and I'm totally going to wear it," he said, as he pulled the ring apart and slipped it on."

"So," I said. "We're both committed to enjoying it and not making it more than it is?"

"I think what we've both agreed to is that I won't turn it into a hookup, and you won't turn it into a marriage."

I laughed out loud, then froze as I looked over Alex's shoulder at the man who stood under the shadow of the cave's rim.

"I think your ancestor approves," I said, and Alex looked around and jumped when he saw Jack as well.

The apparition was smiling and winked at us before dissolving into the shadows.

"Whoa," Alex said, and I could see the goosebumps on his arm.

When he turned back around, he looked at me and asked, "That's what you meant by the spirit had led you, regarding letting me in?"

I nodded.

"How often have you seen him?"

"Just twice in real life like this, but several times in dreams."

"Damn, okay." Alex stood up and moved quickly toward where the horses were tied up. "It's cool and all, but I'd rather not stick around if that's okay with you," he said, causing me to laugh.

"Ah, don't be afraid of ol' Jack."

Alex didn't respond, and as soon as he was outside the clearing, he was on his horse. To his credit, he didn't ride off until I'd mounted Red, but then he galloped back toward the homestead, leaving me laughing out loud behind him.

25

Alex

If Eddie had told me he'd seen Jack's ghost, I'd have thought he was nuts, but seeing him myself, that was beyond freaky. It wasn't like he scared me, but damn I wasn't prepared to run into a spirit while wooing my new man.

Eddie seemed cool with it all, and laughed as I rushed away from the scene. When we got back to the stables, I was still pretty shaken. Eddie followed me to the big front porch, and we sat on the swing together.

"You okay?" he asked.

"Not yet. Still processing."

"If it helps, I think he just wanted us to know he approves of our being together. He's really only been helpful whenever I've seen him."

"So, that's who you saw that day, and you thought I was him?"

"Did you get a good look at him?" Eddie asked.

I shook my head. "No, I was freaking out too much."

Eddie chuckled again. "Well, he looks like an older version of you."

"That's even more freaky."

"Maybe," Eddie admitted. "But, you are his direct descendant. I doubt it's too much of a surprise that you resemble him. Hell, I know I look like a lot of my mom's ancestors. Maybe not the spitting image like you and Jack, but I can see myself in a lot of their photographs."

"Do you have any pictures of Jack?" I asked.

Eddie shook his head. "No, unfortunately, I don't have a picture of him, or his brother Sampson. The only picture we have is of the oldest brother Levy, and we only have that, because they took his picture when he became the lawman in Alamito."

"It's a lot to take in," I admitted, and Eddie slipped his arm around my back, resting it on the swing.

"I understand. I was really overwhelmed the first couple of times myself, but, hell, think of it this way, how many people get to see their own ancestors?"

"Who'd want to?" I asked, causing Eddie to laugh out loud.

"Good point. Anyway, back to the topic we were discussing before Jack interrupted us. I like you a lot, Alex, and I really am looking forward to getting to know you better."

I couldn't help but smile, and leaned over to kiss his sweet mouth.

"Eew," I heard instantly, as Drake came out of the house.

I cocked my eyebrow at him, and Eddie laughed. "We've been caught."

Luke came out behind his brother, the skeptical look he often had on his face when he met a stranger was back in full force.

Drake broke the silence by asking, "Dad, is Alex your boyfriend?"

Eddie looked at me, the smile never leaving his face. "Yeah, he even got me a promise ring, wanna see it?"

Both boys looked at us skeptically, but then came over to look at their dad's ring.

When Luke spotted the ring on my finger, his face lit up. "Did Daddy give you my ring too?" he asked, and I chuckled at his expression.

"Yep, it fits perfectly too."

Drake looked at his brother with what appeared to be jealousy, and asked, "You knew Dad was gonna give Alex a ring?"

His little brother seemed to love the thought, and nodded. "Yeah, but he didn't tell me he was his boyfriend, just that he wanted to give him my ring."

Drake pouted, and I reached over and patted his head. "So, I should probably ask you both then, do you mind if I court your papa?"

The boys looked at me for several moments before saying anything. I could tell they were struggling with how to respond, but finally Drake said, "Are you gonna hurt him like our mama did."

I felt Eddie tense next to me, but I didn't react to it.

"That's why I bought your daddy that ring. I promise to try not to hurt him or you two, but I'll be honest with you, when two people start dating, there's no guarantee it'll work forever. Here's what I know. When two adults really like each other and really respect each other, they can be both friends and boyfriends."

Drake took his brother's arm and pulled him back into the house.

Eddie looked over at me, his expression a mixture of amusement and concern. Several minutes later, both boys came out and stood before us. Drake looked me in the eye, and said, "We both agree to let you date our dad, but only if you promise to let us know if you are going to break up with him. We don't want him to be sad like he was when mama left."

Out of the corner of my eye, I saw the emotion swarm over Eddie.

I reached out and shook hands with each of the boys in turn. "I tell you what. I'm going to go inside and get cleaned up before supper. Why don't you and your dad spend some time together talking this out." Both boys nodded as I stood to leave.

"Wait," Luke said, before I could go far. "Aren't you gonna kiss him goodbye? Uncle Flex and Uncle Mitch kiss every time they are going to be apart."

I chuckled. "I wanted to, but I didn't know if it would bother you."

"If you're boyfriends, it's okay," Drake said, though I could tell he was embarrassed.

I leaned over and kissed their dad, and winked at him so the boys couldn't see me.

"I'll see you boys at dinnertime," I said, and took my leave.

26

Eddie

T HE BOYS SAT ON either side of me, and we swung for
several minutes while I figured out what to say.

"So, this is pretty big stuff, huh?" I asked.

The boys nodded.

"I'd have told you, except we only just decided to be
boyfriends before you came out. I guess it's good, though, for
you to be aware of it right at the beginning."

The boys didn't respond, so I decided to address the elephant
in the room.

"So, we never talked about your mom and me splitting up.
She left so long ago, and I didn't know if she was coming back
or not, or I'd have brought it up before."

I didn't figure the boys would respond, and I could tell this
was making them sad.

"Here's the deal, I loved your mom with all my heart. Sometimes people don't feel the same way. You don't know this, but we got married when we were really young, then you two came along shortly after that, and I was so happy that I was going to be your dad. You know, like we've talked about before, your mom was using drugs, and those drugs made her get confused about things. She loved you two very much, but the drugs made her forget that."

Luke leaned over onto me. "Did the drugs make her forget she loved you too?"

The question hit me hard. I thought my youngest understood things better than I did, and the emotion of it took me a moment to overcome. I wiped the tear that fell from my eye and nodded. "Yeah, son, I think that's exactly what happened."

"Is that why she wanted the divorce?" Drake asked.

"Yeah, and she met someone who likes drugs the same way she does. He doesn't make her think about love and family, and all that stuff."

"Dad?" Luke asked.

"Yeah, son?"

"I hope she don't come back."

I couldn't help the tears now and didn't try. "I'm sorry you feel that way, Luke. I wish it was different."

"She's never been a real mom to us, you've been our mom *and* our dad."

I nodded, totally overcome with emotion, but both kids had seen the reality of our situation.

"I hope I've been enough."

The boys both hugged me, then we all just sat on the swing together.

When Emma Jean came out and saw us, she smiled. "So, I heard some of the serious stuff going on out here. I've put a bowl of ice cream out for each of you on the counter. Drake, could you bring one of the bowls to your daddy? My mama always said hard talk should come with something sweet. I think all three of you deserve that."

Drake did as he was asked, and the two boys went to the countertop and had theirs, while Emma Jean sat across from me.

"That was pretty intense," she said.

I chuckled. "I should've had that conversation a long time ago."

"Nah, honey, things like that come to a head when they're supposed to. You've got two amazing little men in there."

I nodded, still too emotional to say much.

"I think they approve of you and Alex too," she said, and smiled.

"I wouldn't have sprung it on them like that, but we got caught up in the moment. Jack made an appearance while I was showing Alex the mine. It gave him a fright, so we weren't really thinking straight."

"Wow, so he's seen Jack now too?"

I nodded. "But, it appears Jack is pleased about us seeing each other. Seems we have permission on all accounts. Alex's mom said as much before we left."

Emma Jean shook her head. "Well, you know Jimmy and I like him as well, and I know your grandparents would've approved, especially with his link to the property. They were both suckers for all the woo-woo stuff, and that goes doubly so for your grandma."

I smiled. "She really did talk about all that a lot when we were little. We were fascinated by all her stories of ghosts, the Chupacabra and all that stuff. This just makes me miss her all the more."

Emma Jean smiled. "We all miss her, son, but you can bet she's looking down on us all and smiling. This whole thing would please her, especially you and Alex. She even had a couple gay friends that would occasionally visit her here on the ranch. I believe she'd grown up with them."

"Really? I never heard that story."

"Well, it wasn't discussed much. I think for her it was more because their death had been too painful, but also, because we all thought you were straight."

I laughed. "Oh, well, whatever I am, I'm sure liking Alex."

"Me too," she said, patted my knee and took my ice cream dish, before standing up. "I'm gonna go get those boys to help me clean up, then I'm going to send them back to the duplex to play with their dogs while I finish up. I think they could use a little downtime while they process all that's happening."

I nodded. "I think I'll take Red back out to check the fences, not that I don't trust Flex, but I'd like to double-check his work. Speaking of Flex, where is he?"

"Oh, he and Mitch had to run into town."

I laughed, "In other words, they were looking for an excuse to get away."

Emma Jean touched her nose, and winked. "I think you're on to the real story there."

I smiled as the older woman went into the house, and waited a moment, before climbing back onto Red's back.

My life had taken a ninety-degree turn, and I was reeling from the changes. Despite all that, I was proud of my boys and completely taken with this new relationship. I was still wary of it, but regardless of what was to come, I was confident Alex could be trusted, and for now, that was all I needed to know.

27

Alex

L IFE SPED UP AS I'd predicted after we got back from El Paso. Renting the ranch for a full three months enabled me to take my time with the filming. That was awesome, since I rarely had that sort of luxury on my other films. Usually, I was bouncing around, dealing with things in the background, so we were on location for a minimum period of time.

Even if I wasn't dating one of the ranch owners, and enjoying that part thoroughly, I'd be enjoying the relaxed pace this location allowed me.

We fell into a pretty good routine. I'd spend the night at the duplex when I could get away from my evening duties at the house. Some mornings I'd ride out with Eddie to check the fences. Sometimes, when I'd keep Eddie in bed, enjoying his sleepy body, it caused him to get out late, so I'd sleep in after he left, and then I'd get the boys ready for school.

Those were my favorite mornings. The boys had come to accept me as part of their lives, and I'd begun to enjoy their morning banter, and the constant prodding it required to get Drake to do what he needed to do to get ready and out the door on time for his bus.

If I was really lucky, Eddie would show up just in time to see the kids off, then when they were gone, we'd fall back into his bed, and I'd fuck his sweaty, horse-smelling body into ecstasy, before I got up to face my own busy schedule.

I loved it when he smelled like a cowboy. I'd always had a special place in my heart for rodeo riders, and some of them were real cowboys, working on ranches and farms all across the Southwest, but I'd never dreamed I'd have one of them at my disposal, and god help me, I never wasted an opportunity to enjoy putting that tight body of his to use.

The first week of December, my director called me and announced he'd found someone for the final actor role. The character for Jack in the story needed to be someone who represented both sides of the international line, and as a result, we were struggling with who could pull it off. After they left, I knew we had the right man for the job.

That night, I'd planned to spend with Eddie and the boys in the duplex, but my meetings with the director had run over, so I didn't get to see Eddie after supper.

I got up early the next morning, however, hoping I'd see my hunk and possibly get to ride with him along the fences.

When I got to the stable, I was surprised to find our leading actor awake and petting the horses.

"You're up early," I said, startling the man.

He laughed after regaining his composure. "I don't sleep well the first couple days I'm in a new place. I'm also a fan of horses. I grew up with them, so I thought I'd come down and meet these."

I smiled. "They are nice horses. I was just about to ride out and meet my boyfriend as he checks fences. I'm sure he wouldn't mind, too much, if I brought you along."

The guy looked surprised. "You have a boyfriend?"

"Yep, he's one of the owners of the ranch."

Before I knew it, the actor had come over to me and pulled me into a kiss.

"What the hell, man. I just told you I have a boyfriend."

"I'm sure he wouldn't mind," the guy said as I pushed him back.

"You'd be wrong about that," I heard the voice behind me say, and I turned to find Eddie sitting atop Red looking at us.

I pointed at the guy. "Listen, we aren't in an open relationship, and right now, I need your nose to stay unbroken, so why don't you head on back to the house while I explain to my..." I looked up at Eddie and could tell he was steaming. "...to my angry boyfriend, why he came up on me kissing another man."

The actor blushed, thank god. At least he knew he'd crossed a dammed line, and disappeared out of the stable.

I looked over at Eddie, expecting to see an angry cowboy looking back at me, only to find him smiling from ear to ear.

"What? I thought you'd be pissed!"

Eddie hopped off Red and came over to me, pushing me back against the stable wall, and kissing me square on the mouth.

When he pulled back, he said, "I can't be mad at my boyfriend for telling a very handsome actor to keep his paws to himself. Besides, it was hot seeing you stand up for us."

I looked at him through slanted eyes. "I was preparing for a total forgive-me session." I chuckled.

"How about we get nasty behind the stables instead?" he asked

He pulled me over to the tack room, dropped down and un-zipped my pants. As he took my cock into his mouth, I moaned. "Damn, I need to hire more actors to come onto me if this is what happens."

Eddie pinched my ass hard and I squeaked. The chuckle he made while sucking me off resonated throughout my body.

Eddie ran his hands over my ass, and coming back up, he flipped me around and bent me over. I was surprised when I felt lube being smeared over my ass, and then him slipping on a condom behind me, all the while kissing my back.

When he entered me, he didn't wait for me to be prepared. I was thankful we'd fucked around a lot, or else it would've hurt like hell.

"You're all mine," Eddie said as he thrust himself inside of me.

"God, yeah, I'm all yours."

He'd never fucked me like this before, possessive, hungry, needy, and *fuck*, if I didn't love it.

"Yeah, Eddie, yeah, fuck me, fuck me hard."

He continued fucking me hard, banging my head up against the wall of the tack room.

Just as I was about to climax, I felt Eddie pull out, and he turned me around again, pushing me onto my knees. After pulling the condom off, he thrust his cock into my mouth. He fucked my mouth as aggressively as he did my ass. When he pulled back, he jacked off and instantly came on my face.

I came at the same time he did, enjoying the feel of the warm stripes of cum landing on my face and in my mouth.

He shuddered as the last of his cum rolled out of him. He shoved his cock into my mouth again as the last shudder ran through him.

He knelt down next to me, and kissed me. "Don't forget... *right now*, your ass is mine!"

I chuckled as I took a tissue out of my pocket and wiped the cum off my face.

"Trust me, especially after that, I'm not likely to forget anytime soon."

Eddie's smile was electric. "You like it rough, huh?"

"Oh, fuck, yeah. I really did."

"That's good to know. Now, get up, and let's get those fences checked before I have to be back on parent duty."

"Yes, sir," I said, and smiled as I watched my man get my horse out and begin preparing her for our ride.

The rest of the day, I was floating on clouds. Eddie checked all my sexual boxes. Up until this morning, it'd been mostly sweet stuff, and I liked that too, but damn, every so often, it felt good to be manhandled, and this morning felt fucking awesome.

28

Eddie

O KAY, SO I WAS shocked to ride into the stables just in time to see a very handsome man make a move on Alex. At first, I felt a lightning bolt of jealousy, but Alex pushed the man off and put him in his place regarding our relationship.

The sight sent the blood barreling to my cock. When Alex stood up for us, all I could think was how much I wanted him. It might show how little class I had, but damn I needed to be inside him.

I'd luckily grabbed a condom and lube before leaving the duplex, hoping I'd run into him before heading out to do my chores. We'd had sex a couple times outdoors, and I couldn't help but think how much I wanted to do that today, but fucking him like a crazed, possessive caveman was *much* better.

After we got done running the fences, and he'd broken off to go attend to his duties, I began to think of all the different sexual things we'd yet to explore—role-playing being top of that list. *Fuck*, if I wasn't going to change that, now that I knew he liked more than sweet kisses and gentle sex.

As Christmas drew closer, the activity around the film sped up. Sets were being built in the area where the view of the buttes was the best. We'd also done the due diligence about using the area around the river, and the crews built a little adobe hut, very similar to the one that was already there.

It was amazing to watch how quickly the sets went up. Alex seemed so laid back it was often easy to forget he ran a major movie studio, and seeing things come together under his leadership certainly confirmed that.

We all ended up having dinner with the crews under the big cottonwood trees, like Emma Jean had told us they used to do back in the day. The woman positively glowed with all the work, and it was clear she was in her element.

When there were regularly more than thirty people to be fed, Alex hired her an assistant from the culinary school in Alpine. She didn't want the help, but after a couple days, you could tell she was thankful to have the young woman around.

When Christmas arrived, the cast and crew left to spend time with their families. Alex was scheduled to be home as well, but his parents showed up at the ranch. Ellen and Ernesto even brought their newborn with them.

Alex was surprised, but nowhere near as surprised as Luke and Drake. Luke jumped up into abuelo's arms, and Drake grabbed him around the middle.

Señora Zitlal came up behind them, and was immediately embraced by the boys as well. Someone in Alex's family had talked to the boys at least once a week, and after Ellen had her baby, I had to promise that once Alex's production was over, we'd take a trip to see him.

"Is Francesca not coming?" Drake asked.

"She is." Abuela leaned down and kissed him on the head. "She and Lia are having an early Christmas with Lia's parents tonight, but they're coming tomorrow."

I was once again struck by how much my boys had adopted Alex's family as their own.

Alex showed his parents to their bedrooms, giving them the master. With the lack of space, he ended up staying in the duplex with us.

After everyone got settled, señora Zitlal went down and began helping Emma Jean. I already knew they would, but the two women seemed to hit it off like they'd been friends their entire lives.

Shortly after they arrived, Flex and Mitch showed up with our buddy Eric in tow. He'd flown in from Portland to spend the holiday with his family, only to find out his dad had made plans with his girlfriend. His brother had plans as well, so he decided to spend the holiday with us.

I grabbed Eric the moment I saw him, and bear-hugged him for several minutes. "Damn, man, it's been too long. Look at you, I swear you look old and haggard."

Eric cocked an eyebrow. "Down, Badger, down!" I couldn't help but laugh out loud. Badger was the nickname Eric had given me in school, when I went nuts a couple times when I found a couple bullies picking on Flex. The name quickly took root, and I became '*The Badger*' until I graduated high school.

We ended up having the meal on the big front porch. I could tell Alex was happy to have his family here. Señor Zitlal had been chomping at the bit to see the ranch, and I assumed that was why they'd all decided to show up tonight on Christmas Eve.

He ended up asking Jimmy a thousand questions, which the old man relished. Having a massive audience, he embellished the old stories more than I'd ever heard him do before.

When he finally came to the subject of ol' Diamondback Jack, he winked at Alex. "Now, I know you have a particular interest in Jack, since he's your ancestor and all, but I reckon I'll pass the story on over to your young'un there, since he's actually seen his ghost himself.

All eyes turned to him, and I couldn't help but laugh at Alex's surprised expression.

"I'm not the only one to see him. Eddie's seen him too, and more times than me."

I gave him a nasty look. "Jimmy handed the gauntlet to you, movie man. You tell your part, and I'll add anything you miss."

Alex chuckled, but then looked over at the boys, before he began, "Well, it's not like it's really that scary. Eddie was showing me where the entrance to the old mine is, and we'd just sat down. I was convincing him to let me be his boyfriend, when Eddie noticed Diamondback Jack sitting a little piece away from us. He was smiling and winked at us before he disappeared."

"Then Alex ran away like he was being chased by a... well, by a ghost."

Everyone laughed.

"I didn't run away. I just got on the horse and encouraged her to leave quickly."

"Jack seemed pleased that the two of us had decided to try the boyfriend thing out. I have to admit, I was a little surprised, considering how backward things were back then. I'd have guessed he'd have scalped us knowing we were a gay couple."

"Not necessarily," Alex's father chimed in. "There's a family rumor, one we don't discuss often, that Jack was the lover of one of the rancher's sons. The story goes that when his son was here, he walked up on the two of them making out down by the river. The two men didn't see him, and he told my grandpa that he never confronted them, but if what you saw was true, he probably thought it was appropriate, considering."

We all looked at señor Zitlal like he'd just told us he was pregnant. "Jack was gay?" Alex asked.

"Well, bisexual, at the very least. Considering he had two children by then."

"Well, I'll be damned," Alex said

Luke exclaimed. "He said a dirty word," causing the table to laugh again.

Drake looked at me and Alex then, and said, "So, this is like one of those fairy tales. You and Alex are in love, just like Jack and the rancher back then."

I gulped, not sure what to say. How did he get *that* out of this conversation?

I was about to minimize things, when Ellen patted his hand. "Yes, honey, that's exactly what this is like."

Alex gave his sister a nasty look, but what else was there to say? So, instead of saying anything, I turned to Alex with a grin that demonstrated clearly how I'd begun feeling about him, and kissed him square on the mouth.

29

Alex

OKAY, SO THAT HEATED up fast. I was very fond of Eddie, and yes, the thought that I'd fallen for him was definitely a subject that flowed into my mind more often than not, but I usually waved it off as the Latin blood in me that burned hot and passionately. Yes, it was a stereotype, but damn if it wasn't one-hundred-percent accurate when it came to how I felt about Eddie.

Eddie's kiss in front of our families made my heart pound harder, and those feelings I didn't really want to acknowledge swelled just a little more than they already were.

Luckily, the rest of the night was spent cleaning up after dinner, and sitting around on the porch listening to Jimmy, Emma Jean, and Mitch singing old Western songs that were so appropriate for the night.

Before we all turned in, Papa pulled me aside, and asked why I didn't have those three singing in the film.

Of course, we spent a great deal of time working out a plan to recruit them.

When we had a plan of action laid out, Papa chuckled. "You're getting as manipulative as me. Your mama won't be pleased."

"The job seems to require it. They do have the perfect voices for it, though," I said smiling.

He nodded again. "Let me know what they say. Meanwhile, I want to go visit that gold mine and see if Jack will come visit me."

I laughed. "You say that now, but wait 'til you're looking at a hundred-plus-year-old ghost."

"I'm sure it'll be okay, he's family."

"Do you think you could ride a horse, or should I see if Eddie or Flex will let us use the ATV?"

"Definitely the ATV. I'm almost back to my old self, but I'm not sure I'm ready for horseback riding yet."

We went our different ways, each with our mission to recruit Western singers.

The next morning, I stumbled upon Eddie putting stuff away in the stables. "Hello, handsome," I said as I reached around him. "You were gone early this morning."

"Yeah, I woke up early and decided to go get the fences done. You, however, were cute as could be, snuggled up and snoring."

"Hey, I don't snore," I said, pouting. "Well, not much…"

Eddie kissed me, then turned to finish putting the rest of the riding gear away. "Hey, my papa wanted to go see the gold mine, can we borrow your ATV?" I asked.

"Of course, when did you want to go out?"

"To be honest, I'd like to wait until Francesca gets here and we can all go up at the same time. I'm sure she'll want to see it as well."

"When do you think she'll get here?"

I shrugged. "Mama said she'd left early, so before noon."

"Then, let's all go up after lunch. Emma Jean would scalp us if we didn't eat after she's cooked."

I laughed. "Yeah, I agree. Staying on that woman's good side is a wise move."

30

Eddie

I FINISHED UP AT the stables and went back to the duplex to check on the boys, and make sure Jimmy was doing okay. He'd taken kid duty while Emma Jean was cooking, and I did the early chores. Unfortunately, Jimmy was slowing down, and besides the occasional outing with guests, he tended to stick close to home. Of course, that made him the perfect babysitter, although I was sure he was putting some seriously ornery thoughts into the boys' minds. I figured after catching the boys in some scheme like capturing a jackrabbit, empty-handed, or outrunning a road runner, I had Jimmy to thank for the idea.

I pulled the ATV out and wiped it down in anticipation of taking the Zitlals out to the mine. By the time I was done, it was time to get back to the house for lunch, so I piled Jimmy and the boys into the vehicle with me and drove over.

We were immediately met by two overly excited five-year-olds, and their mom, Lia.

My kids jumped out of the ATV and toward their new buddies, determined to show them around the homestead.

"Hey, you guys be careful," I yelled. "Drake, Luke, remember the twins aren't used to this area, so don't go far."

I hoped they heard me, but there was no evidence or reaction to indicate they had.

Lia walked over and grabbed my hand for a handshake. "Do you think they'll be okay?"

I sighed. "Well, they are boys, so I don't guarantee anything, but Drake and Luke know their way around the place, and we've pretty much gotten rid of all the snakes, so yeah, I *think* they're fine."

She smiled. "I wish we could come out here more often. I think the boys would love it here."

"Then, you should. I think my sons have adopted yours anyway. They haven't stopped talking about them since we got back from El Paso."

"If you mean that, then I'll take you up on it, especially seeing your setup here. My parents even have a slightly used camper we could hook up in your park."

"Wow, that sounds perfect. Have you been inside the house yet?"

Lia looked a little green and I laughed.

"It's overwhelming, huh?"

She nodded, then smiled. "They are so amazing, friendly, full of laughter, fun, and the absolute opposite of my family."

"I completely understand," I said, chuckling.

"I tell you what, why don't you and Francesca use the lodge instead of the house. As it is, I'm sure the boys will have to sleep on the floor, and this way, you have a little separation."

She looked skeptical, so we went in the same direction the boys did, and up to the lodge. When we walked in, Lia's eyes lit up. "Wow, you wouldn't expect this from the outside. I thought it'd be run down and old looking."

She smiled throughout the tour and found the perfect room where she and Francesca could stay, and the boys could be right next door.

I showed her where the sheets and blankets were stored, and where to toss them after they were done.

By the time we got back to the house, Emma Jean and señora Zitlal were serving lunch. All four boys were washed up, and sitting at a table that'd been set up just for them, and they'd already started eating.

Lia told Francesca about the lodge, and how the boys wouldn't have to sleep on the floor, and Francesca hesitantly agreed. I felt bad for Lia. She was going to have to adjust to this family, but hopefully, giving her a little space would help her breathe a little before that happened.

After lunch, Emma Jean volunteered to watch the kids, so I could escort the Zitlal family, including Ellen, who'd talked her husband into staying back with the baby, to see where their ancestor had lived.

Eric and Flex showed up right before we left, and so we included them on the adventure.

Señor and señora Zitlal took the ATV, while Ellen and Lia rode in the back. Francesca, Alex, Flex, Eric, and I rode over, leading the way to the cave.

We hadn't been back since the experience with Alex and me, so I was surprised to see tracks around the hedge that hid the opening. Luckily, none were in the clearing itself, showing whoever was out here didn't actually find their way in.

I mentioned it to the group, and asked that they hold back while Flex and I looked around to ensure no one was still lurking in the area. After a quick ride around the mountain and into any hiding places that could be seen, I pulled my phone out, got pictures of the tracks, including close-ups showing what types of sole each had, then I escorted the family into the opening.

"Wow," they exclaimed.

"It's like going back in time," señor Zitlal said.

I smiled. "That's what my thoughts were as well. I don't think it's changed any since Jack was here."

"This is so cool," Ellen said behind me.

After they wandered around the opening, looking at the old mining equipment and the stuff that had been used for cooking over the fire, I showed them into the cave. They were shocked to see Jack's bed in the corner and even more surprised to find how discreet the entrance to the mine was.

"Have you been into the mine?" Francesca asked.

"No, it's not safe. If I thought anyone could get into it, we'd probably have to cave the entrance in, or block it some way or another, but since there's no evidence anyone's found it yet, we haven't been too concerned."

"It looks like someone is pretty close though, what do you make of those tracks?" Alex asked.

"I think we need to have your security start doing a sweep out here while y'all are filming," I said. "I'll call the sheriff and send him the pictures I took when we get back to the homestead. Regardless, this is your chance to see where your ancestors lived. Don't let a few footprints put you off. Clearly, they haven't found their way in yet, so there's no need to be too concerned. It's pretty well hidden, as you can see."

I could tell the group had mixed feelings, but they were happy to explore. Next to Jack's bed, señor Zitlal found a small carved figurine the shape of a man. It'd been carved out of stone.

"Have you seen this before?" he asked me, after bringing it to where I stood.

I walked out into the light and was surprised to see a small sculpture... of me. Alex looked over my shoulder and began laughing.

"What?" I asked as I turned around.

"It appears I'm not the only one who looks like my ancestors."

"You think this was from back then?"

"I'd bet on it, and now we know he had feelings for one of the rancher's sons, I'm guessing that's a sculpture of him."

"Well, I'll be damned," I said, staring at the little figurine. "Jack had some skills with carving. The detail is pretty amazing."

I passed the little figure around as the Zitlals, Flex and Eric each took turns looking at it.

When they gave it back to me, I slipped it into my saddlebag for safekeeping.

"To be honest, I've never explored that part of the cave. Was there anything else over there?" I asked.

"No, just some ancient bedding and what looked like it must've been a straw mattress," señor Zitlal replied.

After a few more minutes while the family looked around, we rode toward the view of the buttes since that was one of the prettiest views on the ranch. By the time we headed back, it was beginning to warm up. Even in December, it could get hot during the day.

Everyone went their separate ways after that. Emma Jean informed us dinner would be ready at six. "Mitch and his assistant, Mrs. Ruth, are expected around five," she told us. "So if we could all be back together by then, we can let the kids open presents before we start dinner."

I'd had a hell of a time finding something for Alex. Eventually, I'd ended up calling his sister Francesca, and she recommended a few things like his favorite tequila, a type of chocolate from

Guatemala, and a few other odds and ends. However, the moment I saw Jack's carving of, well, I'm guessing his lover, even though it looked like me, I knew it was the ultimate gift for him.

Señora Zitlal wanted the kids to stay with them, so I went back to the duplex myself, found a small box, and stuffed it with tissue. I gently cleaned the little carving, removing the years of dust, making the features stand out even more. Then I rubbed it down with beeswax and put it into the little box. I was just about to find wrapping paper when I caught movement out of the corner of my eye.

When I turned, Jack was sitting on the edge of the sofa watching me.

It was still such a shock to see him so plainly, and for the first time, I was seeing him in my living space.

"You gonna give that to him?" he finally asked.

I nodded, the hairs sticking up on the back of my neck.

"Good, I'd planned to give it to my guy."

Jack looked nostalgic. "He'd been so patient after my son showed up, so on the nights we were apart, I carved that for him. I wanted to give it to him as a thank you for letting me have time with my son, even though it was killing us both to be apart."

"Did he look like this?" I asked.

"Yeah, he was taller than you, maybe a whole foot taller, but you definitely resemble him."

"I had no idea. I think Alex is surprised he looks so much like you."

"We have distinct features us Zitlals. He just inherited those from me."

"Did you love him?" I asked, unable to resist knowing more about this man and my ancestor.

"I didn't think I'd be able to love again. I'd loved two others before him. First, the kid's mom and then a man who'd ended up dying while we were stationed at Fort Davis. When I came to work out here, it just happened, then it got hectic with the bandits, and, well, before I had a chance to tell him how I felt…"

"Do you know what happened to him? There's no history I could find, just that his oldest brother inherited the property."

Jack shook his head. "He's lost to me too."

We stared at one another in silence for several beats, before I asked, "Why are you here?"

"I don't reckon I'm supposed to tell you much. To be honest, I don't rightly know myself. Just, I'm here 'cause I'm needed."

"It must be strange to see your descendants like this."

Jack chuckled. "I've been around a while, young man, ain't much strange to me no more."

He stood then and looked toward the door. "They are already there," he said.

"Who?" I asked, confused at the change of topic.

"It's just a matter of time before you'll be having your own showdown. I've been keepin' them away from the mine, but I can't keep 'em out forever. You need to be careful, and you need the mine's help as well. If you don't want to end up like me, you'll need to stand together to defeat them."

I was about to ask more questions, but just like that, Jack was gone.

It was disconcerting having a conversation with a ghost. In all the ghost stories I'd ever heard, there was a cold chill or a breeze, but with Jack, it was just like he was a normal person hanging out with me. Nothing strange or odd, except he had a tendency to just disappear.

I registered the warning in the back of my mind to share with Alex and Flex later on. Meanwhile, I found the wrapping paper and wrapped the little box that held the figurine.

It was a quarter to five when I finished, and as I headed out the door to join the family, I thought I saw something out of the corner of my eye. I turned, expecting to see Jack, but instead, I saw what had to be Jack's lover, my whatever-great-uncle. He winked at me and disappeared.

Fuck, if this didn't get weirder by the minute.

The kids opened their presents first before we ate, then we had our ridiculous feast. Alex exclaimed that he thought Christmas at his parents' house was bad. I agreed, and said, "I can honestly say, I've never seen this much food for a holiday in my entire life. Emma Jean, Señor Zitlal, you've outdone yourselves."

Needless to say, we were all stuffed to capacity after the meal, and despite how delicious the desserts looked, none of us had any room for them. Instead, we let the kids go outside to play, while the adults gathered around the tree and opened our gifts.

When everyone had finished, I pulled a little box out, and with everyone watching, Alex began to unwrap it.

When he pulled out the little figurine his papa had found today in the cave, cleaned and shined, several of the family gasped.

Flex looked at the figurine in Alex's hand, and said to me, "I can't get over how much it looks just like you."

"Apparently, we have pretty common features," I replied, thinking about what Jack had told me earlier.

When they showed it to me, I knew it belonged to Alex and his family. "I think it's the last thing Jack carved before he died."

Alex stared at me in disbelief. "I can't believe you'd give this to me..." Then, he looked around his family, and said, "...to us."

I smiled. "I think he planned to give it to his lover, but unfortunately, time ran out before he could. Regardless, I really think it belongs to you now."

Alex pulled me into an embrace then kissed me in front of the entire room. "It's the most wonderful gift in the world, knowing it came from him, and that he carved it for the one he loved. Add to that, it looks so much like you..."

Alex was getting emotional, so I smiled. "I know for a fact..." I pointed at the figurine in his hand, "...they are happy you're getting it."

"How?" Francesca asked from across the room, breaking the spell between Alex and me, and I chuckled.

"Let's just say the spirits are moving today."

"You saw him again?" señor Zitlal asked, and I smiled.

"Well, among others, but let's not get into that. I already feel like I'm half out of my mind for believing all this, and I'm the one who saw it."

A chuckle ran around the room, but as I scanned the faces, I didn't see skepticism. Lia looked confused, but that was because she didn't know the whole story, and I'd be damned if I told a medical doctor I was prone to seeing ghosts. She'd have me diagnosed and medicated before the holiday was over.

The next day, everyone left for home. Alex had to go back to El Paso to get a few things squared away with the studio before filming started. I missed him like crazy while he was gone. This was the first time we'd been apart for more than a day or two since we'd gotten back from El Paso. I was briefly concerned about what it'd be like once he was gone for good. I didn't let the thought fester, though. We would enjoy each other until it was time to part company. I wouldn't let my overanalytical brain stop what I was enjoying so much.

Things were progressively getting more chaotic. While he was gone, different crews prepared for shooting, but when he got back, he came with actors, actresses, costume designers, musical experts, and a host of other people who I had no idea what they did.

I quickly pulled the boys back to the duplex to prevent them from disturbing the actors. When the kids were in school, I'd go over, and as inconspicuously as I could, do the ranch's chores. Dealing with the horses, checking fences, and various other things that had to be done to keep things from falling apart. I could tell when this was over, I'd have a shit-ton of work to do to catch up on what wasn't being dealt with. None of that bothered me, considering how much fun it was to watch the organized chaos unfolding around me.

I barely saw Alex, and when I did, he was usually talking to someone or giving someone directions. One evening, I walked by the stables just in time to see Alex finish talking to a group of actors. As he left, he started to walk toward me, only to be caught by the director. He looked over at me, regret etched on his face, and waved.

That was the most interaction we'd had in over a week. I missed him in my bed, hell... I missed him in my life. I had to admit, nothing was lonelier than having him near me, but unable to access him. The thoughts of what it would be like when all this was over began to crowd my thoughts, and it was becoming more and more difficult to ignore them.

By the time filming started, I'd decided it would be best if the boys and I stayed at Mitch's motel, and got out of the way entirely. It had become almost impossible to keep the boys from going over, and I had to threaten their lives more than once to get them to stay away.

The school in Alamito had long ago shut down, and the kids from here went to a different school from the one the boys attended. This meant I had to get up earlier than usual to get the boys to the ranch early enough to catch their bus or I had to drive them all the way to Alpine.

Emma Jean and Jimmy were embroiled in the chaos as well. Jimmy was on hand as a representative of the ranch, and Emma Jean was the cook, so I had to feed the kids myself too. I was so happy Alex's production was doing well, but except for the eventuality of losing Alex, I was looking forward to it being over.

The main shoot, as Alex called it, took a full month and wasn't over until mid-February. After that, the main actors left, and the pandemonium reverted to simple chaos. One day, Alex came to the motel and excitedly pulled me into a bear hug, telling me the main shoot had gone extremely well.

He'd arranged with Flex and Mitch for them to keep the boys, and he took me out to eat in Alpine. "I've missed you like crazy," I admitted.

"Yeah, I kept thinking I'd find time to hang with you, but as it is, I don't think I've gotten more than three hours sleep a night since the shoot started."

I reached over and took his hand. "When will it settle down enough for us to get some sense of normalcy back?"

Alex looked at me and shrugged. "I'm sorry, Eddie, I should've warned you. Sometimes the main shoot can be easy, and I don't have to do anything other than just hang out. Other times, it's just as intense for me as it is for everyone else. I didn't think this one would be so crazy, but truth is, with the international relations like they are, I should've known."

"It's not that I'm upset. I just miss you, and..." I whispered so only he could hear, "...I'm horny as hell. I've gotten used to having you in my bed."

Alex's expression changed to naughty, and he leaned close. "Well, I'll have a little time off before the second shoot starts."

"Then let's take advantage of the break."

I leaned over closer, and said, "I want to fuck you so hard, you won't be able to walk for a week, then I'm going to make you come over and over."

I leaned back just as Alex was swallowing hard.

"Check," he squeaked, causing me to laugh. We'd only gotten our meal a few minutes before, but Alex got them to put it in to-go packages and we rushed back to the duplex.

"Remind me to get Flex and Mitch a gift for keeping the boys tonight," I said, as we all but broke the speed of sound getting back.

31

Alex

THINGS DID GET BACK to a routine. I still didn't have much time to spend with Eddie, at least not as much as I'd have liked. We sailed through the second shoot and were able to get the special effects done fairly quickly. The filming with a model of the set was being done back in Juarez. We'd put that off until the very end so I could finish filming here and make sure the crews broke down the sets and returned the ranch to its normal state.

By the time things were said and done with the ranch, it was early May and it was getting hot as hell. Because the intensity of the shoots had settled down, I'd been able to spend most nights in Eddie's bed over the past two months. Luckily, the crews didn't get up early, so usually, I could spend time with him, or get the kids ready for school while he was running the fences and managing the chores.

It was almost like we'd become a real family by the time we were ready to break down the sets.

In our advertising, we'd used the song Mitch, Emma Jean, and Jimmy sang, and it was beginning to climb the charts in Mexico as well as the US. My three singers, however, just shook their heads when I brought it up, saying I was being silly. I tried to tell them there would be a lot of people who'd want the three of them to sing for them once the movie was released. I'd already had interest from several streaming sites to use the film rights. I could already tell the movie was going to be a hit.

My life had become so integrated with these people, I was honestly beginning to worry how I was ever going to get back to my old life traveling for productions. I tried not to think about it too much, but I didn't think I'd survive without loving on Eddie, and being with the rest of his family.

It was summer break for the kids when I had to go back to Juarez for the final touches. I decided I'd be a bit devious, trying to get Eddie to come with me to El Paso for the summer. I recruited help from his cousin and Emma Jean.

One evening after the crews were gone, we were eating on the porch, and I asked Eddie if he'd consider coming with me to the hacienda.

"Sure, I'm sure Flex doesn't mind taking fence-running duties for a few days."

I shook my head. "No, I mean for the summer, until school starts back for the boys."

32

Eddie

Alex, I'm sorry, but I have duties here. We need to make sure the fences are repaired, and I'd like to get the cattle pastures extended, so they can find enough to eat through the dry summer. I'm only just now going to be able to do that, now that your crews are done with filming."

The conversation was overwhelming me. I started to argue again when Flex interrupted me. "We've already talked about all that. Jimmy knows a couple workers who can do the fencing, and now that the motel's traffic has decreased, Mitch and I have decided to move out to the house full-time, so we can do what we need to, to make it our home."

"So, you're finally ready to move in?" I asked perplexed.

Mitch smiled. "It's a compromise thing. I'll spend summers out here, as long as I have Ruth to run the motel while I'm gone, then we'll spend the winters in Alamito. That way, you and Flex can take turns with the ranch's responsibilities."

Flex laughed at my confused expression. "I know you're going to want to spend time with Alex and his family," he said, "so Mitch and I have agreed to make it so you can, and won't have to worry about things here at the ranch while you're gone. Remember, it's a partnership, cousin."

I didn't really know how to react. I didn't want to leave the ranch, it was my home, but I didn't want to be without Alex either.

I looked at the boys and asked what they thought.

"I think it'll be fun," Drake said. "Francesca and Ellen told us they'd help us with our rodeo skills, and abuelo said we could help him in their garden, since he can't do it by himself any longer."

"They even said they'd pay us," Luke said.

I looked at Alex with narrowed eyes. "I feel like I'm being set up here. When did y'all plan this out?" I asked.

Alex chuckled. "Well, to be honest, I conspired with Flex and Emma Jean. My parents must've been doing their own conspiring with the kids. This is the first I've heard of all that."

I sighed. "I need to think about..."

Emma Jean came out carrying a huge casserole dish. "You need to stop thinking about it and go be with your man. This ranch has survived generations without you, and it'll survive a few months more. Besides, you need a break, just like anyone. Go to El Paso and be with Alex."

I stared at her in shock. "I can't..."

"You can, and you will." That came from Jimmy, who'd been quiet the entire conversation.

"Boy, I watched yer grandpa work his life away running this ranch. I think if he and yer grandma had spent more time on family and less worrying about which cow to breed with which bull, yer moms wouldn't have hated this place so much. I understand it gets under yer skin, and you love it, but you can't lose sight of yer loved ones neither. Go on and spend a few months with these new family members. Let us take care of the doings 'round here."

I stared at the food on my plate as the rest of the table moved on to different conversations. I did know what it felt like to be alone, without support, and without family. I thought that was why I clung to this place so much, so hard. I loved it here, no doubt, but I also knew I loved Alex.

I thought about how much fun the boys had with the Zitlals last fall, and how much they wanted to learn to do rodeo stuff. Flex and Mitch were smiling as they talked to Emma Jean about the refurb projects they were planning on the house now that they'd be here full-time.

Alex was teasing Drake about some girl he'd met at school, and Luke was making kissy noises at him, causing Alex to laugh then chastise him, but then laugh again. I knew they were right.

I needed to let go of the iron clasp I had on the ranch and let myself go, if only for a few months.

"Okay," I said, startling the table into silence. "Okay, I'll go, but only for the summer, and, Flex? If you need me, you have to promise you won't hesitate to call. This is my place, my home, and it's hard for me to let it go even for a short time, but I'm game, especially since summer is so damned hot."

I looked at Alex, who was positively beaming at me. "Not that El Paso is much cooler," he replied.

Before the boys got to me with an excited tackle, a quick appraisal of the faces around the table showed approval.

33

Alex

Even though I'd schemed to get him to agree, I didn't think it'd be this easy. Eddie loved ranch life, and I knew nothing was further from it than my family's hacienda. That being said, right after Eddie agreed to stay with me for the summer, I called Ellen and Francesca. We began setting up ways he could work with the horses, knowing how much he loved riding. I hoped it'd encourage him to enjoy being away.

Just like last time, the minute we walked into the house, Mama and Papa were all over the kids. Every moment of their days was planned, and I could tell the kids were enjoying themselves immensely. Unfortunately, even with the horses, Eddie clearly wasn't having as much fun.

The final work on the film took me away every day, leaving Eddie alone in the big house. I knew if something didn't change and fast, I was going to lose my opportunity with him. I loved my job and couldn't imagine giving it up to live on the ranch, nor could I imagine living without him curled next to me at night.

The solution came about surprisingly one afternoon, while Eddie was visiting me at the studio. The special-effects director was going over footage of our hero plowing through the bandits, leaping from the horse when he ran out of bullets, and tackling the bad guy to the ground.

Our stunt man had come down with the flu right before we were planning to film the scene, and Eddie, hearing our dilemma, said, "I can do that. I used to sneak up on Eric and Flex when we were kids and do that very thing to them."

"Seriously?" the director said, and I immediately refused.

"Aba," I said to the director. "I just got him to stay with me, and now you're trying to kill him. This is something that should be done by a professional, not my boyfriend."

The director looked nonplused. "I agree, but we're going to have to put off filming until Hernando recovers."

Eddie came over, put his arm around me, and said, "Baby, I've been a roughneck my entire life. I love doing crazy stunts like this. If I were in danger, I wouldn't do it, but like I said, I've done this a thousand times. I'm sure Flex and Eric would both tell you, I can do it so I don't hurt anyone. Although they hated it, I know how to roll so I don't hurt myself, or the one I tackle. Let me show you with one of your rodeo dummies you have out there. If I don't do it to your satisfaction, I'll leave well enough alone."

I hesitantly agreed, already planning in my mind for the Emergency Room visit. Eddie climbed up on the high-strung Arabian horse we used for the scene and let him prance around nervously. Within seconds, Eddie took off like a bullet toward the dummy. Just as he was about to reach it, he leaped off, soaring through the air. He grabbed the dummy, rolled and landed with it securely tucked beneath him.

"Damn," I said, and had to calm myself down, because fuck if that wasn't the hottest fucking thing I'd ever witnessed. Suddenly, I wanted to be the one who ended up underneath him.

The director grinned at me. "Let's try it with a real person, shall we?"

I still wasn't convinced, but Eddie was a grown man and could do what the hell he wanted, even if I didn't want him to.

They lined the stunt doubles up, this time going through the entire shoot, where the bad guy was shooting at the hero, and damn if Eddie didn't nail it again.

"You're hired," the director said, and just like that, my boyfriend was performing the stunts we needed to finish the film.

I still didn't like it, in fact, I hated it, but Eddie lit up like a beacon. The night after he began his role as a stunt double, we made love more passionately than ever before. Who would've known my gentle man would love the rough and tumble adrenalin rush of pulling stunts for the studio?

As fate would have it, Eddie's skill as a stunt double was serendipitous. Multiple shots that we'd filmed while at the ranch ended up being lost in transport. So, we had no choice but to rebuild the set here in Juarez and reshoot the scenes that couldn't be recovered.

Fate intervened further, and Hernando's flu turned into pneumonia. He was hospitalized for several days, which meant if Eddie hadn't been able to take his place, even if I'd found someone to replace Hernando, we'd have been weeks behind.

Needless to say, Eddie became the hero of our household. Papa being his number-one fan. Señor Zitlal, the hard-ass studio owner he was, was never okay with overruns. Whenever there were issues with shooting films, costs skyrocketed quickly.

34

Eddie

I WAS BORED OUT of my head the first week I was at the hacienda. Alex, Francesca, and even poor Ellen, who was overwhelmed with being a new mom and trying to manage her job at the studio, tried to entertain me.

They put me to work on the horses, but they had two people hired to manage them already, so I was in the way the minute I stepped into the stables.

I tried hanging out with my boys as they were learning various rodeo stunts, but besides being a bystander, I was a third wheel there as well. I was about to throw my hands up and either get a job or go back to the ranch, when Alex invited me to the studio with him.

Secretly, I'd always loved pulling stunts. When I was a kid, I used to watch shows about Evel Knievel, and I'd pretend I was him jumping cars, or doing other outlandish stunts. By the time

I was in high school, I began practicing stunts on the horses out at the ranch.

Luckily, for me *and* the calves, I never tried with a real one. Instead, I began tackling my cousin and friend Eric. At first, it was just me pouncing off the horse and onto them, but later I tackled them from the horse as it was galloping.

I'd also taken a skydiving class from one of my mom's many boyfriends who loved doing it, but even though mom never let me jump from a plane, I learned how to roll when I hit the ground. Combining the two enabled me to enhance my skill of grabbing one of the two boys, and rolling them to the ground.

Oh, by the way, Flex and Eric hated it, and cursed me up and down when I did it, but now it seemed I would be able to put the skills I'd learned a decade before to good use.

After convincing the director and my overly protective boyfriend that I could do this without injuring myself, or the other stunt doubles, I was immediately pulled into the filming.

Damn, I'd forgotten how much I loved doing this. I doubted I'd have ever done anything like this on my own, mostly because I had kids and responsibilities, and I wouldn't do anything to put myself at risk when they depended on me so much.

Luckily, the dangerous stuff had been filmed at the ranch, and I was safe enough. I didn't worry too much about the stunts. I knew nothing we were doing would injure me, at least not too badly.

I couldn't think of a time when I'd been happier. My boys were more than occupied, Alex and I made love like jackrabbits, and I was doing stunts that kept my adrenalin pumping, and made me a hero with Alex's family, not to mention how much my kids were enjoying watching my stunt work.

Before I knew it, the summer was almost over, and Alex was just about to put the wraps on the film.

The movie premiere was going to be held at the San Diego Film Festival in October, so it honored both sides of the international line, and promoted collaboration between both cultures.

The night Alex announced the film was complete and ready for distribution, the family had an enormous party at the hacienda. Luke and Drake, as well as Lia's twins, were dressed in mini-tuxes and given the duty of escorting guests into the party. I couldn't help but be proud of my boys as they not only escorted world-renowned movie stars and billionaires into the party, but were great helping the younger boys do so as well. If it hadn't been for my kids fitting their roles so well, I would've probably felt completely out of place with this overly fancy crowd of people.

I'd been dressed in a ridiculously expensive tuxedo as well. Alex placed my hand on his arm and introduced me to each of the guests as his stunt-double boyfriend. I wondered how he'd have introduced me if I hadn't fallen into that role. What I knew for a fact was that after loving on this man for just under a year now, he didn't care that I was a backwoods redneck. He treated me like his equal. That message was clear every time I was with him, no matter who we were hanging out with.

I hadn't gotten close to any of the actors during filming, but several of the production crew and I had gotten to know each other well, especially when I lent a hand at building sets, or helped them find resources. When Alex finally let me off his arm, I was able to hang out with them and the other stunt doubles, and found I enjoyed their company as well.

Lia and Francesca found me, and told me they were taking all four boys into the house to tuck them in for the night. I was just about to go with them when Aba, the special-effects director, caught me, and asked if he could have a word. Francesca smiled, and I knew she was aware of what Aba had to talk to me about. I gave her a wary look, and she waved at me as they left to find the boys.

Aba led me to the gazebo at the edge of the garden, where there were fewer people. We sat down, and he asked, "I haven't spoken to Alex about this, and I'm sure I'm going to get a tongue lashing for it, but you are a natural with stunt work. Hernando is retiring. His wife has given him an ultimatum. Quit, or she was going to leave. So, I'm wondering if you'd like to join my crew full-time?"

"Wow, Aba, I don't know what to say. I own a ranch and have kids, so I can't really travel all over Mexico filming. Besides, you know Alex would blow a gasket if I tried. The man was like a helicopter mom the entire time we were filming this summer."

Aba laughed. "Es verdad," he agreed in Spanish. "Alex wants what's best for the company, and his papa is already in agreement that you are perfect. Luckily, we don't have to have you on location very often. You could work here in Juarez when we do the special effects and stunt shots here. If we want you on location, I can guarantee we'll never need you more than a week at a time. Besides, shooting on location is a lot of fun, and you can even bring the boys with you to experience Mexico in a way that wouldn't normally be possible."

I leaned back against the iron seat and sighed. "It sounds awesome actually, and if it wasn't for my responsibilities, I'd say yes with no hesitation. Give me a little while to think about it. When will you need me again?" I asked.

"We expect to film our next movie in Baja California, late next spring. I won't need stunt doubles until summer."

"I've heard Baja is beautiful, and the kids would be out of school by then. Let me think about it," I said again. "I'll let you know."

I could tell Aba already thought he knew I was going to say yes, and I probably was, but I needed to make sure I didn't put my kids or the ranch in a bad situation.

That night as Alex lay in my arms, I asked him what he thought about me working for him in an official capacity.

He looked shocked, then annoyed. "Aba should've talked to me about this first."

I laughed. "Does he have to talk to you about other people he hires?"

Alex looked even more annoyed and shook his head. "No, of course not, but you aren't just anyone, you're my... well, my boyfriend," he said.

I continued smiling and kissed his pouty lips. "Seems to me, it's my place to talk to you, not his. He's just doing his job."

Alex sighed. "You really are good at what you do, but those guys get hurt. We even make them sign an agreement with damages built-in, and they have to agree not to sue us beyond what we give them. Eddie, we do that because it's expected that at some point, they *will* get hurt."

I leaned back on the bed. "I know the risks, and no, I won't do the really dangerous stunts. I won't put my life in danger. Still, the lower-level stunts, the stuff you do here in the studio, that's something I can do without worrying about my safety."

"So, you've already decided to do it?" Alex asked.

"Not yet." I chuckled. "I need to talk to Flex to make sure I can get away when I'm needed by Aba, but I do think I've decided I'll come out next summer to help with your next film in Baja. If that's okay with you."

"What if I said it isn't okay with me?" Alex asked, and I leaned up again, so we were face to face.

"Then I'd say no."

"Really?" Alex seemed surprised.

"Yeah, really. This is *your* company Alex, it's what *you* do and what *you* love. Part of the reason I think I'd enjoy doing stunts is so I could spend time with you, be a part of this life, *with you*, but if it bothers you, no, I'm happy with my already-busy life working on the ranch."

Alex sighed deeply and flopped onto the bed. "Selfishly, I want you to say yes, so you can be a part of this life, but if something happened to you, especially if it's because you were working *for* me, I don't think I'd ever forgive myself. Part of me just wants to keep you locked away, so I know you're safe."

I burst out laughing. "Dude, you don't know me well if you think I'm a fragile thing you can tuck safely in your castle. The reality is, I love the rough life. Hell, I could be kicked or gored by a cow or horse at any moment. I chase off javelinas, move rattlesnakes, hunt Barbary sheep, and chase off bears and mountain lions for a living—not to mention, we have a real-life bad guy who wants to kill us still at large—so, I seriously doubt I'm in much more danger jumping off horses, or whatever I'll be doing in Baja."

Alex didn't look at me, but continued looking up at the ceiling. Finally, he asked, "When do you plan to give Aba an answer?"

"I want to talk to Flex about it, but I'm thinking next week."

"Okay, let me talk to Aba about what he has in mind, and then let's regroup. If it's the same level of stunts you did this summer, I won't object, but if he wants you jumping out of buildings or the more insane stuff, I can honestly say, I'm going to fight against that."

I leaned over and kissed him. "You really are an old mama," I said. "I can't imagine how overprotective you'd be if you had kids."

Alex smiled wickedly. "I think I'd be a great dad. In fact, why don't we try to make babies tonight."

As we made love, I could tell something had shifted in our relationship. Not only had we disagreed about some major life stuff, but we'd come to a consensus about it, respectfully and collaboratively. That was something new for me, and damn if it didn't make my heart even fonder of this man.

That night, I tossed and turned. I kept having nightmares where I could hear Alex calling for me, begging to help him.

No matter what I did, or where I turned, I couldn't find him.

Finally, after running and searching all night long, I heard Jack's voice say, "Find him before it's too late."

I woke up exhausted. I put my hand over his side of bed wishing he hadn't left early. I really could've done with kissing and holding him for a few minutes after such a horrible night.

I worried about what the dream might mean, but to be honest, it was so haunted-house-like, that I just assumed that I was worried, because I was falling in love with him.

I got up and did what I could to shake off my feelings of concern. I was clearly overreacting, which wasn't something new to me. I tended to overreact to everything when it came to the people I loved.

35

Alex

The summer was drawing to an end. Eddie's boys had to be back at school in mid-August. I was already missing them, and they hadn't even left yet.

I had several things I needed to finalize at the studio, and I figured I'd be able to take a couple weeks off to spend with them at the ranch. When I told Eddie that I thought I could spare that much time, he was genuinely excited. "I have several chores I can put *you* to work doing. Think of it as the stunt-double equivalent of me working for you."

I knew I'd be working late tonight, so Eddie had invited Lia and Francesca's boys to accompany them to a movie to celebrate their last days in El Paso.

After finishing up several phone calls, I was getting ready to go up to the apartment to crash for a few hours, then get up early to work again. The more I could get done, the more likely I wouldn't get called back before my two weeks were over.

I'd just stripped off my shirt when the burglar alarm went off.

Shit, I immediately thought. *This is gonna cost us*. The last time we got broken into, the policía had needed several bribes to pursue the criminals and continue keeping an eye on the studio.

I got the call from the alarm company a few moments after the alarm went off, and I told them I could meet the policía when they arrived.

I made sure the apartment door was locked, turned off the lights, knowing it was best for them not to know anyone was here and waited.

Less than two minutes later, the front door to the apartment burst open, and three dark figures came into my room flashing lights.

"¡No dispares! ¡Soy el dueño!" I shouted, assuming it was the police.

The last thing I remembered was being struck on the head.

36

Eddie

W HEN THE MOVIE WAS over, Lia and Francesca came back to the hacienda with us. Señores Zitlal had asked us to go back for cookies, so they could see the boys and hear what they thought of the movie.

They were just about to leave when señor Zitlal got a call on his mobile.

Laughing at some of Luke's antics, he left the room only to return a few moments later in a panic.

"Ninos, can you go into the kitchen and bring out the rest of the cookies? These are almost all gone."

I looked at the heaped plate of cookies sitting on the table and knew this wasn't going to be good news.

When the kids were gone, señor Zitlal spoke quietly, so the boys couldn't hear. "That was the Policía de Juarez. Someone has broken into the studio. When they went to find Alex, his apartment door had been broken down, and he is missing."

I had to sit down, I couldn't feel my feet, and I knew I was on the verge of a panic attack.

"Why...? Why would anyone do that? Was he kidnapped? Are they going to ransom him? What...? I don't understand."

Lia came over and put her hand on my shoulder. "It's okay, Eddie, just breathe. We'll get answers soon, but you need to take some long breaths. The boys will be back any moment."

That shocked me out of my panic. "Yes, the boys... but..."

"Shh, I know, just focus on your breathing," she said.

When the boys came back in, Lia announced that they could each have one more cookie, and then she began escorting them toward their bedrooms.

"Are we spending the night, Mama?" one of the twins asked.

I heard her say yes, although I knew they were planning to leave before the news about Alex hit.

After Lia returned, we went into the large living room and sat across from each other, waiting for news. Of course, none came. In the wee hours of the morning, señor Zitlal called the chief of police in Juarez, asking for an update.

When he came back, he informed us they had recognized one of the perpetrators. When he told us the name, John Princeton, I was struck with guilt. This was *my* fault. *I* was why Alex was in danger.

"It isn't Alex they're after," I said, feeling the room begin to spin around me. "It's me."

I immediately called the sheriff in Alpine and told him that Alex had been kidnapped while in his Juarez studio, and that the police there had confirmed it was John Princeton who'd kidnapped him.

Of course, I was told they couldn't do anything, considering the crime occurred in Mexico, but that they'd be on the lookout for him if he crossed back into their area.

My next call was to Flex, telling him to be careful while out working, and I told him about Alex and Princeton. He was worried about me, but assured me there was no sign of anything there. Señor Zitlal came in while I was speaking and told me they were going to send the same security team back out to keep an eye on the place, at least for the time being.

Ellen and Ernesto came over shortly after the kids had eaten breakfast. Ernesto helped Lia keep the boys entertained. We were hoping we could keep them from knowing about Alex, until we had more information to tell them. Besides, none of the adults were going to be able to help them cope, since we were all still reeling from the news ourselves.

A representative from the police department came to the hacienda, which showed just how much sway the Zitlals had in Juarez for them to cross international lines. The man sat down with all of us and explained that they thought Princeton was acting alone. The undercover policemen they had working with the cartel said there was no indication they knew what was happening. In fact, there was some indication that the cartel was angry this had occurred on their turf without them being notified.

I didn't know enough Spanish to understand the officer, so Francesca interpreted for me. "They think that's good news, because the cartel won't be tolerant of someone on their turf. More likely than not, Princeton and his men will be in danger themselves."

After the policeman left, señor Zitlal came back into the room and informed us they had an ongoing relationship with the Juarez cartel, and it was really good news that they weren't the ones behind this.

"So, where does that leave us?" Ellen asked. "What do we need to do next?"

"I need to go to the studio. If the leaders of the cartel want to meet with us, they'll only do it there, where they know they are safe from US officials."

I could tell that señora Zitlal wasn't happy, but she didn't intervene when Francesca, Ellen, and their father left for the studio. I was determined to go as well, but all three said no. "You aren't someone they know or trust, and if they think you are why Princeton broke with them, they might decide to take it out on you."

I sat back down. The sick feeling never leaving me. The kids came into the room, and I knew immediately that Drake and

Luke understood something was up. When Drake confronted me, I confessed that Alex had gone missing, and we were all trying to figure out where he was.

The boys nodded soberly and came to sit next to me.

"Why don't you try to get some rest Eddie," señora Zitlal said. "I'll stay with the boys."

"I won't sleep, señora," I said. "I'll take them into the games room and let them play while we wait."

She nodded. I knew she wanted to be with the boys to keep her busy, but I wanted them with me, safe where I could see them. Loss and emptiness seemed to flood me. It'd been a long time since I'd felt like this, not since my ex-wife and her bad-news boyfriend had come to the ranch last fall, but now the stakes were higher. Alex's life hung in the balance, and I knew without a shadow of a doubt that was one-hundred-percent because of me.

I ended up dozing off in the darkened games room as Drake and Luke battled in front of me. I woke up to Lia tapping my shoulder, and gesturing me into the hallway.

"The cartel has contacted the family," she said quietly, so the boys couldn't hear.

"They aren't involved, and they have people out looking for Princeton themselves. They did say that he has been trying to get them to help capture you for some time. Because the cartel has a relationship with the Zitlal family, they've refused. They even warned Princeton not to get involved, but he went against them on this."

"What's the word with Alex?"

"They expect we'll hear from them soon, and they told us we'll probably be told if we want Alex back, we'll have to trade him for you."

"*Shit*, I guessed that's what this was coming down to."

"Eddie, what's this all about?" Lia asked, looking at me in a way that showed she thought I was somehow involved in the criminal underworld.

I sighed. "It's why I came here the first time. My ex married Princeton, the man who kidnapped Alex. She hates me, and I'm guessing she's gotten her new husband to help her get rid of me."

"I don't understand. Why does she hate you so much?"

I laughed bitterly. "Lia, I can't answer that. It's odd, after all this time, she's still so hung up on revenge." I could tell Lia still didn't understand, and I shrugged. "My ex..." I hesitated a moment, trying to figure out what to say. But, how did you explain to someone how an addict thought? How did you explain that by helping her, she began to see me as her greatest threat? I couldn't find the words, so I just said, "She said I wanted to control her, because I didn't want her to do drugs. She hates me 'cause I worried about her."

Lia sighed and pulled me into a hug. "It'll work out. Just hang in there," she said, and walked back down the hallway.

The ultimatum came early the next morning. Señor Zitlal got a call from an unrecognized number. When he answered, Alex was on the line.

"Papa, I'm okay," he said.

The older man immediately put the phone on speaker.

"You know he's alive." Another voice instantly replaced Alex's. "Bring the faggot to the ranch, or you'll never see this one again."

In the background, we heard someone hit Alex, and he moaned out loud.

"If you hurt my son again…" Señor Zitlal said in a low voice, "…I swear you'll be hunted down like game, and your death will be drawn out and painful."

The man laughed. "We aren't afraid of an old man," he said. "Bring him to the gold mine by five tonight. We'll be waiting… and no cops. If you try any shit, we'll kill him."

They hung up then, and everyone turned to me.

"We have to do it," I said immediately. "They aren't joking. They'll kill him."

I got up and headed into the room to gather my things and prepare for the drive home.

"Wait," señor Zitlal said. "We aren't just going to walk into their hands. They'll kill him *and* you if we do, and likely anyone who comes with you. I'm going to make a few calls, but you need to be ready to leave in an hour."

I nodded. "I want to leave my kids here. I'd prefer they weren't in the middle of this. If something happens to me, Flex, my cousin, is their godfather, and he'll get custody of them, but for now, I just want them to be safe."

I broke down then and turned to leave. Señora Zitlal came up behind me and pulled me into an embrace. Moments later, I felt the arms of the others around me. "You aren't doing this alone, son," she said. "And, of course, the boys will stay here where they're safe."

Francesca stepped in front of me. "Don't worry, we've been in similar situations. You can't work in Mexico and not deal with the criminal underworld. Princeton is an idiot, he's alienated one of the most powerful cartels in Mexico, and that, if nothing else, will work to our advantage. He can't go south, at least, not without putting himself at serious risk, and now that US law enforcement knows he's in Texas again, knowing they have evidence he's kidnapped Alex, and brought him across international lines, they are screwed there as well."

"How do they know?" I asked, feeling sick all over again. "If they were involved, they'd likely go in with guns blazing, putting Alex at risk."

"They know, because we've been keeping them informed," Francesca said.

"They'll fuck this up. They'll put Alex at risk," I said, the tears falling from my face. "It's better if I go in alone, let them trade Alex for me. Let me..."

"What?" Francesca said angrily. "Let you sacrifice yourself for him? What about your kids, damnit?" she asked, and I fell into a nearby chair, all the energy going out of me.

"I'm why he's at risk. It's my fault."

I'd somehow managed to keep the panic at bay, but now it was confirmed this was about getting me, I couldn't hold it back any longer.

We all sat together in the room while señor Zitlal made his arrangements. When I finally got myself together, I walked to the games room where the kids were playing, and pulled them into an embrace.

When I pulled back, I said, "I need you to stay here and stay safe. Will you promise me you'll be good and kind?

Both boys nodded, but the tears began to flow. I should've known they would pick up something was happening.

I embraced them both, and before I could lose my resolve, I got up, kissed each on the top of their heads and went into the living room to meet señor Zitlal and drive back to the ranch.

To my surprise, we didn't drive all the way, after all. The driver the older man had hired drove us to the little airport we'd flown out of when we flew to Florida together. "This'll be more comfortable and faster than driving all the way to Alamito," he said, as we boarded the flight.

Once we were on the plane, he said, "Okay, I'm going to level with you, Francesca is wrong. I don't have US law enforcement involved—not on this case. I pulled favors from some of my... well, let's call them *colleagues* from Juarez. They are going to meet us at the airport in Alpine. Don't ask questions, don't look at them, don't ask their names. Just be silent and let me handle everything."

"How will they know where we're going?" I asked, and the older man chuckled.

"These are my private security men. They keep us from being murdered at almost every film location we are on. At this point, they know your ranch better than you do, but again, son, I can't reiterate how important it is that you do not acknowledge this, now or after it's all said and done. These men are the best at what they do, but there are many reasons why the cartels fear them."

"Are they the same as your security detail I met before?" I asked, and señor Zitlal shook his head.

"It's very unlikely you've ever seen these men, unless they wanted you to."

That was all he needed to tell me. I wasn't sure why, but knowing we had someone meaner and likely more dangerous than John Princeton and his gang, made me feel much better about the outcome.

As señor Zitlal had said, we were met at the airport by several scary-looking men. We were escorted to the back of an older model vehicle with heavily tinted windows. If I'd seen the vehicle on the road in Alamito, I'd have assumed it belonged to a couple of local drug dealers. The subterfuge was perfect, somewhat intimidating, but certainly not a big enough statement to cause Princeton's gang to be suspicious, if they were watching for us.

I was surprised when the vehicle took a government road on the neighboring reserve bordering our property. They drove along the rough road, until they came to the ranch's property line. There was a small building that sat on the state's side of the line that I always assumed was a storage place.

After one of the scary-looking men got out and unlocked the building's door, we were quickly escorted inside. The interior was dark compared to outside, and it took me a few moments for my eyes to adjust. When they did, I was shocked to see a man who was my height, same hair coloring, and could've been a relative of mine.

"You are to stay here," the same guy who'd unlocked the door said. He showed us several monitors that each showed various parts of the inside of the building. "This is the video footage from our body cams. You'll be able to watch our progress from here," he said, then after we were seated, the entire crew left, except for one man.

He handed señor Zitlal a phone. "Call this number, tell them we're here, and are coming to make the trade."

Señor Zitlal complied. He put the phone on speaker as it started ringing, and when a grumpy voice answered, he said exactly what he'd been told to say. The voice was irate. "How did you get this number?"

The man took the phone from señor Zitlal. "That isn't your concern. What you need to worry about now, señor, is whether you get to survive after taking your prisoner without our permission. The trade will take place in thirty minutes sharp. If we don't see Alex, we'll kill you all and send your body parts to your family piece by piece."

He hung up and pocketing the phone, left without another word.

Señor Zitlal and I watched as the men got into ATVs and drove toward the mine's entrance. How they knew where it was, I couldn't figure out, until I remembered the footprints. Then I knew. They'd been the crew to check out the place before the Zitlals had arrived. I wasn't sure I was impressed with or afraid of the older man sitting next to me. Regardless, if this worked, I'd be happy to have Alex back, and I honestly didn't give a fuck how—or who—rescued him.

We watched the men get into the ATVs, drive toward the cave, and when they got close to the entrance, they stopped. Precisely at the time they said they'd make the trade, they drove up to the entrance and waited. The man disguised as me got out of the vehicle, hands in the air, and began walking toward the entrance.

We heard them yelling something in Spanish, and a few moments later, a scared-looking John Princeton and another man came out carrying Alex. He was clearly unconscious, and I jumped up to get a better look at the screen. Señor Zitlal gently pulled me back down on the stool, and said, "Be patient, they wouldn't kill him, especially since they think the cartel are helping me get him back."

They laid Alex down outside the bushes that hid the entrance. We watched as the man who was supposed to be me was taken into custody by Princeton and an older man who didn't look like he belonged there.

The men immediately grabbed Alex and ran with him to the ATV. Within seconds, we heard gunshots, and I was sure the poor guy pretending to be me had been killed. To my surprise, though, he came back out through the bushes a few moments later.

In Spanish, I heard him tell the men something that I assumed meant the kidnappers had been killed. The leader, the one who'd clearly been in charge since picking señor Zitlal and me up from the airport, turned his body cam off. I watched him through the other men's cameras as he went through the opening, then returned a minute later.

We watched them as they took Alex back into the opening and laid him on the ground next to Jack's bed. The leader took his body camera and placed it in an inconspicuous part of the cave so we could watch Alex, then he and his men came back toward us.

When they reached us, they gave us a basic set of instructions.

"The cops are on their way to the ranch. One of our men is working as their undercover, and he contacted the sheriff ten minutes ago, telling him you had landed and were on your way to the ranch house. All the times of arrival and records have been changed to indicate you arrived according to what they are being told. So, as far as you are concerned, you landed twenty minutes ago, and are now headed to the house. Nothing you've seen here ever happened. When the sheriff investigates, they will find Alex, alive, but unconscious. They will also find a symbol of the Juarez cartel, which will demonstrate that it was their doing that put this to rest."

"Wait, are the cartel going to begin harassing us now?" I asked, and got a nasty look from señor Zitlal.

"We aren't the cartel," the man said. "But this was all done with their blessing. Now, don't ask any more questions," he said, and gave señor Zitlal a direct look before walking out the door.

We got back in the sedan and drove toward the main road. When we arrived, a limo was there to meet us. We got out of the sedan and into the back of the limo. The driver was clearly part of the rescue team.

When we got settled, I waited for señor Zitlal to chastise me. Instead, he patted my knee. "You are going to have to do a little acting now. Let your concern for Alex guide you, and you'll need to be surprised when you hear the men were killed."

I nodded. I was so shell-shocked. I was sure I'd be able to just be myself and not have to worry about acting. Besides, after seeing Alex unconscious, I could only think about him and getting him back safe.

The limo arrived at the ranch, and I jumped out before the older man. I ran toward the house, only to be met by the sheriff. I immediately came to a stop. "No, you can't be here!" I exclaimed. "They'll kill him, they'll kill him."

The sheriff came over and pulled me into an embrace. "Shh, we got this, he'll be okay."

"No... you can't be here."

I didn't have to pretend I was crying. I wanted them to get to the mine soon and get Alex, and the fear I had for him was enough for the tears to flow freely.

They ended up putting both señor Zitlal and me into the back of one of the deputies' cars. I was sure they assumed we'd be trying to get to them, or jeopardize their mission.

Once the tears had begun, I couldn't stop them. I wept unashamedly as we waited for them to return.

Emma Jean came and stood next to the car, her face haggard as she kept vigil with me.

We heard the helicopter before seeing it, but the deputy who'd put us in his vehicle came over to us and told us they'd found Alex alive, but injured. He was going to be flown to the hospital in El Paso, because his wounds were so severe.

"I want to go with him," señor Zitlal said, but the deputy shook his head. "I'm sorry, sir, but there's no room in the helicopter."

I could tell the older man was beside himself with worry. He wasn't acting either.

He turned to me. "We can take the plane back to El Paso," he said, but the deputy shook his head again.

"We need you to stay and give a statement about what happened."

Señor Zitlal raised up to full height. "My son is being airlifted to a hospital, because he is suffering from life-threatening injuries. I'll be damned if I sit here and give a statement when he is in danger!"

Another tear slipped down his face as the sheriff came up behind him. "It won't take long, sir, then you can go."

The man seemed to crumple then. "Tell me where they are taking him. I'll call my wife and daughters, they can meet him there."

The sheriff nodded, asked where they were taking Alex via his walkie-talkie and when they gave him the name of the hospital, the older man phoned his wife and told her they were airlifting him now, and where to meet him. When he hung up, he allowed himself to be led to the porch of the house.

The sheriff interrogated us briefly, asking if we'd spoken to the cartels. Finally, he sighed clearly satisfied with our responses, and said, "Okay, if you two can come into the house, I want to tell all of you what we found with Alex."

When señor Zitlal was clearly about to complain, the sheriff said, "They have a right to know what we found señor. Just give us a moment more, then we'll let you get back to your son."

The older man was clearly upset that his path back to Alex had been blocked, but he followed us into the main house anyway.

Flex immediately pulled me into a hug. "God, Eddie, we were so worried. When the sheriff called to tell us you were on your way here, and to stall you if you got here before they did, Mitch and I rushed over. What's going on?"

The sheriff took over the conversation. "I'll let him explain all that later, but for now, I have news that you all deserve to hear."

We all stared at him. Even after seeing what I had, I was still curious about what he had to tell us that I didn't already know.

When I sat down next to Flex on the sofa, the sheriff said, "There were two people dead at the scene when we arrived. They look like they were shot just a short time ago. We have confirmation that the Juarez drug cartel are taking credit for their deaths, not only because we saw a symbol painted on the wall of the cave, but because they sent word to the Policía in Juarez that they were going to handle them.

We are trying to track them down now, but the part you really need to know is that Princeton is one of the ones killed, but so was the preacher from Alamito. We can't be totally sure about this, Flex, but this all but confirms he was the one who shot you, or at least was responsible for the shooting."

Flex looked sick and relieved at the same time. "The Juarez police said there was a third man. Do you know where he is?" I asked, then I thought about it. "Is it possible the third person was my ex-wife?"

The sheriff shook his head. "We don't know. Señor, but if you're willing to send us video coverage from the studio that night, we can see if we can determine their identity."

The older man nodded. "I'll have my assistant send that to you right away. Now, if you don't mind, I need to get home to my son."

When the tears fell from his face, the sheriff relented. "I'll have more questions, but you're free to go."

He nodded, then turned to me. "Eddie, do you want to ride with me?"

I jumped up. "Yes, please. Sheriff, what's Alex's condition?"

The sheriff stood and shrugged. "Serious, it's serious. I'm guessing he'll need extensive surgery to recover."

I gasped, and señor Zitlal pushed me out the door and toward the limo.

The sheriff escorted us to the airport, lights and sirens on, so we could get there at top speed.

When we got there, the plane was ready to leave. Once we'd boarded and buckled in, the plane took off.

The moment we were securely in the air, señor Zitlal looked over at me. "You did well, but don't tell Alex or my family what really happened. The men you saw, they are specialized in keeping people like us safe. Mexico wouldn't be a real option for us to work in without them, not to the extent we do."

"Why did you let me see all that?" I asked.

"Because you love him, and because he loves you. If it had been my wife, I'd have wanted to see it all."

I nodded. "I did want to, and I won't share your secret."

The moment we landed, we were rushed into a waiting car and toward the hospital. We were met by señora Zitlal, Ellen and Francesca. After we were embraced, I asked where the boys were, and Francesca told me both Ernesto and Lia were at the hacienda with them. "They'll be safe there," Francesca added.

I caught señor Zitlal's gaze and knew at least while my kids were in the Zitlal residence, no one would go near the place.

Alex was still in surgery when we arrived. He'd been assessed during the helicopter ride and was taken into theater shortly after landing.

I paced the floor until señora Zitlal took my arm and pulled me into their family huddle. The tears came unbidden again. When I was able to get ahold of myself, I apologized. "I'm sorry, I'm being so dramatic. I'm trying to keep it together."

"Don't be silly. None of us are being dramatic," Francesca said, wiping her own tears.

"Son," señora Zitlal said. "Don't apologize for loving our boy."

Of course, that sent me into another fit of tears.

Several hours passed as we sat in that dreadful place. Once there were no more tears to shed, I went to the window, pulled my phone out, and called the hacienda. When Lia answered, I told her we still didn't have answers, but that I needed to talk to my boys.

Within moments they were on the phone.

"Hey, guys, sorry I didn't call you earlier, but I was trying to get to the hospital with Alex."

"Is he gonna be okay, Daddy?" Luke asked, and I had to hold back the tears again.

"I don't know, honey, he's still in surgery, but once I do know, I'll call you back, okay? I didn't want you to think I was hurt, though. I didn't even get to see anything. The sheriff was at the ranch when abuelo and I arrived, so I was never in any danger."

The line was silent until Lia came back on. "They are relieved, Eddie. I can see it in their faces."

"Okay, I'm going to go, but I'll call when I know something."

"Tell Francesca I love her."

"She knows, but I'll tell her anyway."

When I hung up, I had to sit down and let the tears flow again. I'd fucked this up royally. My kids had thought I was going to die, and in the end, I hadn't done a damn thing to help Alex. Now here I sat, waiting for news about a guy I was still only dating at best. Yeah, his family were being sweet and letting me be a part of this, but I was still just a sideshow. The way I'd been crying, I was acting like I had a claim on the man that I just didn't have.

Yes, I was in love with Alexandro Zitlal, but he'd never given any indication that he was in love with me. As I stood in the hospital with his family, Alex fighting for his life, it became evident that I didn't belong here. I was the overly dramatic boyfriend, who wasn't pushing my way into the family circle, and that thought made my stomach hurt.

I was about to leave when I saw the physician come out to speak with the family. I quickly went back to the group and felt my knees buckle when he said the surgery was a success. "Alex has suffered a severe beating. There are no major bones broken, but he does have a few broken ribs, but they aren't going to jeopardize his life. He *was* bleeding internally in several places. We've managed to stop all the bleeding. Our biggest concern right now is the head injury. We had to operate to release the pressure on his brain.

"Was there brain damage?" Francesca asked.

The surgeon shook his head. "It's too soon to tell, but we think we got the pressure relieved before it became too bad."

When he left, we were all relieved. They were all planning how they'd manage visitation, and I slipped off, determined to extract myself from them. It was time for me to stop acting like Alex and I were more than what we really were.

I went to the cafeteria, ordered a coffee, even though it was late. I knew I wasn't going to sleep, regardless of the hour.

It was early enough that I doubted Lia was in bed, so I called. When she answered, I told her that Alex had pulled through, and the surgeon had given us good news. "Would you let the boys know?" I asked.

"You already have," she said. "They weren't able to sleep, so we were in the games room watching *Star Wars*."

"Daddy?" Drake asked. "When will you be home?"

"I don't know, kiddo, probably tomorrow morning. Why, what's going on?"

"Nothing, I just wanted to see you."

"I know, son, but right now, I need to let Alex's family do what they need to do. If they aren't ready to come home tomorrow morning, I'll get a cab and be there when you wake up."

When the line fell silent, Lia assured me that they were both nodding.

When I hung up, I was surprised to see Ellen standing next to me.

"Are they okay?" she asked.

"As okay as they can be."

"Are *you* okay?" she asked, and I choked out a bitter reaction.

"Never been so *not* okay in my life."

"Well, join the crowd," she said, and came to sit beside me. "What's going on? I noticed you slip away after the surgeon left."

"Sorry, I was trying to get out of the way. I'm embarrassed that I've been so overly dramatic."

"You haven't been overly dramatic. Your lover just got out of surgery. I think your responses have been pretty much expected."

"Well, see that's the point, isn't it? Ellen, I'm not Alex's lover. I'm just someone he's been seeing. I'm someone who almost got him killed, and I absolutely have no right to be acting like I'm anything but just someone Alex is screwing."

"That's all a bunch of horse shit!" she exclaimed. "Alex is crazy about you, you're crazy about him, and we're all crazy about your kids. Pretending you're just someone dating Alex is disrespectful and hurtful, if you want the truth of it."

I sighed. "Ellen, Alex has never pretended we are anything more than boyfriends. I don't mean to be disrespectful or hurtful, but it is what it is. When you add in the fact that I'm why he's in the hospital bed, it makes it all that much worse. I really should leave. I don't belong here."

"The hell you will." I looked up and into the furious face of Francesca. "I don't know what this pity party is you've got going on, buster, but you're going to get over it, and you're going to get over it right now. My brother is lying in a hospital bed, because a couple thugs put him there. Those thugs haven't got a damn thing to do with you, except maybe they wanted to put you in that hospital bed too… or maybe even worse. My brother needs you, and I don't know if he's told you this yet or not, but he'll definitely need you and want you when he wakes up."

I was about to blow them off. I knew they loved Alex, and they assumed we were more than we were. I wasn't going to argue with them, not while he lay in bed, overcoming serious injuries.

Ellen must have seen my resolve, because she reached over and grabbed my hand. "Listen, I doubt he's told you how he feels. He's a dork like that, bottles his emotions up like an idiot, but here are some facts for you. Alex *never* brings home men he's dating. In fact, before you, they never lasted long enough for him to *bring* them home."

Francesca chimed in then. "Alex hasn't even tried to hide how he feels about you and your boys. We've all seen how he looks at you, how he can't keep his hands off you. We know when our brother is in love, and that's what this is."

Ellen patted my hand. "Eddie, he's all but adopted your two sons. Every morning, he's up early, fixing them breakfast. He intentionally spends time with them, seeks them out even when he gets home from work."

Francesca chuckled. "Before Luke and Drake came into our lives, we'd never seen him show the slightest interest in kids. Hell, we'd all come to the conclusion that if we had to rely on him, there'd never be nieces or nephews. You know we're right. You can't *not* have noticed how he feels about your boys."

I sighed. "I know all that, but I can't help but feel responsible for Alex being here, and without anything... well, formal, it's hard to justify being here."

"Do you love him?" Ellen asked.

I looked at her, shocked at the blunt question. It forced me to reel and find an answer that might help me avoid telling Alex's family how I really felt. Something, anything that might help me save some elements of my breaking heart.

"Um..."

"Eddie, this isn't a hard question. Do you love him?"

I felt the tear slip down my face. I was surprised I had any tears left in me. The knot in my throat prevented me from saying anything, so I just nodded.

"If you love him, then give him a chance to tell you the same."

When I didn't respond, both women flanked me and hugged me from either side.

"You've got Alex duty first," Ellen said. "Mama and Papa are checking on him, then we're going to drive them home, let them sleep in their own bed tonight, and one of us will come and relieve you in the morning."

I nodded and followed them up in the elevator to the recovery room where they were keeping Alex. We were told he'd be in recovery for at least a few hours before being transferred to the ICU. Once there, one of us would be allowed to stay with him.

The family waited with me until we knew he'd been transferred. They told the nurse I'd be with him until tomorrow morning. I could tell the nurse wanted to argue that it was family only. The way the entire family looked at her, though, made it clear it wasn't up for debate.

After they left, the same nurse wheeled in a sleeper chair and a blanket. "You let me know if you need anything else," she said.

"When will he wake up?" I asked, and she shook her head. "Not for a while. We've got him sedated. He needs time to heal, and the medical coma will help his head heal faster."

I nodded. "Okay, I'm good, thanks."

She smiled and disappeared. Throughout the night, the nurses came in to check his vital signs or give him medication. I didn't sleep. Instead, I lay awake watching Alex sleep.

He was really banged up. His face had multiple bruises. I saw his back when they moved him in the night, and it was black and blue as well.

I thought back to when Flex had been shot and how helpless I'd felt then. Now I was looking at another man I loved more than my own life, lying in an El Paso hospital bed.

I got up around two in the morning and called my mother.

She answered the phone groggily, and I didn't wait for a greeting. "Are you behind this kidnapping?"

"Edward, what are you talking about?" she asked.

"I'm asking you, did you hire a bunch of thugs to take me out?"

She was quiet, which told me all I needed to know.

"Mother, it's time you get the fuck out of my life. I'm telling the sheriff you're involved, and I'm going to get a restraining order against you."

I was about to hang up when she said, "I didn't."

"What?" I asked.

"I didn't hire anyone to hurt you, or even Flex for that matter."

"Then what did you hire them to do?" I asked.

"I'm not at liberty to say."

I stared into my phone, the bile churning in my stomach. "Fuck you," I said, and hung up.

I was done with her. For the first time in my life, I was empty emotionally where she was concerned. She'd all but confirmed she was involved.

I was relieved by the Zitlals the next day, and took a cab back to the hacienda. As I'd promised, I was there before the boys were out of bed.

Both of them tackled me when they saw me and wept for several minutes, refusing to let me go.

We sat on the floor in the kitchen until they no longer clung to me.

When Drake finally pulled back, he said, "We were so scared. We thought you weren't coming back."

"I know, I know…" I consoled. I couldn't really deny his statement. I was pretty sure when I left them, I wouldn't be coming back either.

We spent the day in a pile. They refused to let me out of their sight, so they watched TV while I slept. Around six, the Zitlals returned home with enough pizza to feed a nation. Even then, the boys refused to leave me, until I got up to go with them.

We sat around the kitchen bar, eating the pizza. Señor and señora Zitlal were as exhausted as me, and they went to bed shortly after we finished eating.

We weren't far behind, and I was glad that my bedroom had a king-sized bed and large TV, because I needed a lot more sleep, and the boys were far from comfortable letting me out of their sight.

I woke up around three in the morning, with the boys asleep on either side of me. I got up to brush my teeth and turn the TV off. When I came back, Drake was watching me.

"What's up?" I asked.

"Did they kill the bad guys?" he asked.

I looked over at Luke, who was still asleep. He was still a little young for this conversation. I sat next to Drake and nodded.

"So, they won't come after you again?"

I shook my head.

"Did they kill Mama too?"

I looked at him. "Why do you think they'd kill your mom?"

"She hates you. She's always hated you. When we were little, she'd say stuff like one day she'd kill you."

I shook my head. "No, she wasn't there."

"Did they kill him?" This time, it was Luke who spoke. *Shit*, I thought to myself, I'd hoped he wouldn't be part of this conversation.

"Which him?" I asked, knowing which one he meant, and stalling for time.

"Her new husband."

I sighed and nodded.

The boys looked at one another, but didn't respond.

"What's going on with you two?"

"We prayed that he wouldn't kill you, that God would take him first," Luke admitted.

"It's not right to pray for people to die, but thanks for the prayers to keep me safe. I think they must've worked."

"They worked for Alex too," Drake said. "We were worried he wasn't going to make it. We knew it was Mama's husband."

"How did you know?" I asked, and both boys shrugged.

I sighed again, not sure what to say. The conversation had so many pitfalls, it was impossible to avoid adding trauma to the situation no matter what I said, so I decided to skip saying anything other than, "you're safe, I'm safe, and now Alex is safe too. I don't know if your mom was involved or not, but tomorrow I'm going to call the lawyer and make sure she can't come around us again, at least not without getting arrested. Her husband and the bad guy that shot Flex are both dead. So, now we're safer than we've ever been."

I noticed the two look at each other strangely, and I laughed. "You two are as easy to read as Alex. Spit it out, what's on your mind now?"

"What about Grandma?"

"What about her?"

"Is she still gonna come after you and Uncle Flex?"

I put my hand on Luke's head and kissed his forehead. "No, I'm going to ask a judge to make her stay away too, and if they find out she was involved with all this stuff with your mom's husband, they'll arrest her and put her in jail." That seemed to mollify the boys. "Have you been worried about your grandma?" I asked.

Neither boy said anything, but I could tell the answer was yes.

"Okay, so here's the deal, I didn't want Grandma around either, but I didn't want to keep you away from her in case you wanted to get to know her. Of course, she pushed us out of her life when she and Uncle Flex were fighting about the ranch, so I didn't even think about her that much, or how you felt about her. To tell you the truth, I thought maybe you'd forgotten her."

"She was always mean to you, even when you were with Mama and helping her with chores and stuff, she'd say mean things to you."

"Did she ever say anything mean to you?" I asked.

Both kids shook their heads. "She didn't really talk to us much," they admitted.

We sat on the bed for several moments, before I said, "I'm gonna tell you something your great-grandma told me once before she died. We were talking about my mom, and how she didn't like me very much, and my grandma said, '*Well, son, blood family isn't something you can choose, you're stuck with what you've got, but that being said, your real family sometimes isn't blood at all. Sometimes it's who you meet and learn to love that is your real family.*'" I could tell this had gone over their heads. "Your real family is Emma Jean and Jimmy, Flex and Mitch. So, you see, family isn't just me and your mom, or your grandma. It's also all the people you've learned to love, and who've learned to love you back."

"Like you love Alex," Drake said.

I smiled. "Yeah, like I love Alex."

"We love Alex too," Luke said. "When can we see him?"

"I don't know," I admitted. "He's hurt really bad, and the doctor said they don't know when he'll wake up, but when he does, we'll all three of us go over so you can visit him."

We crawled back into bed, and as the boys fell asleep next to me, I thought about the conversation I'd had with Francesca and Ellen. The boys had connected to Alex on a level I hadn't even acknowledged, and if I thought back over it, it was all because of how he interacted with them. I wasn't ready to admit

Alex loved me, or saw me as more than just his boyfriend, but I couldn't pretend he hadn't become important to my children.

37

Alex

SOMETHING KEPT BEEPING IN my dream, causing my head to scream with pain. I began trying to wave the sound away, like it was some sort of fly buzzing around my face.

Moving my hand wasn't easy. In fact, it was like moving through water, as if something was weighing it down.

I managed to open my eyes and immediately regretted it. The lights were harsh and intense.

I heard my sister's voice then. "Alex, are you awake?" she asked, but something was in my mouth and I couldn't respond.

I moved to pull whatever it was out, but my hand was stilled before I could reach it.

Alex, this is your nurse. I need you to leave that alone while we extubate you," she said, and I thought this must be some horrible nightmare.

I must have fallen back to sleep, because a few moments later, I woke up with my parents and sister in the room. I tried to ask where I was, but my throat felt like I had a bad case of strep throat.

"Don't try to talk yet." It was the nurse again. "Give him some time to heal, and then he should feel better," she said, and disappeared.

I must have dozed off, because when I opened my eyes again, the room was empty, except for... was that Eddie?

"Eddie," I managed to say, and he rushed over to me.

"Hi, honey," he said. His face was the most wonderful thing I'd ever seen. Like a fresh breeze on the hottest of El Paso summers.

"Where am I?" I asked.

"You're in the hospital," he said, and pushed my hair back on my head.

"Why?" I whispered, feeling myself getting drowsy again.

When I woke up again, Eddie was there, but so was the rest of my family. I just stared at them. I was beginning to remember who put me here.

"I was beaten up," I said, and my father nodded.

"Yeah, really bad," he confirmed.

I looked over at where Eddie was standing, and said, "They were going to kill you."

He nodded. "I know, but they didn't. I'm still here."

"I wanted to kill them," I said, but the talking was hurting my throat again.

He nodded again. "Yeah, I wanted to kill them too."

I smiled at him and let myself drift off again.

38

Eddie

A LEX'S RECOVERY WAS PAINSTAKINGLY slow. The doctors confirmed there was no brain injury, but he was still unable to do much for several days after waking up. The doctors kept telling us it was because of the damage he sustained, and that he'd heal soon enough.

When he was finally able to stand on his own, I brought the boys in to see him. They'd been worried and hung on everything anyone said about his recovery, so knowing Alex was up to handling their visit, I didn't hesitate to let them see him.

I was pleased that Alex's face lit up when he saw them. "Where have you two been? I figured you would at least come spring me. Do you know yesterday they made me eat green peas?"

Both boys stuck their tongues out at the thought of eating green peas.

"I swear you are the same age as them," I said laughing.

"You're just jealous, old man," he said.

"So, I want all the dirt. What's happening at the hacienda? Have you registered in school yet? Come on, it's a gossip desert in here."

Both boys were talking a mile a minute, telling Alex they'd gone back to the ranch and registered in school, they'd stayed with Emma Jean, but that I'd stayed here with him.

Alex looked over at me and smiled. The sight made my heart beat a little faster.

Of course, they had to tell Alex about every detail of their lives. Soon enough, I could tell Alex was tiring. "Okay, why don't you two run down to the cafeteria with Francesca while we give Alex a break."

After they left, I wandered over and rested my hand on his. "I may be wrong, but I'm thinking those two missed you."

Alex chuckled. "I miss them too. When do I get to go home? I'm supposed to be in your bed at the ranch, not in this uncomfortable thing."

"Any day, you just have to pee on your own, then you're free to go."

"Hell, why didn't anyone tell me that. I can go pee right now."

"Um, I think the doctor, at least two nurses and your mom have all told you that. If I remember correctly, you told them you weren't ready."

"That's slander and fake news," he said, and tried to get up.

"You know you can't go chase the boys around, even if you do get up to pee, right?"

He stuck his tongue out at me, but winced when he sat up.

The nurse came in and said, "It's going to hurt, because your ribs are still pretty beaten up, but come on, I'll help you."

"I need to pee," he said. "Y'all told me if I can pee on my own, I can be sprung from this joint."

The nurse laughed. "That's pretty much the only criteria."

Alex struggled through the pain, stood up, and managed to walk to the restroom with the nurse's help.

When he came out, he said, "Fuck, when the hell did it become such a damned triumph just to be able to pee on my own?"

"Um, since you were beaten by one of the most notorious drug dealers in Texas," Francesca said as she came back into the room with the boys behind her.

"Did you go pee?" Drake asked.

"Yep, like a freaking champ," Alex said, which earned him a fist bump.

"So, you're coming home now?" Luke asked.

"No, not yet, it's probably too late today," I said. "But, probably tomorrow."

Both boys cheered and danced around Alex's bed.

The nurse came back in laughing, and said something about the party being here in this room.

"Papa Alex is coming home tomorrow," Luke said, without acting like calling Alex papa wasn't one of the biggest milestones in all our lives.

My face must've bloomed, because when Francesca made eye contact, she grinned from ear to ear.

"Is that so," the nurse said. "Well, if that's the case, I'm gonna have to kick you boys out so your papa can get enough rest that the doctor will let him go."

That put a damper on the excitement. "Do we have to go?" Drake asked.

"Yeah, I'm afraid so. If Alex is too tired, they won't let him leave. You know how those pesky doctors are," Francesca said.

I leaned over to her, and said, "I'm totally gonna tattle on you," causing Francesca to laugh out loud.

"Okay, boys, you're with me…"

Both kids moaned at the same time. "What? I was gonna say, to go spoil our dinner with ice cream, but if you don't want to, I'm sure your abuela would be pleased."

"*No*… ice cream, ice cream." They both started harassing Francesca.

She ruffled both kids' hair. "Why don't you hang out with Alex while I run these naughty wild men across the street to the ice cream place. Once their dinner is completely spoiled, we'll be back to pick you up."

I just shook my head while the three of them left.

"I swear, she's as bad an influence on them as you are."

"What?" Alex exclaimed. "I'm like the best influence on them they've ever had."

I chuckled. When I looked at him, I sighed. "So, the Papa Alex thing is new."

"I wondered if you were the one to put them up to that."

"Nope, that was all Luke. I doubt he needed anyone to put him up to it. Does it bother you? I can have a talk with them if it does. He doesn't quite have a handle on this whole 'just dating' thing yet."

Alex's face fell. He didn't respond, so I came over and sat next to him. "What?"

"Well, we aren't 'just dating', are we? It feels like we're more than that."

"It does to me too, but you haven't brought it up, so…"

Alex reached over, and even though I could tell the move hurt him, he took my hand. "I'm not going to profess my undying love in a fucking hospital room, but Eddie, you're really important to me, more important than I can even express."

I smiled and leaned over and kissed him. "That's good, Daddy Alex."

His eyes grew huge, and if he hadn't just been injured, I'm sure he would've pushed me.

"Papa, not Daddy. That's got a lot of different meanings."

"Better change your thinking 'cause if I don't correct them right now, there are a couple boys who are totally gonna start calling you that."

"Damn," he said, and I chuckled.

"Takes some getting used to."

"I don't have to get used to your sons thinking of me as a parent, Eddie, but what do you think of it?"

"I think it's probably too soon, but they didn't really ask my opinion. They have minds of their own as you well know."

He didn't respond to that, but instead stared at the ceiling letting the conversation lay where it was.

"I want to talk about this again, but not here. Are you staying at the hacienda for a few days while I recover?"

"No," I said, shaking my head, "I'm sorry, Alex, we've gotta get back, but we can come on the weekends, if you want us to."

He pouted. "I wanna go with you to the ranch."

He looked so much like one of the boys, I almost laughed, but seeing this wasn't really funny to him, I held it back.

"I've talked to your mom and dad about that, and we all agree, you need to be somewhere that someone can keep an eye on you, at least until you are squarely back on your feet."

When his frown deepened, I leaned over him, and said, "I want you more than anyone else, ever. If it wasn't what was best for you, I'd have already scooped you up and hauled you back to the duplex, but I have to get back to work, and your mama needs to dote on you some while you recover. They were so worried about you, Alex."

His face shifted, and I knew he understood what I was saying.

"As soon as I'm back up on my feet, I'm coming for my two weeks at the ranch though, you can't deny me that, so don't try."

I laughed and kissed my sweet boyfriend on the lips. "If you don't come on your own, I'll come... *kidnap you* myself."

Alex reached up and touched the part of his head where the surgeon had drilled through his skull. "Just don't hit me over the head, okay?"

"Okay, I promise, no hitting you over the head."

39

Alex

L YING AROUND RECOVERING WAS like watching paint dry. Eddie had been right, Mama needed time to dote on me, just so she'd know I was okay. After a week of it, I was absolutely done.

"I'm going to the ranch," I announced Sunday, during our family dinner. "I'm recovered enough that I can get around almost like a normal person, and I absolutely cannot lie around any longer. If I do, I'm going to go mad!"

Mama looked at me, and I could tell she wanted to argue, but for some strange reason, she held her tongue.

"I'm thinking this has more to do with you missing a certain cowboy and his two kids, but what do I know?" Francesca laughed, and Lia elbowed her in the ribs.

"What?" she asked. "It's what we're all thinking."

Lia just shook her head, and reached over to move one of the twins' glasses from the edge of the table, effectively ignoring her fiancée's response.

"I do miss them," I admitted. "More than I thought I ever would."

"Have you told Eddie how you feel?" Papa asked, and I shook my head.

"No, not like I should've," I admitted.

"He almost left you at the hospital, because he didn't feel like he belonged there," Ellen chastised me. "It took both Francesca and me a lot of heavy conversation to convince him our block-headed brother cared enough about him that he shouldn't feel that way."

I sighed. "I know. I kept thinking I was going to die, and that I'd never get to tell him how I felt."

"That reminds me." My father must've felt sorry for me changing the subject.

"I talked with the Policía de Juarez, and they said they couldn't make out the third figure, but they believe it was a man, and not Eddie's ex-wife."

I nodded. "I think he'll be happy to hear that, considering she's the mother of his kids."

"Yes, they already contacted the sheriff in Alpine to let him know."

"Are there any leads to who it might be?" I asked, genuinely concerned. One kidnapping was enough for a lifetime.

"No, they still aren't certain. While you're in the area, I'd suggest you talk with the sheriff, and see what he thinks. Maybe those who knew Princeton's gang will have more insight."

"I wish we could all put this behind us, but unfortunately, as long as there are any of these… well, these bad guys at large, I think there's still some risk."

"I've been thinking about that. Why don't we spring for security to remain on the ranch for at least a few more months until things settle down? I'd prefer my grandchildren are protected."

I looked at my father like he'd grown horns. "Your grandchildren?"

Both Mama and Papa laughed. "Like you don't already think of those children as yours. Even if you haven't proposed yet, we all know it's just a matter of time."

"Papa, you're jumping the gun a bit here. I haven't even told him how I feel about him yet."

"That's because you have lost your touch, but I'm guessing you'll remedy that soon enough, and when you do, I hope you both agree to have your wedding here."

"Papa, it's too early for all that."

"What's too early? Do you love Eddie?"

Mama put her hand over his and shook her head. "Love must happen at its own speed, mi amor. It can't be rushed even by overbearing fathers. But, mi hijo, your papa is right, if you love this man, you should let him know, and you should also figure out how to make him yours, so he'll never again wonder if he belongs in your life, whether that's during the good times or the bad."

The twins saved me by spilling their drink, and making their mom jump up and begin cleaning. I looked over at the little one and winked. I'd already begun thinking of them as my nephews. Knowing that I couldn't begrudge my parents or sisters wanting me to hurry up and make the two boys, they'd all come to love, family.

I managed to talk Papa into letting me use the private jet to fly to Alpine. If I hadn't still been in pain, I doubt he'd have agreed, but because I was, and more likely because he wanted me to seal the deal with Eddie, he did. Thank God, because I couldn't imagine I'd ever survive on a four-hour car journey. I'd seriously improved since being released from the hospital, but my ribs still felt like someone was kicking me anytime I moved the wrong way.

Eddie met me at the airport in Flex's truck, saying his old one had long ago lost its suspension, and he didn't want me to have to bounce my way back to the ranch. I kissed him, thanking him for being so sweet.

When we got to the ranch, both boys hugged me like I hadn't seen them in a year. The hugs hurt my ribs, but I'd be damned if I'd ever let them know that. It just felt good that someone wanted me back in their lives as much as these two did.

I settled into the same routine I had before, by helping get the kids to school while Eddie did the morning chores. It just felt so right, like this was where I belonged. I slipped into the routine so easily, it was as if I'd always been doing it.

My days were filled with everything, from helping Jimmy clean and polish the tack in the stables, to helping clean the duplex after the kids had gone to school, anything I could do and not feel like I was stabbing myself in the sides due to the broken ribs.

Evenings were my favorite, since that was when the family gathered together. More often than not, Flex and Mitch would come out, and we'd talk over homecooked meals made by Emma Jean.

Eddie's ex-wife had been arrested for conspiracy to murder around a week after I got to the ranch. The sheriff had come over and explained that she and Princeton had worked out an entire scheme against him. She'd even gone so far as to take out a life insurance policy on Eddie just before their divorce.

We were still unsure how the preacher fit into the equation, but we assumed Eddie's mother was somehow involved. After Eddie had called her asking if she was involved in my kidnapping, she lawyered up and refused to speak to the police. Eddie got a restraining order against her, mainly because she refused to show up for the trial, but there was an ongoing investigation, and he was sure she was involved. He'd already told the police about their conversation, and the sheriff agreed it was suspicious that she didn't deny her part in all of it from the beginning.

I was biding my time until I could get back up on a horse, because frankly, I wanted to propose to Eddie and do so in a fashion that befitted a proper cowboy, but every time I tried to climb onto the back of the mare I'd all but claimed as my own, I had to stop, because the pain in my ribs was still too intense.

Before my visit was over, however, Eddie surprised me by pulling up to the main house, where we were all gathering to eat, with a beautiful surrey pulled by his horse Red.

"What's this?" I asked, and he smiled. "Well, you've been trying to get on top of your horse for two weeks, so I figured, since you were going to have to go back soon, maybe you could enjoy a ride around the ranch in this."

The family and I walked around the beautiful carriage-style surrey, admiring its beauty. "Where did you get this?" I asked.

Eddie smiled over at Mitch. "Mitch knew someone in Alamito that collects them. Usually, they sit inside an old warehouse collecting dust, but when I said I'd clean it up and oil all the parts, he agreed to let me use it."

"It also helped that the old man is gay, and when we told him it was to woo his man, the old romantic almost jumped up and down," Mitch added.

I smiled. "So, this is my wooing?"

Eddie leaned over from the seat and kissed me on the lips. "I sure as h..." He looked over at Luke and quickly changed what he was going to say. "...heck, hope so."

He jumped down and helped me into the passenger seat, which hurt my pride more than a little, since it still hurt to climb into things, and I wouldn't have been able to climb into the seat without his help.

He waved everyone off and drove around the back of the stables toward what I assumed were the buttes.

When he neared the volcano, he stopped. "I wanted to bring you back here to talk to you, but if the place brings up too many bad memories, we can go someplace else."

I shook my head. "No, I don't really remember being here. I was beaten up someplace else, so they must have brought me here later on. The only memories I have of this place are the ones with you and seeing Jack."

"Good," he said, and pulled the surrey over to the entrance of the mine.

When we walked through the entrance, I immediately saw that Eddie had prepared for us to be here. There was a small table with a tablecloth covering it, two candles, and plates. When I sat down at the table, he rushed back to the surrey and grabbed a basket I hadn't even noticed, and brought it in, setting it on a little side table he'd brought for serving.

My heart began to beat, knowing where this was headed, but I didn't let on. I was just enjoying being wooed, as he'd called it.

He lit the candles first, then served us each what appeared to be Emma Jean's empanadas.

"So, I see Emma Jean was in on all this," I teased, and he winked at me.

"Best food in Brewster County," he said. "Besides, you can eat empanadas with your hands, and empanadas are like the food they used to eat in mines all over the world. It only made sense to serve them, right?"

I leaned over and kissed him. "Totally right."

He walked over to where a small radio sat and turned on a song I immediately recognized as *Besime Mucho*, an all-time favorite romantic tune we'd used in the movie we'd filmed here.

"Wow, you're pulling out all the stops. Where did you get this?" I asked.

"Your sister sent it to me. It's the soundtrack for your new movie." Then, he shrugged, and said, "It felt appropriate."

I stood up and pulled this amazing man into a hug and began to dance slowly to the romantic melody.

When the music ended, Eddie knelt in front of me, pulled out a ring box handing it to me, and asked, "Alexandro Zitlal, I'd never have believed it possible to love someone as much as I love you. It would honor me more than I have words to say if you'd agree to be my husband."

I couldn't help my response. Tears slipped from my eyes, and I reached down, willing Eddie to stand back up. If I could've, I'd have knelt with him. He stood up and I pulled him into a kiss, before I pulled back, and said, "Eddie, I love you so much, and fuck, if I could've gotten onto that damned horse, I was gonna propose to you myself, but for me, the answer is yes, yes, and for the rest of my life, and with all my heart, it's yes again!"

I was pulled into a tight embrace, and tried not to wince.

"Oh, sorry," he said, and when he could tell I was okay, he kissed me again.

"Have you told the boys?" I asked, after Eddie began to lead me back to the table.

He laughed. "Oh, man, who do you think picked out the ring?"

I hadn't even paid attention to the ring. I looked down at it and laughed. It was similar to the promise ring I'd bought him, but in the middle was a raised image of Xochiquetzal, Aztec goddess of love, and on either side of it sat two stones. I guessed they were the birthstones of each of the boys. When I asked Eddie, he smiled and nodded. "They wanted to be part of this as well."

It was late when we got back to the house, but unsurprisingly, both boys were sitting next to Emma Jean, waiting for our return.

"Did you say yes?" they both asked as they ran to the door.

I sat on a chair and showed the boys the ring. "It fits perfectly," I told them. "It appears I'm gonna be Papa Alex for real."

"Are you going to adopt us?" Drake asked.

I looked at Eddie who shrugged.

"I'd like to if that's what you want."

The kids hugged me and had a hundred questions—about the wedding, where we were going to live and stuff—which I had no idea how to answer.

Eddie laughed. "Boys, he just said yes. We don't have plans yet, but you can be a part of planning it all if you want to," he said, and it mollified them enough that they were willing to go to bed.

Both Eddie and I tucked them in, kissing them both on the forehead before turning off the light, and coming out to the living room where a very excited Emma Jean embraced us. "Poor Jimmy stayed up as long as he could, but we already knew you were going to say yes," she chuckled. "I'll give him the official news, though. Alex, we are so happy to have you in our family, and this one deserves to be happy for a change," she said, patting Eddie cheek.

When she left, we sat on the couch, making out, and celebrating our new engagement.

"There's a lot to plan, and I warn you now, my family are going to be so freaking nosy about it all. You'll have to stand up for what you want, or my mother and sisters will take the entire wedding over, and neither of us will have a say."

Eddie chuckled. "I don't care when or where I marry you, Alex. I just want to marry you. But, if you're willing, I'd like to have a small ceremony in Jack's cave. It seems we owe him for all this. Not only because I think that whole snake trick at the river was a setup to force us closer together, but because he kept you safe and warned us when things got bad."

"I agree, and I think my family will want that too, considering our connection with Jack."

That night we made love gently. It still hurt too much to do anything else, but as we touched and kissed each other, the message was clear. Our love was real and solid. It was a love to last the ages.

40

Epilogue - Eddie

A LEX WASN'T JOKING. THE wedding planning was taken over by his family. Thank God, neither of us cared how the main ceremony was held. In the end, it was a grand thing that took place in the gardens of their hacienda. Dignitaries, bigwigs, even the leaders of various cartels across Mexico showed up for the party. I didn't know any of them, but Alex or his family introduced me to everyone that showed up.

One in particular, however, I recognized immediately. The man was introduced to me as señor Romeriz, a business owner in Mexico City. When he noticed I'd recognized him, he winked at me, then introduced me to his husband. "Family are the most important thing in our lives, protect them with everything you've got," he said, before moving away and talking to other dignitaries in the room.

Señor Zitlal looked over and nodded at me when he left, and I smiled. This was our secret, one I'd never share, but damn if I wasn't really happy that man was a part of our lives.

The main wedding was fun. The kids enjoyed it too, and there was a lot of activity leading up to the wedding and after. It was fun to watch my little family, Flex, Mitch, Emma Jean, Jimmy, and even Eric interacting with the elite. Everyone took an interest in them, especially since they'd been featured as singers in the film.

Mitch, Emma Jean, and Jimmy even sang a love song together at the reception, which was met with intense applause.

The part of our nuptials that inspired me the most, however, was the small ceremony we had with our immediate families in Diamondback Jack's cave. Señor Zitlal performed the ceremony, which was more of a blessing than a wedding.

When we both pronounced our love, we turned to see not one of us had a dry eye. Even the boys were emotional. Of course, señor Zitlal pulled the kids to the front, and had each of them pronounce their relationship with Alex, and Alex with them.

For me, even though it wasn't the legal part, it was the aspect of our relationship that cemented us together for all time.

Two things happened after the wedding. One, señor Zitlal presented us with a signed copy of my ex-wife's agreement to let Alex adopt the boys. When I asked if she was tortured, he shook his head. "No, she readily agreed. I had my lawyers speak to her directly. In the end, she was going to prison, so she didn't have much to lose."

"You know, I've known that woman a long time, she must've negotiated something."

Señor Zitlal chuckled, "Oh, yeah, she wanted you to pay for her legal team, and various other things, but we put the skids on that. We did agree to create a small account with money in it that she can use while in prison."

I shook my head. "She's such a piece of work. She tries to have me killed, then she wants me to pay her legal fees... So, you paid her off?" I asked.

Señor Zitlal shrugged. "It seems to me it's a small price to pay to ensure she's out of your life for good."

I nodded. "And for Alex to be the boys father, I couldn't think of anything they... well, or I would like more."

"Then, I'll have the attorneys get to work setting it all up."

"By attorneys, do you happen to mean Francesca?" Alex asked, causing his father to laugh.

"Well, she is the best one we've got."

"Did Francesca talk to my ex?" I asked, shocked.

Señor Zitlal laughed. "Of course, she wouldn't have let anyone else handle something this important to her or us."

This family never ceased to amaze me. It was decided then that the boys and I would all take the Zitlal name. In fact, when I asked them if they minded, they were ecstatic about it. To be honest, I was too. I loved the idea of having the name of my man and his family who loved me... us unconditionally, instead of a man I barely knew, and who'd tossed me aside like a piece of crap.

The second surprise came a couple weeks later. Señor Zitlal asked that both of us join him at the studio in Juarez. When we walked into his very fancy office, he sat us down in front of a large monitor he had sitting in one corner of the room, and he turned it on.

It took a moment for the screen to focus, but as soon as it did, it was clear we were looking at Jack's cave. Alex was lying in a bloody pile on the floor. Jack was sitting on the floor beside him, stroking his head. Alex looked at me, then at his father. "How did you get this."

I didn't wait for señor Zitlal to respond, but kissed Alex instead. "Some things are best not known," I replied, earning a smile from my father-in-law.

Señor Zitlal hit a couple buttons, and the image disappeared, replaced by one of Alex and me when I proposed to him. My eyes grew large, and I was glad Alex wasn't feeling well enough to make love as I'd planned originally.

"Okay, that's freaky," Alex said. "Remind me not to fool around anywhere near that cave." I laughed.

"I was thinking pretty much the same thing," I admitted, earning a cocked eyebrow from señor Zitlal.

When I looked at him, questioning why he was showing us the video, he smiled and zoomed in behind us, inside the darkened cave. It took a moment for us to see them, but once the image was adjusted, you could see two distinct characters sitting in the cave, watching us. If you didn't look too closely, it looked like older versions of Alex and me.

The hairs on my arm rose with goosebumps. "They're back together," I said, and felt the tears slip from my eyes. "It must've had something to do with us coming together."

Alex looked at me, skepticism in his expression, and I laughed. "Don't be silly, you know there's strange things happening down there. Besides, doesn't it make you happy to think Jack and his lover found each other after all this time?"

Alex smiled and asked, "You really do have a Latin streak running through you, don't you?"

"That and a lot more, but mostly I think it's about having found the love of my life as well as knowing our ancestors have found each other again."

We climbed the stairs to Alex's apartment, which had been fixed and was now fitted with a steel door, and various locks that would prevent entry without some serious equipment. We made love for the rest of the day.

Alex and my lives surprisingly fit together. If you'd have asked me two years ago if I'd ever find this kind of love, I'd have told you in no uncertain terms, "People like me don't get storybook endings."

There were no words to say how happy I was to have been wrong about that.

LOVE'S HEIRLOOM

Steve sees ghosts, Eric feels disconnected from the world. Can these two find solace in each other's arms?
Continue the Big Bend Series with Love's Bequest

Available at your favorite bookseller.

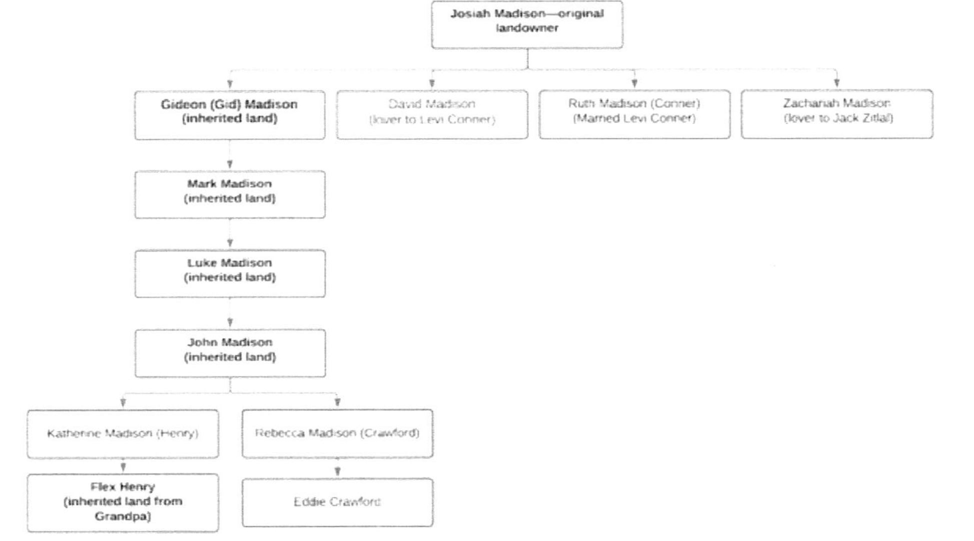

Josiah Madison—original landowner
Gideon (Gid) Madison (inherited land)
David Madison (lover to Levi Conner)
Ruth Madison (Conner) (Married Levi Conner)
Zachariah Madison (lover to Jack Zitlal)
Mark Madison (inherited land)
Luke Madison (inherited land)
John Madison (inherited land)
Katherine Madison (Henry)
Rebecca Madison (Crawford)
Flex Henry (inherited land from Grandpa)
Eddie Crawford

Join Blake's email list to get advance notice of new books and receive his occasional newsletter:

www.blakeallwood.com

<table>
<tr><td>

MM Romance
By Blake Allwood

<u>Transitions Series</u>
Aiden Inspired
Suzie Empowered (MF Romance)
Bobby Transformed

<u>Chance Series</u>
Love By Chance
Another Chance <u>With</u> Love
Taking A Chance <u>For</u> Love

<u>Romantic Series</u>
Romantic Renovations (1)
Romantic Rescue (2)
Romantic Recon (3)

<u>Melody Series</u>
Melody of the Heart
Melody of the Snow

<u>Road to Rocktoberfest Anthology</u>
Changing His Tune - 2022

<u>Coming Home Series (2023)</u>
A Long Way Home
Family Home
Down Home
…and many more

<u>Novellas</u>
Tenacious
Moon's Place

</td><td>

Romantic Fantasy
By Adam J. Ridley

<u>Big Bend Series</u>
Love's Legacy (1)
Love's Heirloom (2)
Love's Bequest (3)

<u>The Witch Brothers Series</u>
Emerald Earth
Diamond Air
Ruby Fire
Sapphire Water

</td></tr>
</table>

Blake Allwood was born in west Tennessee, then moved to Kansas City MO after earning a degree in Early Childhood Education from Graceland College in Lamoni, Iowa. He met his husband Shaun in 1995 and they officially married in 2015, once gay marriage was legalized; although they still consider Valentines Day 1995 as their true "anniversary date". Twenty-two years later (2017), after fostering 12 children together, he and his husband sold their home, purchased an RV and began traveling the country with their two dogs.

Typically, Blake can be found relaxing in the RV or by the fire with his laptop and their Jack Russell Terrier, Buddy, curled up between his legs demanding attention. Denver, their Siberian Husky mix is often asleep at his feet or playing tug of war with Blake's husband.

Most of Blake's stories are inspired by the places they have visited in their ongoing travels. His first book, ***Aiden Inspired***, was released in 2019 and he has now written over 20 books. In

2023 he is releasing the ***Coming Home*** series which is comprised of ten-plus sweet contemporary romance novels that are based on a fictional town in his home state of Tennessee.

Blake also writes under the pen name of Adam J. Ridley for his urban fantasy fans looking for stories revolving around gay characters. His first series is The Witch Brothers Saga, starting with ***Emerald Earth***.

bibliopride.com

Books by LGBTQ+ authors